BLACK BROGUES
&
FRENCH KNICKERS

Jasmin Pink

AuthorHouse™
1663 Liberty Drive
Bloomington, IN 47403
www.authorhouse.com
Phone: 1-800-839-8640

Published by AuthorHouse 01/04/2012

First publihsed in 2003 by
KISMET PUBLISHING COMPANY LIMITED
UK

ISBN: 978-1-4678-7951-4 (sc)
ISBN: 978-1-4678-7952-1 (ebk)

Printed in the United States of America

Dedicated to my family
for their encouragement

A special thank you to Chris
(my cousin and fellow author)
for encouraging me in the first instance

My especial gratitude to
my dearest friend and mentor
Richard Thomas
"MY ROCK"
without whose help and support
this book would never have been completed

PROLOGUE

The driver of the shabby cab was of ethnic origin and reeked of garlic, the pungency assaulting her sense of smell as it wafted around the close confines of the cab. Indian music was belting out of the antiquated radio, making a series of slight sharp noises, as that of paper being crushed. She wished she had the nerve to tell him to switch the bloody thing off but had no wish to strike up any form of conversation with him. It was a miserable, damp evening in May, the rainfall although not heavy, splattered randomly onto the windscreen of the cab. To add to her irritation the windscreen wipers intermittently swished back and forth wiping the droplets of rain away, the final swish making a nerve-shattering squeak as the screen dried off. Thank goodness Gatwick was only a thirty-minute drive away, as the squeak was beginning to grate on her nerves. She tried to detract from the noise by attempting to look out of the window but as fast as she was wiping the condensation away the window would steam up again, thereby making familiar landmarks, indiscernible. Giving an exasperated sigh she sat back in her seat, resigning herself to an uneventful journey.

Jay Patterson was on her way to the airport, it was now nine-thirty p.m., it would be almost ten before she arrived, so she closed her eyes and wondered whether Eros the God of Love would be looking down favourably on her. She hoped he was, then maybe her life would take a turn for the better; after all she was attempting to give him a helping hand by taking the uncharacteristic step of venturing on holiday on her own. On her own? The thought was daunting! Jay's long-term love affair had come to an abrupt end over a year ago, leaving a void in her life that she was finding extremely difficult to fill. It was an ill-fated love affair from the outset, she should never have got involved with a married man and vowed never to do so again. Most men of her age or thereabouts were married and those that were not were usually past their sell by date, had an affliction or were gay. She envisaged that she would be extremely lucky if she would ever find an ideal partner to share the rest of her life with.

However, she still lived in hope and as the saying goes:

"YOU CAN ONLY GET OVER ONE MAN BY GETTING UNDER ANOTHER"!

Chapter 1

Jay arrived at the airport for ten o'clock just in time for check in; her flight was at eleven fifty-five. She made her way to the Monarch airline counter and commenced searching for her passport and ticket only to get flummoxed when she couldn't find them. Her rather large bag had suddenly become a bottom less pit, full of pockets and zipped compartments that she didn't remember having. She kept delving, opening the zippers and closing them, then repeating the process again. Alas, with the same result, she just could not locate her documents.

Tiny beads of perspiration were now starting to appear and glisten above her top lip, she had the foreboding that she may have left them at home when dashing out to the cab, the panic button was now starting to sound in her head. It was now fifteen minutes past the check in time, oh how she hated to be late for anything. There was only one thing for it; she made her way to a vacant bench, laying her suitcase down flat so that she could empty her flight bag onto it, being the only way she could think of to get to the bottom of it. She hurriedly emptied the contents of her bag onto the suitcase, shaking it vigorously to get the last remnants out, only to realise too late what a stupid thing she had done as all her personal belongings had started to roll off her suitcase, leaning over to stop the unremitting flow she regrettably caught the case with her knee which in turn propelled everything across the airport floor. In a frenzy of activity Jay managed to grab the lipsticks, the chewing gum, deodorant and pants and shoved them back into the "Black Hole" that was her bag. However the remainder were still on the move. She caught sight of a tampon making a get away and made a clumsy grab for it, but unfortunately the tampon escaped her clutches, managing only to impede it's capture as she clipped it with the tip of her finger thereby giving it a momentum that spun it through the air, acquiring a life of it's own. She watched, frozen in the posture of a ten-pin bowler, as the small white object went soaring through the air, like a miniature torpedo, following it's progress until it finally dropped to the ground, spinning around and around putting more ground between her and it, until finally it came to a stop, halted by a pair of highly polished black shoes!

Remaining in a crouched position Jay's eyes were transfixed on the destination of the tampon some six or seven metres away, and on the black shiny shoes, the right one of which was gently tapping beside the offending article. She instinctively knew that it was now too late to ignore the tampon; she now had no option but to reclaim it! Dreading making eye contact with the owner of the shiny black shoes (so evidently belonging to a man), she remained crouched over her suitcase, trying to look unperturbed, but failing miserably. Keeping her head still, she slowly raised her eyes upwards from the shoes to the bottom of a pair of navy jeans and so her eyes began their journey onwards and upwards. However, not so perturbed that she could not acknowledge the well-formed thighs, under the tight fitting jeans. As her eyes carried on they became rooted to the so obviously unrestrained prominence between this strangers legs; the large bulge making it clearly evident what side this man dressed! The realisation took her breath away, she could feel her temperature rising and her pulse rate increasing. Contain yourself woman, she muttered under her breath. Anyone would think you hadn't seen a well-endowed man before. Well she hadn't, not one that size any way! She reluctantly pleaded with her eyes to move on again and so progressed to the flat stomach, a shiny black leather belt around his waist with an unostentatious gold buckle securing it, appearing to glint at her in a cheeky sort of way as though having read her guilty imaginings. Progressing as far as the pale blue sweater tucked into the waistband of his jeans when, of necessity, she blinked and in that split second of blindness Mr Toe Tapper took her by surprise as she now found herself staring at a ruggedly handsome face; complete with lopsided grin that made it plainly obvious that he found her embarrassment highly amusing. It was blatantly clear that he had deliberately and calculatingly leant forward, with the sole intention of making eye contact with her. Realising no doubt that it would have taken her an interminable amount of time to traverse his body, as she was certainly making a meal of it.

Jay was transfixed by his stare; even from a distance she could see he had a knowing look upon his face, as though he had read her every thought. With that possibility in her mind, she turned a beetroot red, remembering her pilgrimage along the contours of his lower body. Then, as though someone had clicked his or her fingers, she was once more on firm ground, roused from her hypnotic trance, only to look on in dismay as he leant forward and picked up the tampon. To add to her uneasiness he held it aloft, holding it upright between his fingers for all and sundry to see, calling across to her in a very audible tone saying,

"Madam, is this yours by any chance"?

Well, if the ground could have opened up Jay would willingly have jumped into it. However, she decided to brazen it out, taking a deep breath she made a wild dash over to this beast of man to retrieve the tampon and put a stop to him waving such a personal object about for all and sundry to see.

Oh, oh, BIG MISTAKE!

About a metre away from him she skidded, her legs going from under her and with arms splayed out in front, her body lunging forward, she grabbed him about his firm thighs in an attempt to stop herself falling heavily to the ground. This, however, meant that her face ended up between his legs, which may have been quite pleasant in different circumstances. Her head hit him forcefully, winding him, his legs crumpled, causing him to fall backwards onto the ground. Jay all dignity now lost, red faced and dishevelled, was now in a very awkward position, spread-eagled on top of him.

He was a big man, in more ways than one and he appeared to be in agony. Jay thought that she must of head butted him in his crown jewels. She imagined for an instant at the pain he must be experiencing and grimaced sympathetically, but only for an instant, as now all she wanted to do was to get off this mountain of a man and regain her composure. However, each time she made a move to detach herself from him the more he groaned, she didn't want to add to his pain seeing as she was the cause of it, so all she could do was lay still, all the time apologising profusely, hoping that he would eventually stop groaning long enough for her to remove herself, which he didn't seem about to do.

Time was getting on and she still hadn't checked in, she really wouldn't be able to wait much longer for him to recover; she had also left her luggage unattended. Just when she thought she would have to disregard his pain and make a move she heard sniggering coming from behind her and looking around to her dismay saw a small crowd had gathered – one wise arse shouted out: "I'll give her 9 point 7 for artistic merit"!

The queue of people at the check-in found this comment hilarious, some couldn't help laughing out loud; others were a little more tactful, putting their hands over their mouths to stifle their tittering.

"Oh my God" she muttered under her breath, a little shocked, when she realised that an audience had formed. "Where can I put my face now"?

He must have heard her. Not only had he a big bulge in his trousers, he must have had big ears as well, as he immediately stopped groaning and replied. "You can always put it back where it was five minutes ago, it was rather pleasant".

Like a lightning bolt had hit her, she realised that this bastard was jesting at her expense, his moaning and groaning now stopped as he sat up abruptly, leaning back on his elbows, causing Jay to slide down and sit astride him, glaring into his smug face. Sitting quite still, gob smacked that he had taken full advantage of her humiliation, he was obviously enjoying the situation a little too much as there was a very evident hardening under her. Looking daggers at him, showing her infuriation, using his chest for leverage she forcefully pushed herself off him, there was so much she would like to have said to him but found she would be unable to express herself without swearing, so instead of making a further exhibition of herself, she settled for giving him a killer look, flung her head back and flounced off towards her abandoned suitcase, leaving him prostrate and the sound of his roaring laughter behind her.

Thankfully all her belongings were still where she had left them, several items still upon the ground where they had tumbled, surprisingly nothing had been tampered with whilst she had been making a fool of herself. Jay kept her head down trying not to look back, shoving everything back into her bag as quickly as possible, after putting in the final item, like a cloud had been lifted from her brain, it suddenly dawned on her. All her important documents and money were in the leather bum bag around her waist, which she had forgotten she was wearing as it had swung around and was now positioned in the small of her back. She had hated wearing the blooming thing in the first place, but was advised that it was a necessity, purely to keep her documents and money safe and close at hand. She hated wearing it even more now. What an idiot she was!

She never did retrieve her tampon; she wondered where it was now!

Chapter 2

Jay managed to check in without any more hitches, deposited her suitcase, received her seat allocation and with no further ado, made her way towards the escalator which led to the shops and restaurants, all the time being very wary not to bump into that ape of a comedian again. Only another sixty-five minutes and she would hopefully be boarding the plane, until then she would keep a low profile, possibly even find a discrete place to hide away and have a coffee. Wanting something to read for the journey she went into a bookstore, quickly chose some magazines and grabbing the first book that caught her eye. She handed her money over to the sales assistant, trying to urge her to hurry up as Jay didn't want to hang about any longer than was necessary in the event that she might be recognised due to the fiasco that had occurred a few minutes previously. Purchasing a cappuccino from a café she found an isolated corner and sat drinking her coffee, listening to the dulcet tones of Elvis singing "I'm All Shook Up". Which was very appropriate under the circumstances!

Jay started to slowly unwind, trying hard to put to the back of her mind the unfortunate incident that had occurred a short while ago. Still, when all said and done, he was quite a hunk, even if he was a right bastard. Well, there was no point thinking about him any more, he was off on his travels to wherever that might be, so she turned her thoughts to the magazine now open in front of her.

The hour Jay had to kill before she went on the next step of her journey passed quickly and it was now time for her to go to the departure lounge, checking the overhead screens for departures she found her flight displayed.

LONDON TO MOMBASSA, GATE 21
DEPARTING 11.55 P.M. 03/05/002
ARRIVING MOMBASSA 11.55 A.M. 04/05/02
ON SCHEDULE

She wondered where to go next, not being used to airports, worriedly looking around trying to find some sign indicating where she should go. She wandered aimlessly finally finding an official to ask for directions, who then politely indicated that the entrance to Gate 21 was immediately behind her. What an idiot, she thought, her nerves were obviously getting the better of her; quite clearly the earlier misfortune and the handsome man were still on her mind.

When she came to think of it, the incident was quite amusing, she chuckled silently, thinking that she must have made quite an impact on him one way and another, realising how funny it must have been for the onlookers. If she hadn't been in such a panic about her documents she may have handled it a lot better. That chap must of thought her a right fool. Yes, it was funny, but there was no excuse for him to go getting a hard on like that.

Disgraceful, then again, even that was amusing. It was too late now to drum up the image of that roguish handsome face again, she was off to Kenya and he was never to be seen again!

Jay handed over her passport and ticket to be checked then being waved through towards the security check where she joined the queue of people and waited for her turn to come before she had to put her hand luggage along with her bum bag onto the conveyor belt which was to be screened for anything untoward. She then went through the body scanner and as nothing metal was detected she was again clear to carry on. Fortunately for her she was not among the many people that were picked at random and frisked. Security was extremely tight at the airport, due to the sad event of September 11th 2001, understanding and agreeing with the laborious checks that had to be carried out, Jay would gladly put up with the inconvenience for peace of mind that her journey would be safe as humanly possible.

Now able to meander around the duty free shops Jay window-shopped, looking at and sampling some of the perfumes. She would have liked to have bought a bottle of rum to keep in her hotel room so she could give herself some Dutch courage before she ventured out anywhere but not having any spare space in her bag or wanting to be lumbered down with unnecessary purchases, she passed up the opportunity to buy, hopefully there would be a chance on the return journey to buy her favourite perfume and top up the drinks cabinet at home, that's if she had any cash left, the holiday was costing more than she could really afford as it was.

Her window shopping done Jay followed the signs to Gate 21, deciding against the automatic walkways as they made her feel like her head had to keep catching up with her body, making her dizzy, so she walked. The exercise would do her good anyway as she had an eight-hour flight ahead of her. After what seemed an age, Jay reached the boarding area, there appeared to be hundreds of people already queuing. Where did they all come from? The airport had been quite deserted except for the small crowd that had watched her jumping on a complete stranger; she ought to have put a cap out and collected a few pennies for the entertainment she had provided.

She joined the queue to get her boarding card, waiting patiently whilst the other passengers passed through yet another security check. All bags were being checked again and the random frisking of passengers was once again being carried out. Going with the flow of the slowly decreasing queue until she was almost at the security check and like everyone else there, trying to look nonchalant and innocent, then it was her turn. There were two queues one for men the other for women. Jays bag was taken from her unceremoniously and plonked harshly down onto a long table by, lo and behold, the dreaded butch female; you know the sort, very short-cropped hair, flat chest and no make-up, who was obviously in her element strutting her stuff, dressed up in a unisex uniform. If it wasn't for the fact that she had no trace of stubble, she could have fooled anyone into thinking she was of the masculine gender. She started to manhandle Jay's bag, pulling at it and turning over the contents, inspecting every item within, when all of a sudden this low buzzing noise could be heard; it was sod's law that it was coming from Jay's bag. Taken unawares, stepping back with as much authority as she could muster Butch, as Jay so aptly called her, said, "OK everyone, stay calm, move back away from this area towards the end of the queue"

Jay was waving to her, trying to catch her attention as she was now only too fully aware of what was causing the buzzing and for the second time in less than two hours, was hoping the ground would open up and swallow her.

"You" and pointing in a rather intimidating way at Jay "Will go with those guards and then perhaps we will get to the bottom of this business"

"Please" implored Jay as she was unceremoniously marched off, a guard on each arm, leaving Butch looking perturbed and her bag behind, which had now started to quiver as well as buzz, causing a fair amount of disconcertion amongst the other passengers who were now moving back out of harms way the look of apprehension clear on some of their faces, she could see they were all scrutinizing her it was impossible not to hear them passing judgment.

"She doesn't look the sort does she"? Said a blonde haired woman, looking Jay up and down.

"You never know nowadays". Came a reply.

"Quite a stunner though" added a weedy little

man, rubbing his hands together. "I wouldn't mind giving ***her*** a strip search. Get my drift old boy?" He added nudging the chap next to him.

"Albert, do you have to?" Reprimanded a stern looking woman. "All you seem to think about is what's in your trousers!"

Jay was now beginning to seethe inside. Why, why, why do these things always have to happen to me? This has got to stop before it gets out of hand, Jay thought, managing with a bit of effort to extricate herself from the restraining clutches of the spotty faced youth who passed as a security guard.

"Oi, come 'ere, where do yer think yer going? The guard shouted after her, trying unsuccessfully to grab hold of her.

But Jay had reached her goal, now facing Butch and in a low but firm voice asked, "Why won't you listen to me"? "Do you like your little bit of power"?

"What do you think you are doing?" Butch asked her sternly, standing legs apart, hands on hips looking extremely aggravated that someone had the audacity to thwart her orders as Jay was no longer being restrained.

"If you listen I can tell you what's making the noise, there's no need for a scene" Jay practically begged.

"It's a little late for that, don't you think Madam?"

"Don't be such a damn drama queen". Jay snapped and then realising that she had made a terrible mistake in being so sharp tried a more rational approach. "There's a simple explanation, no need for all this fuss, please give me a chance to explain".

Butch stood with a blank expression on her face, giving the impression that she had no intention of being reasonable. Jay tried again. "Can't we go somewhere where I can tell you discretely, it's a little bit sensitive?

The gay security guard inspected her nails, then facing Jay, raised her eyebrows, tipped her head to the side and huffed in exasperation. To which Jay responded with a cutting a remark. "Being WHAT YOU ARE, I felt sure you would understand, but obviously not". That comment was a major faux pas!

Butch eyed Jay up and down, looking down her nose being even more aggressive than she had before, obviously not liking Jay's inference about her sexuality. With an evil looking grin spreading across her rough, masculine face, comprehension now manifesting itself she turned to Jay, at the same time addressing the captive audience. "Oh, so you know what it is that is making this noise then do you"? Then continuing in the same derisive manner. "Did you deliberately put it in your bag to cause this security alert, inconveniencing not only me but these good people, putting the fear of God into them"?

"No, No, I err," stammered the now very hot and red faced Jay, thinking I am far too old to be talked down to by this bolshy woman or for that matter, anyone.

"OK, then MADAM" Butch continued, emphasising the Madam. "Why don't we tell all these good people what it is you have in your bag"? Butch was taking pleasure in watching Jay squirm, the cow! "Come on speak up, don't be shy. Out with it woman." Evidently a dab hand at making demands.

What a first class bitch you are thought Jay, here goes and taking a deep breath and speaking in an inaudible whisper. "It's a ladies thing".

"It's a what?" Butch exclaimed loudly. "Now come on MADAM, these people didn't hear you"? Wanting to make a point and using Jay as a specimen.

"It's a ladies thing." "You know?" Hoping that Butch would have some compassion and come to her aid. No such luck.

Butch now had the bit between her teeth and was not going to let Jay have her way and in the same perceptible tone. "It's a ladies thing"? "What on earth do you mean"? "Come on woman, spit it out, you've delayed us for long enough."

Jay, finally blowing her top, all thought of dignity now lost she shouted at this pathetic excuse for a woman.

"IT'S A BLOODY VIBRATOR!"

Knowing full well that she had the upper hand and with that self-satisfying grin upon her stupid face said for all and sundry to hear. "Really madam, there's no need to shout, why, all you had to say is that you had a VIBRATOR in your bag, I'm sure we would have all understood."

Her comments were met by raucous laughter from the throng of interested onlookers. Jay couldn't blame them for laughing, it was probably the most exciting thing that had happened to them that week, if the shoe were on the other foot she would more than likely have done the same.

"Well I'd of thought YOU would have understand more than most!" Jay muttered to herself; thinking that Butch more than likely had a twelve-inch "Strappa-dick-to-me" at home that she could use on her girlfriends, that's if she had a girlfriend of course!

"Sorry, did you say something madam", said Butch with that hideous smile spread across her unpleasant face.

"No" said Jay abruptly, wondering when this nightmare was going to end.

"Shall we turn it off then", reaching into the side compartment of Jay's bag, extracting a green vibrator, which was now performing in all its jellified glory in her hand. "My, it is a big one, perhaps if you find you need to travel with your companion in future it would be advisable to remove the batteries first"

She handed it unceremoniously to Jay, who, fumbling with the opening, removed the batteries (remarkably not dropping them), placed it back in her bag then went to get her boarding pass and sit down, hearing Butch say as she went. "Hope you have a good flight."

Jay made a mental note to report the bitch, secretly wishing she'd have the forethought to put the bloody vibrator in her hand luggage!

Chapter 3

She sat in the boarding area and tried to hide behind a magazine, knowing full well that tongues were wagging at her expense. She did have some cause for relief though, at least the vibe hadn't sprang into life and bounced around the airport along with her tampon!

An announcement came over the tannoy – "Can passengers with seat numbers A1 to A26 please make their way to the aircraft"? A number of people got up and filed through the corridor leading to the plane. When they had disappeared, another group of passengers were called, on the third announcement it was Jay's turn and she joined the queue, eventually boarding the Boeing 747 bound for Kenya. She found her seat easily, being in the centre aisle, immediately behind the toilets. There was plenty of legroom but, as she later discovered, only a desirable spot if you needed the toilet every five minutes. She had a quick look about her, noticing that the seat to her right was still vacant and as more passengers were still waiting to board, she decided to sit down to enable them to pass. Taking her seat she delved into her bag and retrieved her reading glasses and a book, no doubt she would have to get up again soon to allow someone to sit in the empty seat next to her.

She opened the book: "MEN, CAN WE LIVE

WITHOUT THEM". The title caught her eye for obvious reasons and as she didn't want to hang around too long in Smith's, just in case HE turned up again, without too much deliberation, she had purchased it. She knew she wouldn't be content without a man in her life, so this book sounded intriguing and who knows may even offer some sound advice. However, Jay did draw the conclusion that the only women that were able to live without men were lesbians, such as the butch security guard; even so she opened the book and started to read.

The plane was slowly becoming occupied and although she was trying hard to read, it was proving difficult with all the hustle and bustle going on around her. Now and again she would peer above her glasses and study her fellow passengers. People are such funny creatures; some had braved the cold weather outside, by wearing shorts and skimpy tee shirts, in anticipation of the expected heat wave that would greet them at their destination. A number of women were done up like dogs' dinners being dressed in all their finery, looking as though they were going to a wedding rather than on holiday. Their faces plastered so thick with war paint that the sun would not have a chance to penetrate through it, along with hair crimped, curled or back-combed and lacquered into place, they looked like pantomime dames. It would be interesting to see what they eventually looked like at the end of an eight-hour journey. More than likely looking like pandas that had inadvertently stuck their fingers into an electrical socket, thought Jay with a little snigger.

Jay was more fortunate than most and lucky enough not to have to wear a great deal of make-up. She had a good complexion and her long, dark eyelashes did not require mascara to emphasise them. She knew that she was pleasing to the eye but was unaware of the affect her sultry good looks had on the opposite sex and if she did actually make the effort, was an extremely stunning woman. Unlike the poor old dear that was chatting away ten to the dozen to a gentleman, possibly her husband, as her lips were so tight, when she spoke she looked like a ventriloquist; with a face stiff like an ironing board, more than likely due to some rejuvenating treatment such as nips and tucks and possibly even Botox as well.

Peering down at her book she read a few lines - could it be true that men think of sex every thirty seconds, yes, she could believe that, in fact she thought about it just as much, that could be because she hadn't had any for such a long time!

There was a bit of commotion and once again she was drawn away from her book and she peered over her glasses, looking at the line of passengers entering the cabin. The cause of the turmoil soon came into view. My God, thought Jay, look at the size of him. How on earth was he going to get up the aisle, let alone find a seat that he could fit in? Oh no, she couldn't believe it, he was heading her way and she had the awful feeling that he was going to occupy the seat next to hers. Please God, please, not next to me. God did not answer her prayers, as this enormous man stood beside her causing darkness to descend upon her as he stood waiting to occupy the seat next to hers.

That will teach me to skip Sunday school and spend the collection money on popcorn, she surmised. “So this is pay back time is it God”? She mumbled under her breath as Fatso interrupted her thoughts with his tight, squeaky voice, due no doubt to the fat compressing against his testicles. “Excuse me miss”. Before she had time to move to one side his bulk cut out the light and he lifted one huge leg the size of an oak tree over her. The rolls of fat quivering like a hundred eels trying to escape the black sack that were his trousers. “Christ, please don’t let him fall on me, I won’t survive”! She prayed inwardly. Then came the other leg, which if at all possible, seemed even bigger than the first! He, Giant Haystacks and Big Daddy rolled into one, clambered over her, huffing and puffing as he manoeuvred his arse, the size of a barrage balloon managing to smother her face and knock her glasses off in the process, which was a blessing in disguise as her specs may well have become embedded into her nose, what with the enormous weight of him pressing down on her. “I can’t breathe, I’m going to die,” she thought. “Please, please, please, God whatever you do don’t let him fart!” Once again, God did not answer her prayers, for he (fatty that is, not God, heaven forbid!), let out a pathetic little pouf, obviously due to the strain of cocking his leg over. Unfortunately the smell was not so pathetic as the sound it had made. Jay now started to retch at the methane that was wafting about her nostrils. Fatty was oblivious to the pandemonium that was going on under his buttocks, as Jay was fighting for air. If I get out of this alive, I will not flout the Church again, she solemnly promised, as she felt as though her life's breath was slowing ebbing away.

She could just imagine her epitaph:

R.I.P

HERE LIES
JAY PATTERSON,
POOR GIRL
WAS SAT UPON,
COULDN'T GET
HER BREATH,
SMOTHERED
TO DEATH!

Just as she thought she was going to pass out he managed to dislodge his bulk and went about the mammoth task of fitting himself into the undersized space that was to wedge him in place for the duration of the journey. Jay needed to breath badly but was wary of breathing in the putrid air around her, thinking how grateful she would be for the above oxygen mask at this time, as she had always been susceptible to retching when subjected to foul smells.

She had fathomed out that this was not going to be a very pleasant trip and blessed having a fairly small frame as this unpleasant man's rolls of fat were lolling all over the arms of her seat, causing her to pull herself in and, unbeknown to her, squeezed her ample breasts together, making a very pleasing cleavage for the men to view on their way to their seats. Who, if caught by their other halves in the act of having a sneaky peek, were given a perfunctory clip around their ears and a cursory shove and urged to move on without delay. Oblivious to the attention she was getting, if Jay had known then she might have put on a roll necked jumper for the journey.

Chapter 4

The Incredible Bulk finally settled himself and promptly retrieved a bag of sherbet lemons from his Tesco's carrier bag. How naff, she thought. You'd think he could have at least gone a bit up market and used an M & S one!

Jay watched from the corner of her eye as this man put his huge fingers the size of German sausages, into a packet of sherbet lemons, which was minute in comparison, withdrawing one sweet, followed by another and yet another, putting them into his slobbery mouth and sucking extremely loudly. His ears acting as a stereo system for every disgusting and stomach churning suck, even down to the saliva sloshing around, was audible and it was making Jay feel a bit queasy, thinking that any minute now she may need to use one of the sick bags. No wonder he is in such a state, she thought.

The aircraft now had its quota of passengers and the exit doors were being closed, she was thankful that she had the sense to request an aisle seat, albeit placed near the toilet, as knowing her luck of late she could very well of had another fatty on the other side of her and then she would have felt like a tube of squeezed toothpaste!

Flight attendants were making their rounds, doing their routine checks and issuing various instructions and comments to the passengers.

"Take your seat now sir, yes we will be taking off shortly", said a skinny blonde attendant as she moved along the rows of people. "Please put your seat in the upright position." "Yes, we will bring you a blanket madam once we have taken off". Then turning to Jay, saying "Sorry Madam but you will have to put your bag in the overhead compartment, it's far to big and may fall into the aisle".

"OK, no problem" she replied getting up from her seat, (which was quite a relief when all said and done, she just wished she didn't have to return to it). Picking up her bag she went to put it in the compartment above her, however that was full to capacity, so she moved on to the next one. Yes, she should be able to get it in there with a bit of a shove. Sometimes she wished she was just a couple of inches taller, being only five feet three inches, especially at times like these, as the only way she was going to get her bag up and into the small space available, was to place the palm of her hand underneath, and with a little jump for momentum, push it up at the same propelling it forward. Where were the flight attendants or even a gallant gent when she needed one?

Jay's bag didn't quite make it the first time, she managed to catch it however and, using the same method as before, attempted again but as she did so the bag slipped from her hand, she managed to catch only one of the handles as it fell, which tipped the bag sideways and for the second time that night her belongings were tumbling out and to her shock and horror, onto the head of the passenger below.

"Clunk" went the hairbrush as it made contact, followed by "bong, bong, ping" as one after the other of her lipsticks dropped onto the groaning passenger, who was now rubbing his head in surprise. She was so relieved at this moment in time that she had secured the vibe in the zipped pocket! "Sorry, I'm so sorry" she kept saying as she tried desperately to stop the incessant flow of her belongings, but to no avail. Mortified, her face frozen in dismay as the final indignity began it's slowly and leisurely decent! The gossamer of black lace shimmied out of her bag and, not only landed on, but covered the whole of the poor man's face below. Jay, suddenly springing into life and throwing caution to the wind, let go her hold on the bag which, promptly and unceremoniously followed the black lace and thudded on the back of this unlucky man's head, who responded by letting out a loud "Ouch"!

"I'm so very, very sorry," said a very red faced Jay trying not to look at him whilst she retrieved all her belongings "I can't apologise enough".

"No, I don't think you can" the man said as he removed the offending article from his face, holding it a bit too familiarly in his hand. Jay looked up at the sound of his voice and stared at him, her eyes wide with realisation as he stared back at her with wicked delight.

"Do you make a habit of picking men up this way", his familiar lopsided grin smiling up at her, which showed that he was enjoying, yet again, her embarrassment and discomfort. He unfolded the black lace and fondling the material between his fingers without reserve. “Very nice, very nice indeed, french lace I believe and black, my favourites. How did you guess”?

Hurriedly snatching her knickers from him, thankful that at least they were clean. “I might have guessed it was you. Have you been sent just to jinx me”? She said through pursed lips as though the mishap was entirely his fault.

“Oh no lady, I think you are doing a very good job all on your own, please let me help you”.

“It’s a pity you didn’t help me before this happened”

“What and miss a view of your navel and the pleasure of having your panties draped over my face?” He spoke louder than was necessary; obviously loving an audience, as he had proved at the check in earlier and he certainly had a captive one at this moment in time.

“You, you” said Jay, trying so hard not to be flummoxed and to think of some witty retort that would alleviate her embarrassment, but yet again this man put her at a loss for words. She felt like clumping him one but the flight attendants had materialised from nowhere and were insisting she sit down. So she swallowed her pride and the need to vent her emotions on him and accepted his offer.

“Yes, I would appreciate it if you could at least hand me my bits and pieces and put my bag away for me.”

“My pleasure.” Picking up her strayed belongings and dropping them back in to her open bag then closing it, he placed it in the compartment with ease “You only had to ask!”

"Thank you" she replied grudgingly "Bastard" she muttered under her breath and with as much dignity as she could muster and her head held high she made her way back to her seat.

As she moved away she heard him ask, "That's ok, you can have a drink with me later to show your appreciation".

Jay sat down in her seat, feeling that the other passengers eyes boring into her back, and putting her glasses on she tried to resume the reading of her book MEN, CAN WE LIVE WITHOUT THEM - If only we could, she thought, they are insufferable!

Chapter 5

"Bing bong" echoed around the plane.

The seat belt sign came on, Jay tried to fasten her seat belt and found that one strap was stuck under the backside of the Bulk next to her. She looked at him; his head was slumped forward on his chest. Christ he's dead, she thought, perhaps he's choked on a sherbet lemon. Then she heard him breath out loudly, his flabby jowls reverberating as his breath escaped his thin pink lips and then breathing in snorting through his nose. She not only had to put up with being crushed in her seat she also had to contend with these bloody awful guttural sounds as he slept. There wasn't much chance of her concentrating on anything much with that going on. She did however; have to retrieve her seat belt. She tried tugging at it, but that was futile with the ten tons sitting on it, she then attempted to make a gap between him and her in the hope that she may be able to get a firmer grip and possibly ease it out that way. Was it easing out? No, was it heck, she needed to get a tighter grip and cringing tentatively pushed her fingers as far under his backside as was decently possible and gripped what she was the strap as firmly as she was able which was followed by a loud yelp as Fatty squealed in amazement, turning his red, sweaty face towards her and winking a pink piggy eye at her. Jay must have inadvertently pinched his backside. Yuk! "Excuse me, I was just trying to retrieve my seat belt and didn't want to wake you, sorry I didn't mean to pinch your ar..", Jay explained, stopping herself before she completed the sentence.

"Oh right" he replied looking a little disappointed.

"Yeah you wish," she thought.

With a great deal of exertion he raised his cumbersome body, the vast cheeks of his backside fractionally leaving the seat. Jay seized the opportunity of the immergence of this small gap to take one almighty tug thus releasing the seatbelt from its restraint, it came away easier than she thought it would making her body jerk back unexpectedly, causing her head to bump into a passing steward. Once again she found herself apologising, explaining that she was only trying to release the seatbelt as it was stuck, grimacing up at him and indicating with a slight nod of her head where the seatbelt had been lodged.

"Are you ok now madam? Do you need any help?" the steward enquired looking concerned, understanding now what had happened.

"No, I'm fine now thank you," but inwardly she thought she was in dire need of help. Why was she so accident-prone? Just one catastrophe after another, at least she was alleviating the boredom for the rest of the passengers that was for sure.

The steward carried on walking up the aisle casting her a sympathetic look as he did so.

She fastened her seat belt and sat back as the safety video was about to be shown on the overhead screen, the flight attendants were now in position to run through the escape and safety procedures. (If you happened to have the jitters about flying these talks do not instil any confidence in you and let's face it, if the plane were to go down everything they were telling you would be quickly forgotten in the panic!). The stewardess nearest her was indicating where the exits were located as the video played and a disembodied voice spoke out, and as though doing an old age pensioners work out the stewardess acted out the words as they were spoken.

"There are six emergency exits", arms reaching forward "two at the rear of plane", arms splayed out the either side "two at the centre of the plane", and her arms flipped back "two at the front". "You should take the emergency landing position, lean forward and put your head between your legs"

And kiss your arse goodbye! Jay thought.

The disembodied voice droned on for what seemed an eternity, some passengers feigning interest, others looking glassy eyed as they stared into empty space, they had all probably heard it before. Others were just blatantly reading or carrying on conversations. Finally and to everyone's relief the safety exercise was over and relative peace restored, it was now time for take off.

Chapter 6

The plane commenced taxiing along the runway, the engines were revving and before you could say "Jack Robinson", the deafening sound of the engines kicked in and the airplane was moving forward at speed, then one almighty thrust upwards making her lean heavily back in her seat. Taking off and landing were not a very pleasant experience for her, once the plane was up above the clouds was the time that she would settle, which she imagined was much the same for everyone on board. The plane was dipping up and down, Jay's stomach following suit, at the same time a loud thumping sound echoed around the plane, several people were beginning to look a bit white and Jay found herself holding onto the sides of her seat as she saw the stewardesses strapping themselves back into their seats. Finally, just as she thought they were doomed, a message was transmitted over the loud speaker. "Please do not remove your seatbelts until the seatbelt light has gone off, do not be alarmed we are experiencing some turbulence" a voice rang out around the aircraft. Yes, I know all about that, I'm sitting right next to a human turbulence factory!! Jay wanted to shout back. The plane dipped suddenly and then soared up again, this continued for what seemed like an eternity but it was really only about five minutes.

"Bing bong"

The seat belt sign went off, Jay released hers and wondered what the in-flight entertainment would be. She didn't have to wait long, because no sooner had the seat belt light gone off, then there was a steady stream of passengers making their way to the toilets. Obviously their bowels had loosened somewhat after the big dipper ride through the clouds! There must have been a queue of about ten people along the aisle beside her, some looking as though they were experiencing some discomfort as they were moving tight legged from one foot to the other obviously trying to contain the urge to empty their bowels or throw up in public. A little boy of about three who was shaking his mothers hand vigorously exclaimed "Mummy, I'm going shit", his mother told him he had to hang on, it wouldn't be much longer and that he mustn't use such words, to which he replied "Daddy says it". As everyone seemed as desperate as this little boy nobody suggested he went first, Jay would not have been at all surprised if there were teeth marks in the lavatory doors, an indication of the desperation to gain entrance to the occupied loos. She couldn't wait to see what would happen if the Bulk decided he needed to go, which wouldn't be long judging by the sounds erupting from every orifice that he possessed. Not very pleasant! There wasn't enough room to swing a cat in an airplanes toilet, perhaps he had a catheter inserted into his little pink shrivelled penis and relieved himself into a bottle strapped to his leg Jay mused wickedly. What a warped sense of humour she had and how nauseating of her to even think of his penis, a shiver of disgust ran down her spine, she must seriously try and occupy her overactive imagination in some other way! Jay therefore retrieved her book and glasses from the elasticised magazine holder in front of her and after straightening out the metal arms of her specs, that had been a bit squashed as they were knocked from her nose when the Bulk had sat on her, she put them on and for the third time since she boarded the plane tried to focus on reading. However, she did not find the book very captivating; there wasn't anything in it that she didn't know already and found herself mentally answering things such as: Why are men confused by love? – Because their hearts are in their dicks! What does a man consider foreplay? – Thirty minutes of begging! Jay amused herself like this for about ten minutes until she uncharacteristically nodded off, waking every so often as her head involuntarily dropped forward; she never slept very well on flights. When she finally awoke from her fitful sleep it was to a gentle tap on her shoulder and a warm, velvety voice whispering in her ear. "Hello, is there anybody there"?

For a moment she thought she was dreaming and drifted back off. Tap, tap on her shoulder again, she jerked up now in surprise and stared bleary eyed towards where the velvety voice had emanated from and which was now speaking again.

"Hey, you are awake then, how's about that drink"?

She gently shook her head and wiped her bleary,

sleep starved eyes so that she could focus better, who should it be, none other than the man that was the start of all her little mishaps. "Oh, it's you", she said and turned away, crossing her arms in front of her and staring straight ahead trying to ignore him, which he was making it impossible to do as he continued on in that seductive voice of his and as much as she had the "hump" with him she found herself being tempted by his words.

"That's nice, especially after I so kindly came to your assistance, come on let's bury the hatchet and have that drink" he coaxed, "I've noticed there are two spare seats behind me, there shouldn't be a problem us having them but only if you want to of course"

Jay gave it a few moments thought as she didn't want to give the impression of being too eager to escape the confines of her seat, which now seemed to be even more restricting as Mr Blobby and his rolls of fat were invading her space even more and she thought that eventually she would be swallowed up in his armpit, never to be seen again.

"You look a little lost for space here," he said nodding towards the Bulk.

"How observant of you", she replied a touch of irony in her voice.

"Come on now, you have nothing to lose by being nice," this handsome man cajoled.

"Ok, if you insist" It would be a relief to get away from the flatulence factory and the risk of being obliterated.

Collecting her belongings she rose from her seat and could have sworn there was a slurping noise as if caused by suction, like that of a rubber sink plunger, as she extricated herself from the confining space. He stood back to allow her to get out, at the same time waving his arm back and giving an exaggerated bow." This way madam, your carriage awaits"

In return for his mimicry, she deliberately stepped on one of the highly polished black brogues. "I'm so sorry" giving him a brief mocking grin that turned her nose up slightly, making her look like a naughty, spoilt teenager.

"Yes, I bet you are, come on you little devil, move it", and although he wanted to slap her cute little backside, this time he would let her get away with it.

They went four rows back to the spare seats; in fact all three seats by the window were empty, which was even better. "This is so much more comfortable, do you think we can have them for the duration?" she asked him with hope in her voice.

"I can see no problem with that, nobody has been sitting here since the plane took off", in saying this he waved to a passing stewardess. "Excuse me miss."

"Yes Sir"?

He gave her a winning smile that would have melted the heart of even the meanest old grandmother. "Would it be ok Honey, if we had these seats for the rest of our journey, only this lady is finding it very uncomfortable next to that gentleman down there. I don't want to get too personal but I think you understand my drift and I'd very much like to sit next to her because, as you may of gathered from her little catastrophe earlier, she needs a bit of looking after".

The stewardess smiled a little too warmly at him and said that there would be no problem and if they needed any further assistance she would be pleased to help.

"Thanks, you are a gem, can you please get us a drink," turning to Jay he asked her what she would like.

"A vodka and tonic would be good."

"Make that two then, thank you."

"OK Sir, I will bring them to you in a few moments" and she went with a spring in her step feeling great that this handsome man had called her "Honey and a Gem".

"Well" he said, "Do you not think it is time we introduced ourselves, although I think I already know you pretty well, after all I have had your knickers draped over my face"!

"You just don't let up do you?" She asked, and not waiting for an answer introduced herself "My name is Jay and yours"?

"Steve, Steve Knight. Jay, yes, I like that"

"Yes, I was called after some bird my dad used to know"

"Ha, Ha, very funny"

She liked his name too, it suited him, dashing and strong that he was, but she wasn't about to tell him that! She was certainly attracted to him and now that she was in a calmer frame of mind she was able to appraise him a little better.

His hair was dark, almost black except for the greying at the temples giving him a distinguished look. Grey hair always seems to have an adverse effect on women; she was glad that hers hadn't yet succumbed to the inevitable. His floppy fringe fell to one side over nicely trimmed and well-shaped eyebrows, giving him a cheeky boyish look. His eyes were something else however, they were so blue, comparing them to a clear summers sky, azure blue, yes that's what they were and they twinkled enticingly when he smiled, the laughter lines at the corners only adding to his charm. A manly nose, straight and not too big, with none of those horrid hairs sticking out, that older men sometimes get. It could be referred to as a Roman nose, it roamed all over his face, no not really, but she couldn't help but jest to herself. His lips were full enough to be called generous but not effeminate and when he smiled his lop-sided grin, he revealed a perfect set of pearly white teeth. Extremely well tanned, either due to sessions on a sun bed or regular trips abroad. His physique, which she had fallen upon earlier in the day (the thought still bringing a blush to her cheek), was firm and as she had unwittingly found out, very well endowed!

Steve returned the scrutiny, having already established that Jay was a real looker. She was wearing casual clothes; a simple white t-shirt that clung to the curves of her ample breasts, the outline of the dark areola surrounding her slightly protruding nipples could just about be discerned. The t-shirt was fairly low cut but in a tasteful way revealing the start of what, he could imagine, was a captivating cleavage. Her tight pale blue jeans clung to her flat stomach and slim legs; he had already noticed that she had a gorgeous tight little backside. There was nothing pretentious about her at all; totally unaware of the affect she had on the male species.

Earlier he had observed the admiring looks and attention that she had been receiving from the men, however not from the women, whose jealousy could not be contained, evident by the none to gentle shoves the men received to make them get a move on. As one woman passed him he heard her say "Don't know what you were looking at, mine are much better", to which he replied, " I know love, but they were blinking at me as I passed", to which he got another shove.

Jay had small petite features in an oval face, large tawny brown eyes with specks of what looked like gold leaf glinting in them and the longest, thickest lashes he had ever seen. They were extremely unusual eyes and exceptionally beautiful. Her lips were full and temptingly kissable. Her dark brown curly hair tumbled unrestrained framing her face and down past her shoulders. Yes, Jay was a stunning woman and not for the first time that, this woman had caused him to have a stirring within his loins.

Chapter 7

The stewardess returned with the drinks trolley and poured their vodka and tonics into small plastic beakers. They lowered the trays attached to the back of the seats in front of them and taking the drinks thanked the stewardess and placed them on the trays.

"This is very pleasant," said Steve "It calls for a toast I believe" and he lifted his beaker in gesture.

Jay lifted the beaker; her hand was shaking. Why? Was it the animal magnetism that she felt between her and Steve or was it just her age? Age more than likely; she was forty-nine going on sixteen. His hand was as steady as a rock as he tipped his beaker towards hers.

"Here's to many more amazing rugby tackles that take my breath away"

"Here's to not making a fool of myself in public and having the p… taken out of me by the town jester – cheers" and she touched her beaker to his which sent, for some reason, a shiver down her body, her hand shook more and the tap unexpectedly turned into a bump, tipping the beaker sideways, sending rivulets of vodka and tonic down her white T-shirt.

"Damn" she cursed.

"Oh dear, here we go again" Steve thought, when he saw the result of the spilled liquid on her t-shirt. “Wonderful, quite wonderful.” The words, unexpectedly, spilling from his mouth. If he was unsure whether she was wearing a bra before he was now positive that she wasn’t, as her shirt was now semi-transparent over one breast, the nipple of which was now standing to attention, due to the ice cold drink. At this moment in time he wished he knew her better, as he was sorely tempted to take her nipple between his teeth and nibble it. She was temptation.

“What do you mean, wonderful”? “I’m blooming well soaked”, she said indignantly. As if a light had gone on in her head, she realised where his eyes had wandered and instantly clasped her hand over her boob when she saw the result of the spilt drink. “I don’t believe it, you are incorrigible”, Jay rebuked.

“I know, isn’t it great”? Steve was not flustered at having been caught out.

This time they both laughed.

“Would you like me to dry it for you” he said pulling a crisp white handkerchief from his pocket and, in an attempt to do so, leant forward, hanky poised.

“No thank you, I can manage quite well myself” she snatched the handkerchief from his hand and dabbed randomly at her t-shirt. “It will dry out in time, but I’ll put a blanket over me until it does, as I can’t stand seeing you with your tongue hanging out like that”!

Steve removed an airline blanket from under his seat and gently tucked it around her, touching her cheek gently in the process. Now it was his turn to shiver, even though it was only her cheek, the gesture seemed so intimate. How he would love to take this funny, beautiful woman in his arms, but for once he wasn't forward. He did not want to frighten her away, but he did want to get to know her a lot, lot better! "So what are you doing going to Mombassa on your own then?"

Jay explained to him that she was fed up with her humdrum life and needed to get away from it all. Steve couldn't understand why a beautiful woman such as her didn't have dozens of eager men beating her door down and he told her so. He wanted to know why she was on her own, Jay told him she was divorced, then a long term relationship ended twelve months ago and it had hit her hard, it was only that she felt able to start living her life again. Jay told him it was something she didn't want to dwell upon, her voice had started getting croaky and her eyes welling up, he didn't press the matter further. Instead he asked her about her family. "Do you have any family Jay, brothers, sisters"?

"Yes, I have two brothers, both older than me, there's George, who has always been a bit of an angel and then there's Paul who's totally different, but they are both great brothers in their own way. George is the eldest and is happily married to Sandra; they have two children. Paul is six years older than me and is married to Penny who is twenty years his junior and surprisingly their marriage is a success, they have two children and a child by his first marriage." "How about you"?

"I have a sister, she's younger than me by ten years, she's just going through her second divorce and usually turns up on my doorstep when the going gets rough. I don't mind, she's my kid sister and I'd do anything for her"

Turning the tables on Steve she asked him why a handsome man like him was travelling alone, she too would have thought he'd have dozens of women beating down his door. He told her that he had been through a messy divorce three years prior, running off with his best friend. His business involved a lot of travelling so it wasn't easy to hold down a relationship and yes, he did have a lot of women coming on to him but he liked to do the chasing those sort of women didn't appear to him and he wasn't the type of man that liked one-night stands. Steve told her that after the business he was currently conducting concluded he would be in London more often, he might then feel it's time for a woman in his life.

"So what type of business are you in Steve?" "If you don't mind my asking?"

"Well, I'm a bit of a trouble-shooter. I find vacant plots of land or property and advise my clients on whether to invest or how to best improve the sites, and if I think the prospects are good, sometimes investing myself. The land is mainly for hotels or holiday complexes; I'm currently setting up a new holiday resort with it's own game reserve, in Zimbabwe. It's almost concluded now, but it's hard work and takes up a lot of my time".

"Sounds very interesting, do you enjoy it?"

"Yes, very much so and, although I say it myself, am extremely good at it. What better occupation, exotic locations, exceedingly good remuneration plus I don't have any overheads".

"How wonderful to be able to do something that you enjoy, I wish I could say the same".

Steve asked what she did for a living to which she replied that she was just a PA, getting some job satisfaction as she took pride in her work, but always thought she could have done better. Steve told her that she mustn't say she was JUST a PA. He said that PA's were essential; he wouldn't be able to manage without one, they were the backbone of successful companies.

Steve could just imagine her sitting at her computer, her dark curls restrained in a tight chignon at the back of her head, perhaps wearing a smart navy suit with a white blouse opened at the neck revealing just a little of her cleavage, just enough to be alluring and definitely not tacky. She'd be wearing stockings of course, which would be neutral and barely discernable from her skin and, only when she crossed her legs to take notes in her role as PA, would the side split of her skirt part, seductively revealing the lacy top, and the soft white flesh above. With this vision in his mind he felt that now well-known twinge that just the thought of her conjured up. If he carried on with these thoughts he would be getting an erection, which could prove to be uncomfortable and hard to explain, as she would definitely not be able to miss it! He therefore went back to their conversation and asked her if her parents were still alive.

"Yes, just my mother, she's almost eighty-two now and still going strong, father sadly died fifteen years ago." How about yours?"

Speaking with tenderness and a distant look in his eye Steve spoke of his parents. "Mine both passed away a few years ago, it was very sad, my father was ninety, he was quite an active old chap and a bit of a wag, still one for giving the ladies the eye and being flirtatious, however he loved my mother to bits and she him. They had been together for well over sixty years, and then he died suddenly of a heart attack. My mother, bless her, was eighty-nine and she adored him so much that she did not have the will to live anymore; she just pined away, dying six months later and is now where she wanted to be, with the old fellar. If I find someone and only half as in love as they were, then I will die a happy man".

"That is sad, but also wonderful in it's own way, I bet they had some tales to tell, if only we knew what it took to be so in love and happy".

"Well Jay, they told me that sometimes they had to work hard at it but trust was the mainstay, if you don't have trust you may as well call it a day".

"I couldn't agree with you more". "What are you going to be doing in Mombassa?

"I'm just going to finalise a deal on a holiday complex, there's not much to do as the property is already up to a four star rating, really just expanding it and adding more facilities, then hopefully my time will be my own, so if you are at a loose end one day, perhaps you would like to spend some time together?".

"That would be nice, yes I would like that", thinking that's a turn up for the books, all she was going to do was sit by the pool, drink, eat and soak up the sun, now she had more than that to look forward to. He asked her to write down where she was staying. Jay said she needed to get her bag so that she could find a pen and paper. Steve insisted he do it as he said he didn't think she wanted a reoccurrence of her panties falling out again. Her face went pink at his comment, this man was not going to let her forget anything that had happened, but now she didn't really mind, she was getting used to his humour and she loved being in his company, yes he was definitely a bit of alright.

He retrieved her bag and she delved into the black abyss and without a hitch found a biro, tore a piece of paper off the airline magazine in front of her and wrote down where she was staying and handed it over to him.

"The Sandy Beach Resort" he read aloud "Good, you've written the telephone number down, I will ring you once I have got settled and will either pick you up personally or send a cab for you, is that ok?"

"That's fine, I will look forward to it."

Carrying on with the conversation Jay told him about two her children, Rachel twenty-four was now living with her boyfriend in Brixton, much to Jay's disappointment, having moved to Surrey to get away from London so as to give them a better environment to grow up in, only for her daughter to return to a town full of drugs and crime. Richard, her son was almost twenty-two and was upping sticks too, deciding on the spur of the moment to go back-packing around Australia, she'd really miss him, however her children had their own life's to lead, leaving her to get on with hers.

Jay asked Steve if he had any children, he said he didn't as his wife was a career woman so they didn't come into the equation, maybe if they had a child they may still be together, he said he would have loved to have had a son or a daughter but that was life.

As they got to know each other more they realised they had a lot in common, they liked travelling, good food, wine, theatre and shared the same taste in music. They were deep in conversation when a stewardess broke into their conversation. "Excuse me, would you like the chicken or the fish?"

They both decided upon the chicken. Jay thought the fish smelt foul (unusual because the chicken should have smelt fowl, but that's airline food for you she mused). They took the trays of food from the stewardess putting them on the drop down tables, there was never enough room to open up all the food provided, trying to organise it without spilling or dropping anything was difficult so Jay took her time not wanting to do anything that would give him cause to embarrass her again. Both had orange juice, placing it in the little round indent in the table; how this was supposed to stop the contents spilling Jay didn't know. Why didn't they do beakers, like babies had, ones that you could suck the contents out of and no matter how much they fell about the liquid inside did not come out? She supposed that would be too much like common sense!

Like a choreographed performance they undid

the roll from the cling film and the butter from its foil wrapper, they both tore the roll in half, picked up the white plastic knife and lanced the butter. Turning to each other with the knob of butter on the knife they simultaneously said. "This butter is hard"?

If they had looked the same it would have been like a mirror image, they fell about laughing, it seemed so funny to them, and those passengers that could, stared at them as though they were mad, but they didn't care, in fact it made them laugh more, causing a few tut-tuts to be heard. Stuff them; thought Jay we are enjoying ourselves. They ate what they could of the unappetizing meal, the only really edible thing being the roll and butter. They drank the orange juice and declined the offer of tea or coffee. Now all they had to do was wait for the stewardess to come back and remove the remains, which seemed an interminable amount of time, especially as she now wanted to get up and go for a pee.

Finally, relieved of their trays, she could excuse herself. Steve stood up to allow her to pass, at the same time admiring her little tight backside as she wiggled along the aisle. He sat down quickly and wrung his hands together, he had the overwhelming urge to take off after her and squeeze those cheeks until she squealed, but this was not the time or the place – unfortunately!

Chapter 8

Jay stood in the queue there were two people in front of her, she was now desperate to relieve herself and impatient to get back to her seat and the scintillating company she was so lucky to have found. She now felt as though she had known Steve a long time as they had covered each other's history in a matter of hours. So far there didn't appear to be any dark side to him and hoped there wasn't going to be anything lurking in the closet that would burst the bubble. What the hell was keeping the people occupying the loos, they had been in there an age, hurry up before I wet myself, she thought. Both toilets became vacant at the same time and were quickly occupied by the next in line. Not long now, then it's my turn, she hoped they didn't smell, she couldn't stand that. At last, a greasy lank-haired man emerged, pressing against her as he made his way past and back towards his seat, not a pleasant experience! She fumbled with folding doors; it took several attempts before she could fathom out how they unfolded, then when she did, almost trapped her fingers as the door sprang in causing her to stumble through into the toilet. She shut the door behind her and pushed the lock to. Fortunately there was no smell but the dirty sod had peed on the rim and all over the floor and as the space was so confined it was difficult not to step in it. Why is it that some men have an aversion to using toilet paper? Jay thought and answering she with that wicked humour sense of humour - Could it be that God had made them such perfect arses!

However she needed to go and go she must. She unravelled some toilet paper and hurriedly, but tentatively wiped the rim. Even though it was now dry, she could not bring herself to sit down, so quickly undid the zip on her jeans pulling them down at the same time as the small thong that she was wearing. (Thongs had taken a bit of getting used to initially as they felt like they were going to cut her in half, however Jay found they were essential if she was wearing tight clothes and didn't want a visible panty line "VPL" as advised by her daughter Rachel). She perched precariously above the toilet, her jeans wrapped around her knees restricting movement, having to steady herself by placing her hands on her thighs, similar to the stance of a Sumo wrestler, then squatting over the pan she emptied her bladder with a sigh of relief. She hadn't thought she had drunk so much; she could have been urinating to get into the Guinness Book of Records. She likened herself to a pig she once saw at a Farm, it peed what seemed like gallons, a never ending stream that cascaded down the incline that it was standing upon, creating a large pool of steaming froth at the bottom, although not a steaming froth she felt the amount could not have been far off what that pig had done! She wiped herself dry with some tissue, pulled her pants and trousers up, zipped and then pulled the chain. The noise was phenomenal as it sucked away the waste, if had been any stronger; she felt it might have pulled her in as well! She washed her hands thoroughly, dried them and getting another piece of tissue, placed it over the latch and opened it (this is something she always did as there were so many people that didn't wash their hands, especially men who had held themselves and in turn peed all over them, she didn't think this action of hers was quirky, just a matter of cleanliness).

She exited the cubicle, without any further complications with the door and made her way back to her seat. Steve stood up, gently cradling her elbow as he guided her back to her seat. He did not pass comment on how long she had been, so he was a gentleman and he could also be tactful if he so wished!

The in-flight video was just about to commence seeing as they were in quiet mode, they both donned the earphones and tuned in to listen to HARRY POTTER AND THE PHILOSOPHER'S STONE. The silence between them was comfortable, even if there had not been a film to occupy them; they had the feeling that it would still have been ok. Jay was tired, she hadn't really had much sleep and it was now almost one a.m. GMT. Her lids were heavy and she drifted off even the sound of the video didn't keep her awake. From the corner of his eye Steve saw Jay's head nod forward and knew she had fallen asleep; he removed his headphones and turned to look at her. He didn't want to wake her, so he gently put a finger under her chin and tipped her head back slowly into an upright position, removing her headphones at the same time. Jay's head lolled to one side and with the dexterity of a surgeon he cupped his hand around it to stop it from jerking and waking her and then rested it back carefully onto the seat, she emitted a peaceful little sigh but did not wake. Steve leant forward in his seat, turning his body so he was now able to look at her in more depth. Her dark curls tumbled around her now peaceful looking face, a ringlet had fallen across her eye and although she was asleep it still made her eyelid flutter, he brushed it away, such soft, shiny curls. His resistance was waning, so he leant forward as much as he dared and breathed in the fragrance of almonds and orange blossom, the scent of her hair was working like an aphrodisiac on him and again he felt the enthusiasm stirring in his loins. What on earth was going on, his mind was asking him, a man in his fifties should have mastered more control! Her full red lips were pouting as if reaching out to be kissed, oh how he longed to do so, but he was going to be patient, he was sure the time would come soon. She looked so young and vulnerable and he found it hard to believe that her children were in their twenties; she must have married early in life.

The ache in his trousers had eventually subsided only to be replaced by the feeling that he wanted to protect her. Jay, yes, she was like a little bird and he did not want her to fly away, he felt such warmth for this tiny little woman a feeling he had thought he would never experience again! Now that he had relaxed Steve too was feeling the affects of the journey, reluctantly he reclined back into his seat but before he closed his eyes, he once again cupped Jay's head and positioned it gently onto his shoulder, he leant into her and positioned his head on top of hers, it was the only other intimate thing he dared do at this stage. He fell asleep with the fragrance and warmth of her hair caressing his senses.

Chapter 9

Jay stirred to the sound of bottles rattling against a trolley.

For a few moments she wondered where she was, she felt something heavy on top of her head and opened her eyes slowly. As her sight gradually restored and she was able to focus, she remembered that she was on the plane and that Steve was beside her. Her head having somehow found it's way onto his shoulder. The heaviness she was feeling was Steve's head pressing down upon hers. The pleasure she felt at this realisation was insurmountable. Jay did not want to break the spell, she was cocooned in the depth of luxurious warmth and hated to have to disturb this moment. However, her neck was seizing up due to being in the same position for too long. Jay knew she had to move which would eventually wake Steve up too; she hoped he wasn't one of those people that got grumpy when woken unexpectedly.

Hesitantly removing her hands from under the blanket that Steve had placed over her earlier, she looked at one hand and then the other a little surprised for there was definitely another hand upon her thigh and it definitely wasn't hers. Cheeky beggar, she thought, but she wasn't upset by the discovery!

Jay tentatively nudged Steve in the ribs with her

elbow, “Steve” she whispered “Steve, would you like a drink?”

“Err, what?” He replied somewhat sleepily.

“Steve, they are coming around with the drinks now and my neck is a bit stiff, I need to move”, she said squeezing his leg gently.

Steve sat up abruptly; at the same time removing his hand from her thigh. Shame, thought Jay. He looked towards Jay who was now rubbing the back of her neck.

“Sorry honey, how long have you been awake?”

“Only just, that’s the first time I’ve slept well on a plane, must be the company I’m keeping”, Jay said, pleased that he wasn’t grumpy.

“What do you mean?” he said defensively “Am I that boring?”

“No, I didn’t mean that silly”, she didn’t want to tell him exactly what she meant, she wasn’t going to give too much of what she was feeling away, she was having difficulty keeping her feet on the ground as it was. She couldn’t bear to get hurt again and was worried that in such a short period of time she already felt a little more than friendship towards Steve, so before she gave too much away she quickly changed the subject. Neither seemed embarrassed by the closeness that they had experienced together during those few hours of sleep, it had just seemed like a natural progression of the things to come.

Nature was now calling Steve, so he excused himself, asking her to order him a V & T if the stewardess arrived before his return, standing up he then made his way to the toilet. Now it was her turn to look at him as he sauntered along. He was very smart, taking care with the way he dressed, noting the expensive Versace designer jeans that still looked well pressed, even though they had been slept in and clinging very agreeably indeed, outlining the curvature of his well-rounded, muscular buttocks. Mmmm, unexpected lewd thoughts were going through her mind. She wished she knew him better. She would have loved to have accompanied him into the loo and pressing her body into his, wrap her arms around him, grasp his ample tool and guide it whilst he peed. She wondered if he would like that sort of thing or was she just depraved! Steve returned and sat down beside her.

"You were quick", wishing she could say something amusing like "Hope you shook it well" but refrained, he may not appreciate her sometimes coarse sense of humour. It was easy to spot the men that didn't shake it well enough, they would emerge from the loos, totally oblivious to the fact that their trousers were like blotting paper and that the excess urine was slowly spreading across their crutch, which would eventually end up looking like a map of Asia!

"There wasn't a queue", he explained.

You may have a dick the size of a donkey but you obviously don't have a bladder the size of pig, she reflected, her lips curling at the corners in amusement.

"What are you grinning at?" Steve wanted to know.

"Nothing" she lied "I'm just happy at the thought of sunning myself by the pool".

"Oh", he sounded a little disappointed that she could not share her thoughts with him, but he recovered well. When the stewardess arrived with the drinks trolley he ordered them both a V & T and as he took them from her he said. "Thanks honey you are a star."

The stewardess gave him a cheesy smile and Jay was sure that if Jay hadn't of been there next to Steve, she would more than likely have tried her luck and made a more noticeable pass at him! Instead all she said, with that stupid grin on her face was, "My pleasure sir".

"My pleasure sir." Mimicked Jay in a whiney voice and pulling a face.

"Now, that's not nice" Steve said, "You're not jealous are you?"

"No. Why on earth should I be jealous?" she replied a little to sharply, as there was indeed a little pang because he was addressing someone else as honey and not her. Why shouldn't he (logic coming to the rescue), he was a free agent after all said and done?

Steve was perceptive of the change in her attitude and knew, somewhat gratifyingly, that his comments to the stewardess had bugged her, as Jay had now turned towards the window, shoulders' hunched making out she was looking at the sights below. He could imagine the expression on her face and that she would be looking a little bit miffed.

"Come on sweetness" he said cajoling her "Let's have these drinks and make a toast to you having a wonderful holiday and my sharing most of it with you"

If Jay had been a dog her little ears would have stood to attention, wondering if she had heard him right. Sharing most of my holiday? She mulled the idea over. Fantastic, bloody, bloody, fantastic, her thoughts were running away with her and she was absolutely delighted with the possibilities. Turning back towards Steve she picked up her drink, this time being extremely careful not to spill any and touched his beaker with hers. "To a great holiday" they said as one.

The final hour of the journey came all too quickly for Jay as she didn't want to leave Steve's company; she wished the flight was another eight hours, but that was not possible, knowing full well that she would eventually have to say goodbye to him at the airport and then go their separate ways with, of course, the possibility that she would not see him again, she sincerely hoped that was not going to be the case and that he was really genuine.

The seat belt light came on and a very crisp, hoity-toity voice spoke out:

"Good afternoon ladies and gentlemen, this is your Captain speaking. On behalf of my crew and myself we hope you have all had an enjoyable flight with Monarch airlines. We will shortly be arriving at Mombassa Airport. Please be advised that the temperature outside is 32 Degrees Celsius, 93 Degrees Fahrenheit, the humidity is at 58%.

"Some warmth at last", Steve said rubbing his hands together.

"Yes, the heat is going to hit us when we get off the plane. Won't it be wonderful?"

The Captain continued his speech. "You should

now adjust your watches, Mombassa is four hours ahead of GMT time. The time now, therefore, is eleven a.m. There is still at least six hours of sunshine to soak up, make sure you use plenty of protection, as the sun is intense. We will be landing in approximately ten minutes, ensure that your seats are in an upright position and seatbelts are fastened. We wish you a very enjoyable stay and look forward to welcoming you on board a Monarch Airline again, thank you."

Chapter 10

The landing was as smooth as it could possibly be and everyone was rushing to get their bags and belongings out of the luggage compartments. Why were people rushing? They won't get to their destinations any faster; everyone had to go through Customs and collect their luggage, Jay thought, personally she wasn't in any hurry and was pleased to see that Steve wasn't making any move to join the mêlée, it was pleasing to note that he had patience as well as charm! Jay didn't want to get up and rush off, wanting to stay as long as she could and in as close proximity to Steve as she could. She had the feeling that Steve had the same thoughts thought.

The inevitable had to happen though, soon they were collecting their things and fortunately her bag was sitting on the spare seat so they didn't have to struggle for that thank goodness. Steve took hold of her bag like the gentleman that he was and continued carrying it as they made their way along the aisle towards the exit.

"Goodbye and thank you" said Steve to the stewardesses as he went forth into the belting heat and glorious sunshine"

"Have a good time", said the girl with the cheesy smile.

Jay gave Miss "Cheesy Smile" a steely stare and

ignored Miss "Honey you are a Gem" and quickly took up position next to Steve, as if to say this man belongs to me, and descended the stairway by his side.

The heat was stifling after the coolness of the airplane, there was not a flicker of a breeze and Jay could feel the perspiration accumulating immediately between her cleavage; her hair was getting damp too, wishing that she had put shorts on instead of jeans. Those passengers that had worn them from the start of the journey were not as silly as she had first thought. Steve on the other hand didn't look as though he was feeling the heat at all, even though he was dressed in jeans and a jumper (albeit a cotton one), but then he was more used to these climates; she hoped she didn't look dreadful. Steve certainly didn't think so, on the contrary the beads of perspiration had made her hair curl even more, clinging to her forehead in a squiggly fashion like someone had doodled absent-mindedly with a thick magic marker. Her t-shirt was becoming translucent between her breasts; he surreptitiously hoped that she would get a lot hotter, the moistness from her body making the whole t-shirt see-through. He could but wish!

They boarded the airport bus, cram-packed like sardines with no air-conditioning. So many smelly, dirty bodies, she hoped for Christ's sake she didn't pong, it was a concern as she was now sweating buckets. She decided against reaching up to the hanging strap above her head, as a recent deodorant advertisement sprang to mind. Everyone was dancing, waving his or her arms high in the air except for one girl, who hadn't used the correct deodorant. This unfortunate girl obviously had sweat marks on her dress and was dancing with her arms plastered, from the elbow up, to her sides and was only waving her hands about in a circular motion in time to the music, looking a bit of a tit. Jay did not want the embarrassment of letting Steve see her sweaty armpits so she took the much more enjoyable way out and clung on to the black leather belt that was around Steve's waist, he did not object!

They alighted at the terminal, joining the queue for Customs; it was taking ages. Why was it that no matter where she queued, whether it be Tesco's or the Post Office, she always managed to get in the queue that took the longest, even after she had made what she thought was a smart decision by moving to a shorter queue, the one she was originally in would miraculously gather momentum and disperse, leaving her still queuing, sod's law! This was the same scenario, but unlike at Tesco's etc., she was in no hurry and she found that for once in her life patience came easily to her.

Steve, looked down at Jay – "Oh, by the way, little bird I have something of yours"

"And what may I ask is that?"

He took on the stance of David Copperfield, waving his hands back and forth over each other as though he was conjuring up some mystical happening. "Abracadabra, do not fear. What do we have behind this ladies ear?" Putting his hand to the back of Jay's ear, just as dexterously as any magician pulled something from behind. "Voila!"

he grinned mischievously.

"Bloody hell" said Jay, snatching the missing tampon from his grasp and depositing it safely in her bag. "I wondered where that had gone, I'm never going to live that incident down am I?"

"No, I don't think so, it will be a story to bandy about at the Rugby Club." He said teasing her.

"You git." Affectionately landing a gentle punch on his arm.

After passing through Customs without any hitch they collected their luggage, thankfully all in one piece. Steve found a trolley, placing both their suitcases on it. Jay noticing that Steve's was an immaculate burgundy colour, possibly crocodile skin. She was a little ashamed of the drab, old battered canvas hand me down suitcase that her mother had given her. Steve made no inference to the state of it and treated it as though it contained precious china, lifting it with ease to it's resting place.

They made their way outside and stood for a while watching, as they, along with several other travellers, were greeted by the locals in their national costumes, some adorned with magnificent headdresses, their faces painted in an array of colours, lifting their legs up almost to their chins and flaying their arms about in rhythm to the drumming of bongos, the hollow echo of a steel band. There was also singing from the native girls, it was a spectacular sight and made her feel that she was really going to get into the swing of this holiday when, all of a sudden, one of the native dancers sprang out at her. He waved his arms frantically, lifting his legs and jumping high in a frightening display, yelling something indecipherable at her. She sprang back in surprise and fell against Steve who immediately wrapped his arms protectively about her tiny frame.

"Well, hello my frightened little bird" she clung onto him and he could feel her heart pounding beneath her bosom which she unknowingly pressed into his abdomen. "I'd be enjoying this, if it wasn't for the fact that you are once again standing on my shoes!"

She reluctantly drew away from him, looking down at his now, dust covered black brogues, no longer shiny and looking out of place on this immaculately clad man. "Sorry Steve, but he made me jump, it was so unexpected"

Once again they ended up in fits of laughter, if this was the enjoyment she could expect with him, she could barely wait for him to join her, if indeed he did.

Jay now had to find the Rep for the Travel Company, with whom she had organized her trip. Steve, gentleman that he was, pushed the trolley alongside her and assisted with her search until they eventually located the Rep, standing alongside several others and holding her Agents holiday board. The Rep welcomed her, checked her itinerary and pointed her in the direction of where the coach was waiting to transport her. Steve stayed with her until they reached the coach, lifting her suitcase with ease from the trolley and putting in the compartment at the side of the coach. The Porter standing by, looking dismayed and very disappointed when Steve did not tip him. Even though he hadn't done any portering for them, he had the audacity to think he still deserved one. Life is tough ain't it!! She thought.

"Well, this is it then", she said sadly.

"Yes, I will contact you as soon as I can", he promised.

"I'll look forward to it."

Steve bent down and pecked her formally on one cheek and then the other, she was a little disappointed to say the least and unbeknown to her so was Steve, for some reason known only to himself he had once again refrained from holding her and kissing her as he really wanted to.

Jay boarded the small eight-seater coach, took a seat at the rear and looked out the dusty window but Steve was nowhere to be seen. The remaining seats were occupied almost immediately and before she knew it the coach was speeding away, leaving a cloud of red dust in its wake. She once again, looked out the window in the hope of seeing him, wishing that the cloud of dust that was obliterating her view would disappear. Then just as her hopes were fading, the dust started to diminish, like a curtain being drawn down it found it's way to the ground where it belonged, revealing Steve in blurred magnificence, waving to her, putting his fingers to his lips blowing a kiss to her. She waved back elated, tears of happiness seeping from her eyes. He waited, he bloody well waited, God bless his little cotton socks, she thought the feeling of warmth flooding through her veins; perhaps he really did care. All she could do now was wait for him to contact her!

Chapter 11

Jay watched until she couldn't see Steve any longer, she turned and looked out the side window, a little disappointed was it because she felt as though her heart was like lead or because the view was not that spectacular? Being a third world country, the roads were rough and bumpy, litter was scattered and rubbish piled high; a banquet for the many dogs that were delving into the mounds. She imagined that rodents of all shapes and sizes would be rife making the stockpiles of waste heave at night. The locals however seemed unaware of the squalor and the smell it permeated, no wonder there is such a lot of disease when basic cleanliness was absent!

The ramshackle coach had no air-conditioning, seatbelts and virtually no seats, as every time they drove over a dip in the road Jays would wiggle loose, almost causing her to end up on the floor. They certainly didn't make them like this any more. Thank goodness! The heat inside the coach was stifling, the driver and his colleague certainly didn't mind sharing their body odour, it was awful, she pushed the sliding window open to get some air and although it was warm when it touched her face, it was still fresher than the air inside. Little pickaninnies almost naked, ran alongside, their faces white, streaked by the swirling dust. Some were lucky enough to have hand-me-down clothes, dresses that may have looked pretty once were either too big or too small, the colour or pattern having long faded with age and dust. Most didn't possess shoes or sandals and she wondered how on earth they managed to avoid cutting their feet to shreds on the unforgiving ground. Finding the sweet lollipops she had bought with her, having been pre-warned by a friend that the children here loved them, she proceeded to throw them out of the window, watching as many more children came out of the woodwork as if they had sonar that could detect the sweet fruity smell. Before long she had run out and watched with sunken heart at the little disappointed faces now vanishing into the distance.

Much to Jay's disconcertion a long-legged, flying insect was also drawn by the sweet smell of the lollipops even though the sweets had now disappeared. The buzzing of the insect around her head was insistent, no matter how much she waved her hands about trying to make it exit through the window, it would not oblige. Probably convinced that she still had some secreted about her person. Even though she was worried she may get stung, she carried on flapping her arms about in this futile way, the more she flapped the more the insect buzzed, circling her head, taunting her. It finally came to land on her knee, obviously showing a bit of bravado. Ok you little bugger, she thought, slowly lifting her hand so as not to disturb it, then with the speed of a First Dan karate expert, she bought her hand down, not caring that it would be splattered on her pale blue jeans, a resounding slap rang out and all heads turned to look at her with questioning looks upon their faces.

"Blasted wasp or something." She explained, rubbing her now smarting leg and wiping the gunge from her hand with a tissue, glad that she wasn't a Hindu having to put up with crap from creepy crawlies!!

They drove past several villas and hotels, which all looked sad and badly maintained, the white-washed walls, now greying, the chipped plaster baring the burnished mortar and what were once beautiful gardens, now brown and dry with neglect possessing little or no flowers. Her heart sunk wondering which one was to be her home for the next week. However, she needn't of worried as ten minutes further on they down a tree lined road, the pungency of the pretty pink and white flowers adorning the walls either side were refreshing and a joy to behold, the road eventually led to the reception of the Sunset Beach Hotel where they were welcomed warmly and handed a whole coconut, complete with straw to suck up the strange tasting milk within and moist napkins to refresh their hands and face. A very nice welcome Jay thought, perhaps it wasn't going to be so bad after all.

After check-in she was led by a chubby, wide-eyed Barry White look-alike, who couldn't help looking at her and smiling, showing off his white, but uneven teeth, what a happy chap, she thought and found the smiling contagious, so they both walked with large smiles on their faces through well-tended gardens with several paths that led off to other buildings. They took the path immediately on the right leading to a double storey white building, each floor having a balcony facing out onto the gardens. Her room was up one flight of stone stairs with fairly basic décor, single bulbs hanging from the ceiling and the odd picture hanging from the walls. Jay was reassured that at least her building was located close to the reception area, although she wouldn't admit it to anyone, she was a little nervous of sleeping on her own in a strange country, having listened to too much scare mongering, especially from her son Richard, who said that being a woman on her own, she could probably end up getting beaten, raped or worse, she could even return home in a black body bag. Such a sweet boy!

The porter opened the door, taking her suitcase inside; there was no need for him to show her around, as there was only a bedroom and a bathroom. She tipped him generously and he showed his pleasure by giving her yet another grin, she would not have been surprised if he had danced away singing a chorus of "You're my everything", but instead he said in broken English "You enjoy stay, I help you next you need" then went on his way chuckling. He was obviously delighted with his tip! Jay closed the door behind him, but before she unpacked she was desperate for the loo only having had one visit on the plane, that one experience had been enough to put her off going again during the flight.

Entering the bathroom cautiously she checked to see if there were any spiders or other such creepy crawlies wandering across the floor, she'd hate to get stuck in the toilet because she were cornered by a tarantula, or similar nasty, shuddering at the thought; she hated spiders! The bathroom was basic, but clean, hurriedly relieving herself she reached for the toilet paper but found sandpaper instead, well perhaps a bit exaggerated, it certainly wasn't what the Andrex puppy liked unravelling. It reminded her of infant school in 1957 where this type of paper was used. If you needed some a request had to be made to a teacher who would ask if you were going to wee or "big ones", if you were going to wee you didn't need paper but if you were doing "big ones then you would be allocated no more two sheets, not very helpful if you happened to have the trots. Although this paper was not much good for wiping a bum it was very good used as tracing paper or for wrapping around a comb to make a tune by blowing through it. What Jay also remembered was that they used to rub it together to try and soften it before use, so this is what she did, but it wasn't too successful, having no choice at this moment in time she tried to wipe herself with the now crinkled paper but the excess drips instead of being absorbed rolled off the paper onto her hand.

"Yuk!" – "Bloody rotten paper" she blurted out with irritation, "Will have to use the tissues I bought until I can find some decent stuff".

Jay washed her hands using soap that smelt like candle wax, it was hard and didn't lather (again reminding her of school days), it would have to do until she unpacked her M& S toiletries when she had a shower. She dried her hands on the white hotel towel that was remarkably soft, which was a pleasant surprise, wondering how many people had opted to wipe their backsides on them, giving the toilet paper a wide berth. With that thought in mind she decided she would not use them for drying her face from now on!

Sauntering into the bedroom, where a massive double bed took up most of the room, pity she would be the only one in it. A mosquito net draped back, tied with white ribbon to either side, flower petals were scattered over the cream bedspread and the overhead fan was whirring away. It was pleasing to know that some thought had been given to her comfort before her arrival. There were two bedside cabinets each side of the bed, a large window, complete with mosquito guard, almost the full expanse of one side of the room, this looked out onto the balcony. Turning around was a double fitted light oak wardrobe as well as a long dressing table with mirror, which she walked over to and looked in.

"Aaargh"!!

No wonder she was getting strange looks and that porter couldn't stop laughing, where she had wiped her face with the moist napkin earlier, there were thick red streaks running from her eyes down to her chin. The native warriors would have been proud to have such a display on their faces. That's what you get for driving along the roads in Kenya with the windows open, no wonder she was the only one fool enough to do it, she always learnt the hard way!

Taking off her sweaty, dust-ridden clothes, dropping them in an untidy pile on to the floor; thinking that she'd pick them up later, went into the bathroom, again checking the floor and also the bath for spiders, putting the plug into the bath, just in case one decided to rear it's ugly head from it, turned the shower situated in the bath on and stepped in. "Fucking hell," swearing with the shock. The water was freezing, how could such a hot country have such freezing water! She was in it now, so decided to put up with it for the sake of cleanliness. She shampooed her hair quickly and lathered her slim body, the water turning a reddish brown as the dirt from the day's journey was washed away. When she had almost finished her ablutions and was about to get out of the bath the water started to get warmer. Supposing that with all the hours of sunshine that Kenya is graced with, it must be solar powered and made a note to let it run for at least five minutes the next time.

Wrapping a small white towel around her mass of unruly wet curls then a bath towel around her glistening body, made her way back to the bedroom where she flopped on the bed, leaving a trail of wet footprints on the terracotta tiles. She was now warming up again as the coolness of the shower was wearing off and the oppressive heat was taking over. She removed her towel and lay back naked on the bed, enjoying the caress of the warm air from the fan as it licked her body dry. She pondered for a few moments wondering what Steve would be doing now, wishing that he were here with her. "Well, mustn't lay here too long otherwise

I will fall asleep, need to get down to the pool and make the most of the sunshine," jumping up she went and undid her suitcase pulling out her clothes, putting some away in the wardrobe until she finally located her little black and red bikini, which she donned, subsequently wrapping a long black sarong around her waist she grabbed a towel, suntan oil and made off to find the pool.

Chapter 12

Following the path back towards Reception Jay asked where the pool was located and made off in the direction indicated. Entering the large bar and entertainment area she saw many soft comfortable seats and sofas lining both sides of the dance floor, there were no walls, just large oak beams which supported the enormous thatched roof. The bar was circular; drinks were being dispensed to several guests by the ebony beauties that were working within. Laughter and idle chit chat was being bandied about and several guests welcomed her with a friendly, "Hello, how you doing"?

Since it was an "all inclusive holiday" the drinks were free, so she decided to make the most of the opportunity and ordered a dark rum and coke, fancying a change from vodka & tonic, rum was her usual tipple at home, it got her merry without giving her a hangover the following morning. The rum and coke was dispensed quickly by one of the bar girls and once again Jay enquired of her the location of the pool and was told that it was just the other side of the dance floor, through the archway, she couldn't miss it. One man, who looked to be in his forties, followed her progress admiringly, as she pattered off through the dance area, ultimately to reach the swimming pool.

The pool was glorious, looked extremely clean,

there were sun beds strategically placed around it, large palm trees were towering into the sky with a few smaller trees were situated nearer the beds. There was an open-aired restaurant to one side where several people were having coffee, other than that the area was quite deserted, with only two or three of the many sun beds being occupied. Jay found an ideal position right next the pool, with the branches of one of the smaller trees hanging over, which would hopefully shade her from the heat of the direct sunlight, ideal as she didn't want to get burnt on the first day. Placing her drink beside her designated spot, claiming her right to the sun bed by laying her towel over it, slightly surprised by the obvious lack of Germans, took off her sarong and made her way to the pools edge where she lowered herself into the water, which had been warmed by several hours of sunshine and felt wonderful. Showing her skill off as an able swimmer she swam several lengths, barely causing any disturbance to the even surface as her arms and legs went above and below the clear warm water. The short swim was enough to kick off with as the procurement of a tan was on the main agenda for the remainder of the day, Jay therefore got out of the pool went to the sun bed and made herself comfortable at the same time taking a few sips of her rum and coke, then laying back proceeded to luxuriate in the suns rays as they beat down upon her bare skin. Every so often she would return to the pool when she felt she was getting a little too hot, swim a couple of lengths, returning back to the sun bed for another toasting, turning herself like a chicken on a rotisserie, occasionally having a quick peek at her bikini line to check if the sun was having the desired effect only to be disappointed when there didn't seem to be any difference. During this relaxing period she went over the day's events, laughing quietly at how stupid she must of looked on several occasions throughout the day. Now she had a different perspective on the happenings she could see the funny side and would not have changed a thing, especially since she had met such a fantastic travelling companion. Never in her wildest dreams had she thought she would meet anyone quite like him and so soon. She wondered what he would be doing now and whether he was thinking about her. A tingle went through her body as she remembered their closeness on board the 747 and letting her hand slip to her thigh relived the incident when she awoke to find the warmth of his hand on it, looking forward to further episodes of a similar ilk or perhaps even better. She made a note to check at reception for any messages.

Three hours on, the sun was now slowly going down behind the thatched roof of the open-aired restaurant. Jay thought that she had better think about going back to her room to freshen up and change for dinner. Putting her sarong back on and running a brush through her tangled mass of unruly curls, she collected her bits and pieces and started to make her way back of course this took her to the bar where she decided she may as well stop and have another rum and coke. Several more people were now around the bar, she was a little apprehensive about joining the throng, in case they looked on her as intruding. She needn't of worried though, as on her approach she was welcomed warmly, amazed that they were mainly English guests. She remembered one man from her earlier visit to the bar, being the man in his forties, he had now been joined by another chap about ten years his junior, or so she imagined. They indicated that she should join them, making room for her between them, which she was happy to do as it meant she did not have to sit on her own. These two men were literally falling all over themselves to find out more about her.

"Hi, my names Dave" said the elder of the two.

"And I'm Chris, pleased to meet you," said the other, speaking over Dave in his eagerness to introduce himself.

She took each extended hand in turn, noting Dave had a strong hand shake but Chris' was weak and clammy, she didn't like that at all and discretely wiped her hand on the side of her sarong.

"I'm Jay, you been staying here long?"

"No, we arrived earlier today, got here about ten thirty, been at the bar ever since, can't miss out on all the free booze, you know" Dave offered in explanation.

"I arrived around eleven, flew from Gatwick, I didn't think there was an earlier flight" Jay said a query in her voice.

"We flew from Stanstead, maybe that's why," said Chris.

"That explains it then, did you two come together?"

"No, we've only just met, what about you then? Where's your old man?"

"I'm on my own", immediately she could have kicked herself for giving out this bit of information, as no sooner had she said it, they seemed to rouse themselves, plumping out their chests to perhaps show off their masculinity. Like a couple of rutting stags, battle had now commenced to win her attention, however they were not so magnificent, failing miserably in their attempts to impress, it was highly amusing.

Dave was not slow in coming forward and to get in before Steve did he immediately said,

"Dinner is at seven p.m., you don't want to be sitting on your own". Why don't you join me?"

His power of perception was accurate but it didn't necessarily mean she wanted to join him for dinner.

"I don't want to intrude, I'm quite boring company at the moment", she tried, hoping that she may be able to wriggle out of accepting the invitation, without being too obvious she didn't want to be with him.

"Nonsense, I insist?"

Chris thinking that he was being left out added: "Yes, you must join US" emphasizing the US "It would be our pleasure"

Dave looked a little miffed that he wasn't going to have her to himself, but had no option but to succumb, reiterated Chris's words.

Realising that she would not win she reluctantly agreed and they decided to meet at the bar at six forty-five for pre-dinner drinks, that's if Dave and

Chris were still capable standing after all the alcohol they had consumed!

She finished her drink and excused herself.

"Well, I had better go and get myself spruced up, I also need to finish my unpacking". Taking her leave with a "See you both later".

Jay stopped off at reception, enquiring of the receptionist whether there were any messages for her, only to feel her heart drop like a lead balloon when she was told there wasn't.

With a heavy heart that put a bit of damper on her day she made her way back to her room, at the same time chastising herself for being selfish as Steve was obviously a busy man with a lot of things to do. She should never have assumed that she would be given any priority in his life and then she would not have been disappointed.

Chapter 13

The relative cool of her room added to the empty, lonely feeling she had inside, how she would have loved to fall upon the bed with Steve in a frenzy of unbridled passion, but the feeling of foreboding was now upon her, beginning to think that maybe she had read too much into his attentiveness, possibly lady luck was going to evade her after all and the inevitable would happen, Steve would not be contacting her. It was all too good to be true and fairy stories with happy endings just did not happen, not to her anyway! She tried to shake herself out of the mood she was in, unwittingly speaking aloud. "Stop being so maudlin, he may still be ring, cheer up after all I have been invited to dinner. "A woman of my age should be grateful, going to dinner with a man on each arm, does it really matter that one looked like Barry Humphries' Les Patterson and the other Mick Jagger after a rough night?" " Yes, afraid it does". "You are so superficial Ms Patterson, how could you be so cruel?" she admonished herself, "Just be grateful that at least you will not be eating alone!" Becoming conscious that she was talking to herself out loud, she continued to unpack in silence, pottering about trying to decide what to wear; there was two hours to kill before meeting the dynamic duo, she had plenty of time.

Dusk was drawing in and the outside lights automatically lit up that drew Jay's attention to a window located high up on the wall that she hadn't noticed before, what she saw there made her emit one almighty screech, only to realise how ridiculous it was to scream as there was nobody to come to her aid. The reason for her response was that illuminated by the light dancing upon it, was a massive cobweb the size of a satellite dish and to her horror, smack bang in the middle was a humungous spider, it's black bloated body with long spindly legs busily knitting silvery threads around an unfortunate moth, that was frantically flapping it's wings in a fruitless attempt to escape. Inspecting from a safe distance to see if there was anyway that Cecil, (as she eventually came to call it for the duration of her stay) could get in and possibly scare the shit out of her again, fortunately, as far as she could determine, it didn't seem likely. In the event that it ever did manage to gain entrance she would need a bloody great Bazooka to blow it to kingdom come, as her size fours would not be big enough to splatter it! So logically thinking that as long as Cecil could be seen it meant that he wasn't inside, therefore she could rest easy. She most definitely would not be opening any windows on that side of the building that was for sure!

Eventually leaving Cecil to his dinner, which had now lost its struggle for life, Jay turned the shower on, put the plug in the bath letting the water run for a few minutes, checking that this time it was warm. Once satisfied that the water was an agreeable temperature she took off her damp swim wear, stepped into the bath, the steady stream of warm water greeting her and commenced lathering her body, enjoying the feel of the soapsuds as she smoothed them over the contours of her body. Jay closed her eyes, dreaming it was Steve's hands and not hers that were caressing her breasts, manipulating her nipples until the dark buds hardened in acknowledgement. She lost herself in a fantasy world, her hands stroking her neck, then her breasts, sliding temptingly slowly across her taut stomach, then across the top of the dark downy mound below, back to her ample breasts, pinching the nipples firmly between the imaginary fingers that were Steve's. She let out a little whimper of delight as the feeling akin to a mini orgasm journeyed down her body to between her legs. Her eyes now closed, she was with Steve, his name coursing from her lips "Steve, Oh Steve". She lathered her mound, sliding her fingers between her legs, finding the tiny hard bead of flesh located within the velvety folds surrounding it. Fingering it gently, enjoying the thrill it was instilling in her, she climaxed but at the same time needing more. "Fuck me Steve, Fuck me" now lost in her imaginary lovemaking, she slid her fingers down entering them inside the chasm of her being, working her fingers until she finally reached the pinnacle of her desire. Standing for a few seconds wallowing in the relief she had given her yearning body but even though it had been pleasurable she found she was still wanting, wanting for Steve's arms about her and the warmth of his naked body engulfing hers.

Returning from her reverie, her emotions once

more on a level footing, she finished cleansing herself, got out of the shower and went about the business of finding something to wear. Jay decided on her black and white checked pedal pushers and a lacy black blouse. She found a black bra, then the notorious French knickers, deciding against them, as she only wanted to wear them for Steve, if and when he decided to put in an appearance! She settled for a black thong laying them on the bed beside her other clothes. Sitting down at the dressing table to tie her hair up in a ponytail she noticed that she had actually caught the sun, she was turning a lovely golden brown, the day's sunning had been successful, which made her feel marginally better.

She looked at her watch, surprised that she only had fifteen minutes left to get down to the bar to meet Dave and Chris. If she hadn't of been so hungry she may have decided against it, however she was, so she dressed quickly, added a little pale lipstick to her lips, which enhanced her new tan, a little mascara and a touch of rouge on her cheeks. Looking in the mirror with a nod of approval and a "You will do", she headed out into the evening air and made her way to the bar. The incessant chorus of crickets, or other such nightlife resounded in her ears accompanying her along the dimly lit pathway towards the bar. Moths were desperately beating their wings against the lights trying to find access, the occasional frog would hop in front of her, croaking, causing her to stop in her tracks until it went on its bandy legged way. There was constant rustling in the foliage around her making her shiver, even though the air was still humid, the hairs on the back of her neck bristling at the dreaded thought that something revolting would land her on. After what seemed an age she eventually found her way towards the hubbub at the bar, the merry throng must have been knocking them back most of the day, amongst them was Dave who greeted her and guided her to the bar stool next to him.

"Good evening Jay, you are looking very fetching tonight"

"Thanks and you" being polite but dying to explode in a torrent of laughter.

What a plonker, he had obviously tried too hard to impress, irrespective of the hot climate, he had put on a navy suit, a tad shiny, that fitted like a second skin, it was also a little short in the leg, revealing black patent shoes that had seen better days. Why is it that some men kid themselves that they have remained the same size, as they were twenty years ago, even when it's obvious they need a shoehorn to get into their clothes! A crimson hanky in the breast pocket of his suit, matching crimson shirt with full ruffle, a large gold satin cummerbund and to complete his assemble a navy dickey bow, oh, and not to forget thick gold chain hanging around his neck complete with a Del Boy medallion, wow!!

He had slicked down his thinning ginger hair, now plastered to his head with some cream or such other concoction, giving it a dirty, greasy look, which would eventually block any pores, preventing excess heat escaping his scalp. She could imagine what his discomfit would be like as the evening progressed and couldn't help breaking into a grin.

"You look happy"

"Yes" said Jay "I am"

Dave was looking chuffed with himself, obviously thinking that his attempts at looking suave had its desired affect on her. He would have looked at home as a bingo caller or such like, but dashing he was not, oblivious to the fact that he was the butt of much of the laughter around them that evening. "I have taken the liberty of ordering you a cocktail", handing her a very tall glass filled with blood orange liquid with a red and white straw to suck up the contents.

"Thanks, how thoughtful", she took a sip and was pleasantly surprised by the fruity flavour, with just a hint of alcohol, it was extremely refreshing and before she knew she had emptied her glass and was ready for the next. Dave did not hesitate to replenish it. "Where's Chris, is he not coming?" Jay enquired.

"Oh, I expect he will be here in a mo' ", he replied with indifference.

However, no sooner had she enquired about his whereabouts then Chris appeared. "Hi there people, I'm gasping for a drink, haven't had one for at least twenty minutes". He said ordering himself one.

Dave was looking a bit put out by Chris' arrival, downing his drink swiftly he ordered another so as to avoid having to strike up conversation with him.

Chris was a complete contrast to Dave, he was wearing a lime-green t-shirt, a little sweaty under the armpits, emblazoned on the front in shiny black letters was “SEE REVERSE FOR INSTRUCTIONS”. His shirt hung loosely over navy and lime green striped Bermuda shorts, colour coordinated, so some thought had been given to his appearance, which tickled her sense of humour! His white, skinny legs protruding from below his shorts festooned in a mass of black hair which of course he would not have been complete without the cardinal sin of the dreaded short black socks and sandals. If he had knotted a hanky and put it on his mop of black hair, she would not have been surprised. He had obviously been squeezing his numerous spots, as they were looking very angry and red, some now forming tiny brown scabs where he had made them bleed, he was most probably an habitual nose picker too, she hoped that at no stage during the evening would she have the misfortune to have to touch his hands!

What an evening she was going to have, too such eligible bachelors vying for her favour, if her friends could see her now!!

“Nice to see you have made an effort”. Said Dave sarcastically to Chris.

“Well, one of us had to”. Retaliated Chris and turning to Jay

“But I can see we are both outshone by this radiant young lady here”

Give me strength, thought Jay as she thanked him for the compliment. This is going to be an evening I won’t forget in a hurry and secretly cursed Steve under her breath for not coming to her rescue. Jay noticed the sympathetic looks from the elderly couple opposite; they grimaced at her from behind their hands. She in turn mouthed, “Rescue me” and as they got up they made the point of walking behind her and whispering in her ear said. “We will, later me dear, good luck”, then they left her to her fate as they went to the restaurant. “Shall we get another drink and take it with us to dinner” Jay offered, trying to get it the dreaded meal over with as soon as possible.

“What an excellent idea”. Answered Dave.

“Yeah, I second that said Chris”. Leaning over the bar to see what was on offer, which gave Jay the opportunity to read the “so called instructions” on the reverse of his t-shirt.

1. “100% MALE, HANDLE WITH CARE”
2. “DO NOT PRESS, OR WRING”
3. “RUB GENTLY UP AND DOWN BY HAND”
4. “SIT ON IT AND SPIN”
5. “WHEN SATURATED, REMOVE AND BLOW DRY”

Typical bloody male, he should be so lucky, the only one going anywhere near his knob that night, or any time, would be him if women had any sense. She couldn’t help but conjure up an unpleasant image of him masturbating over a porno’ magazine, then wishing she hadn’t. Was she so sex starved that she had to result to such awful thoughts when all it did was turn her stomach, she quickly obliterated the picture from her mind. She did however wish she had a t-shirt to wear that evening that said: "You're proof enough that I can take a joke" or "Darling, no one could love you as much as you do".

Jay didn't want him to know she had taken the trouble to read the Tommy rot on his shirt so as he stood up from the bar she asked him what drink he had decided upon.

"I will stick with the cocktails, a Pina Collada I think, what about you?" He answered.

"I will try the same"

Dave chose the Sandy Beach cocktail, a combination of coconut, banana, gin and several other ingredients, too many to mention. The drinks arrived, the chaps stood up and proffered their arms and she had no option but to oblige, in so doing they escorted her to the restaurant. They found a vacant table, in tandem they each pulled at the same chair, trying to make it available for Jay to sit down.

"Allow me", said Dave

"No, allow me"

A tug of war ensued as to who was going to pull the damn chair out. Jay completely ignoring them pulled out another chair and sat down. "Shall we order? I'm starving." She said as though she hadn't noticed their conflict. Two crimson-faced men slumped down in their seats, looking daggers at each other. Oh what fun! She thought sardonically, trying hard to concentrate on the menu. Once they had ordered and the food had arrived they sat in comparative silence, apart from the noise of the men as they gorged themselves throughout the meal. Both were acting like a couple of pre-pubescent schoolboys, nudging and trying to get each other to spill something, when they thought she wasn't looking. If she could she would have sent them both to bed without any dinner! They both ate like animals, table manners being non-existent due, more than likely, to the excess alcohol in their systems. Within a matter of minutes Dave had slurped his soup, as a result a snail like trail formed down the front of his crimson dress shirt, looking more like Les Patterson than Les Patterson by the minute!

Dave's second course was the house speciality, an extremely hot lamb curry and as she had predicted earlier, the heat found it's only avenue of escape, globules of sweat were forming on his forehead and by the end of this exceedingly hot and spicy meal his face looked like Niagara falls, streams of perspiration gushing forth, splashing onto his plate making the sauce congeal. She seemed to be the only one aware of this nauseating event finding it impossible to continue eating; to do so might have been fatal, as she was feeling decidedly queasy.

Chris was not much better; it was as though he had racing colours on his knife and fork, he held his head down near to the plate and continually scooped forkful after forkful into his mouth, only stopping occasionally to lick his knife. The only godsend was that he didn't have the curry and therefore his perspiration wasn't splashing everywhere.

Jay polished off her drink and ordered yet another, the men followed suit. She declined desert and sat with some impatience for them to finish theirs, then hopefully she could make her get away. As they were such gannets she didn't have to wait long, Dave let out a reverberating burp and rubbed his stomach in appreciation, she thought any minute now he will cock his arse and let rip, fortunately for her he didn't! Chris unaware of his own bad table manners admonished Dave. "Really Dave, haven't you any scruples?"

"It's just a sign of appreciation, isn't it Jay?"

"Yes, in some countries, I suppose it is", after all, she could hardly say, no, you dirty, filthy, bad mannered pig!

"Well, shall we retire to the bar then" said Chris as they stood up and once again they proffered their arms for her to take. Was there no escape?

Chapter 14

They all managed to get to the bar. How? She had no idea. She had the impression that she was having to hold these two drunken sops up as the days binging was finally having its toll on them. They must have looked a very pretty sight, two great drunken oafs of men, being supported by a tiny, slip of a woman, who herself was now having a bit of trouble keeping upright. Jay put that down to the fact that they were jogging her and not that she had more than enough to drink and hadn't eaten very much at all! It was also some accomplishment that any of them managed to balance on the bar stools, after taking several attempts to do so. Once again the cocktails were forthcoming and Jay was past caring, not registering that she was getting steadily plastered. It was so easy to quench the continual thirst that she was experiencing since she had arrived in Kenya.

The DJ had arrived and was playing Tina Turners' Simply the Best. Jay's body started to sway in time with the music, when someone asking her to dance, disturbed her, turning she saw it was the partner of the lady who had acknowledged her predicament earlier, without any hesitation accepted his offer. He guided her to the dance floor; it wasn't long before Jay forgot she had a partner, losing herself in doing an extremely impressive impersonation of Tina. She loved dancing, feeling good when the track finished and there was a round of applause from the guests in their appreciation of her display. The next song was slow and she found herself holding the hand of the gentleman who had led her into the dance.

"Well, we kept our promise, the missus sent me to rescue yer."

"Thanks, it is appreciated, my names Jay"

"I'm Fred, me wife is Gladys, don't worry girl, we'll look after yer". With introductions he spun her around in time to the music.

Jay grabbed hold of his hand, made a grab for the other, fumbling around in a feeble search only to find that the only thing there was a stump. Surprisingly, possibly owing to the fact that she was three sheets to the wind, she did not cringe at the sight, instead she grabbed hold of his proffered stump, after all it didn't seem to concern him that a crucial part of his arm was missing, Fred proceeded to guide her around the floor with the hard, bony dismembered limb! One more turn on the dance floor and Fred escorted her to a chair at the side of the dance floor, where she was introduced to his wife Gladys who was sitting waiting patiently for her gallant hubby.

"Thanks for the loan of Fred"

"That's ok love, your need was greater than mine, you sit wiv us. We could see 'ow those two 'ave been drooling all over yer". Nodding towards Dave and Chris.

"Yes, they are not exactly Gods gifts are they"?

All three of them laughed out loud.

Gladys was a short, cuddly woman, about five feet tall, even shorter than Jay. She had a rosy, round merry face with laughter lines very apparent around her eyes and mouth, the only makeup that she had on was a touch of red lipstick on her heart shaped lips. Her hair was pure white, cut short and permed into really neat tiny curls and brushed back from her face, she was a typical looking little granny. The pink floral cotton dress that she wore fitted snugly to her ample figure, a thin white belt tied around the area where her waist should have been, however she was just like a tiny barrel with no indentations only bulges. The dress hung just below her knees, chubby short legs protruded from beneath, her small but wide feet wearing beige coloured Dr Scholl's sandals. All in all Gladys was the type of elderly lady that you just wanted to cuddle.

Fred was just as well fed as Gladys, fairly attractive for an elderly gentleman, he too had white hair and possessed mischievous pale blue eyes, like Gladys he always seemed to have something to smile about. His light camel trousers were pulled up over his stomach by a pair of bright red braces, the pink short-sleeved checked shirt that he wore revealed his mutilated arm.

They were such a lovely couple, well into their seventies but still sprightly, informing Jay that they were East Londoners and on their second honeymoon, the pair of them looked really happy together and Jay could not help but feel a little envious.

Fred asked Jay what she was drinking, getting

hers and Gladys's order he sauntered off towards the bar, only to return with Dave and Chris in tow. Fred placed the drinks on the table and standing behind Dave and Chris shrugged his shoulders in dismay and mouthed that he couldn't get shot of them. The three men sat down, Dave and Chris either side of Jay both trying to monopolise the conversation. It turned out that Dave was forty and Chris was thirty-four, both split up from their partners and looking for a holiday romance.

"Well, you can count me out", said Jay, patience now having run out "I'm far to old for either of you, I wouldn't contemplate having a toy boy".

Both sat back in astonishment when they were told her age, both said that the age difference didn't matter to them.

"It may not matter to you both, but it does to me" and with the bravado acquired from having too many to drink, "I prefer a much older man, that's got a bit of class and knows how to treat a woman, unlike you two, who have as much decorum as a baboons with haemorrhoids"!

Chris, his feathers ruffled, slurred his words using expletives that turned the air blue.

"Well, that's fucking grafitude, yer ungrafteful stucked up tart, stay wif yer one armed fucking bandit if that's yer fucking attitude, snotty bitch". Walking off towards the bar shouting more defamatory comments at her, until the management came and removed him.

Dave surprisingly did not make a move, sitting quietly for a few moments, then looking Jay in the eye, "Don't mind him, bloody ignoramus, didn't like his shirt anyway. I'm sorry, if I have offended you Jay, I thought we were getting on ok, perhaps we can still be friends though".

Jay, now feeling a little guilty by her cutting remarks, agreed and when the next song came on, Dave, not taking no for an answer whisked her up and onto the dance floor, where he kept her for several dances, sometimes getting a little too touchy feely, making the "just be friends" quickly forgotten. Jay was very tipsy, however, she still had some sense and didn't want these unwelcome advances, trying in vain to catch Fred's eye so as to indicate she needed him to rescue again but her pleas were going unobserved, as he was deep in conversation with Gladys. Thankfully Dave could not refrain from drinking; eventually leaving them to go and sit at the bar. Jay stayed on the dance floor, shortly to be joined by Gladys, who herself was getting fairly merry, lifting her skirt and waving it about in time to the music, revealing her pink satin bloomers for all and sundry to see. Fred and another couple then joined them; the merry quintet danced, sang and drank well into the night, occasionally being joined by Dave, who was well on the way to ruin. Jay had finally put all her past worries behind her, the thought of Steve was just a pleasant memory, she was too busy having a good time as Fred and Gladys were excellent company. She couldn't remember ever having danced so much; it soon wouldn't be long before she couldn't remember the last two hours either as the drink had certainly taken its effect.

Chapter 15

Jay awoke, choking, being violently ill, she tried desperately to get up from the bed but her head was like lead and just would not leave the pillow, her stomach was aching with the retching, her only relief was when she eventually passed out....

The sun was shining brightly through the blinds, casting horizontal bands across Jay's face, she gingerly opened her eyes, closing them again when the light caught them causing her to wince in pain, her head was throbbing. What had happened to her? Where was she? She put her hand to her throbbing temple, finding an encrustation there, sitting up she swayed. Holding and feeling her head wondering whether she was in hospital having regained consciousness after some terrible accident and that her head had been injured somehow. Her hand moved down over her face investigating the damage, she had dried and congealed blood there to, the pain in her head and the thought that she had been in an accident once more made her feel faint and queasy, causing her to lie back down on the bed only to become aware of an unpleasant smell. She rolled to one side, her face going into a mass of cold goo. Ugh!! She felt dreadful and the smell was appalling. Was this the smell of death? Could she be dying? She wondered worriedly. Jay slowing opened her eyes, dreading the thought of what she may find and she had every right to be. She was mortified at what she saw, for there she was lying in a pool of dark brown vomit, it was on the pillow, on the sheets, over the floor and matted into the mosquito net. “Jay you disgusting bitch,” she reproached herself “How did you get in such a state and look at the bloody mess”.

However, no matter how disgusted she was with herself, it was with a feeling of relief that she wasn’t lying banged up in hospital with horrific head and facial injuries. She tried desperately to get off the bed but she wasn’t functioning very well, her arms and legs were like jelly, so once more she laid back not being able to avoid the vomit. She must get up and get some fluid inside her, she gathered that she must be dehydrated, sliding to the edge of the bed, body still collapsed across it, she flopped her legs over until they touched the floor, now all she needed to was to get her backside to the edge and sit up, then maybe from that position she could stand. She tried once and failed. Why wouldn’t the room stay still? She felt she was going to be sick again and what was worse she felt she needed to go to the toilet desperately, she had to get up now! In due course she managed to stand, steadying herself against the window frame, wobbling and shaking, water she must have water, finding the flask with the filtered water in and taking the lid off sipped at it but it didn’t seem to help, now even more desperate to get to loo not wanting to disgrace herself any further so with great determination she rushed to the lavatory, the speed at which ran was the only thing that kept her upright.

Jay just about managed to remove her pants in time when the world fell out of her backside, splattering the sides of the pan with a whoosh, she then felt the nausea rise up in her again only just positioning her head over the sink in the nick of time.

It was times like these a person could wish they were a contortionist. Jay sat in this most uncomfortable of positions, sporadically erupting from both ends until she was sure it was safe to move. She wiped her backside with the sandpaper, cursing when her finger went through it because it was so wet, she really must run a shower. Whilst it was warming up she had the awful task of trying to unblock the sink. Where did it all these chunks come from? She hadn't had much to eat; it was probably the lining of her stomach. She dug the chunks out as best she could with toilet paper throwing them down the toilet, the rest she had to push down the plughole, when it had finally cleared she brushed her teeth vigorously the taste of peppermint helping to alleviate the nausea a little. When she returned to the bedroom she drank as much of the water as she could, then boiled the kettle to make a strong cup of coffee. Turning around she saw the mess on and around the bed, getting a small towel that she had bought with her she wiped it up from the floor, but it was a wasted effort trying to clean the sheets and mosquito net, in the end she gave up trying, knowing that she would have to go and apologise at reception sooner or later. It was a brown glutinous mess and if she had been sleeping with her backside on the pillow she may have thought she had messed herself, she hoped the hotel didn't think so as she was embarrassed enough as it was! Depositing the sick sodden towel in a plastic carrier bag she tied it securely and placed it in the waste bin. She only hoped that Barry White didn't think it was anything worth taking home because he would be in for a nasty shock!

Still having to steady herself whilst showering she washed all the disgusting vomit off herself, worst was trying to get it out of her hair, which was tangled and lumpy but after a great deal of shampooing and conditioning it seemed ok, at least now she didn't smell. Her mouth still felt like the bottom of a parrot's cage, so she scrubbed her teeth again, swallowing the toothpaste, just in case her breath was still emitting unsavoury vapours.

Beginning to feel a little more stable now, although her head was still throbbing, she sat down in front of the dressing table mirror, looking deathly pale in spite of the tan, made herself a black coffee and drank it slowly, at the same time as downing three Paracetamols. Jay didn't remember much about last night, she could only remember up to the point she was dancing to Tina Turner and a little beyond, but that was about it. How she managed to return to her room and get undressed was hard to fathom out. She could easily have been murdered in her sleep and not known a thing about it, she tried the door, amazed that in her drunken stupor she still had the sense to lock it. Never in all her forty-nine years had she ever been so drunk, she'd only had a couple of rum and cokes, the rest were cocktails and they were mainly fruit juice, she put it down to the fact that she had not eaten very much, vowing never to touch another drop of alcohol again! Glancing at her watch, it was ten thirty, she'd missed breakfast, not that she could have faced anything other than a piece of toast, had better get a move on, the Rep was turning up at eleven to give them all a welcome talk.

After brushing her hair and tying it back, she put on a pair of white shorts and a pink t-shirt, slipped on some flip flops and headed out into the fresh air. Thank goodness the Paracetamols were taking effect, otherwise she didn't think she would make it through the day. Jay stopped off at reception, telling them about her upset stomach and apologising for the mess she had made, saying it must have been something she had eaten and was grateful that the receptionist accepted her excuses without any fuss. Jay then enquired as to whether there were any messages for her, yet again the answer was no. "Well, that's, that then, the bastard, why do men promise things and never follow them through?" Stopping at the bar, on the way to the dance area she asked for a long cold glass of orange juice, then found a seat and waited with the other guests for the Rep to turn up.

"Jayee, cooeee", someone was calling her name, she turned to see Gladys waving at her. "Come and sit wiv us love"

Jay went over and sat next to Gladys, Fred sitting next to her nodded towards Jay. "Morning Miss Dancing Diva 2002, how's yer 'ead then?"

"Don't mention it, I feel dreadful", then Jay recited the nighttime drama. "I don't know how I got back to my room, can hardly remember a thing"

"I took yer back," said Gladys. "Yer could 'ardly stand and tha' Dave bloke was buzzing around yer like a bee at a 'oney pot. If 'e could 'e would 'ave been in yer bed as quick as lightning, so I insisted I took yer back, I waited outside until I 'eard the latch go on yer door then I made me way back to me room. I'm not sure 'ow I managed it cos I was 'alf-cut too, still it was a bloody good evening, yer certainly let yer 'air down girl".

"Thanks Gladys, you're an angel, I don't usually get so tiddly, only had a couple of rum and cokes, the rest of the evening I drank cocktails"

"Well, tha's it then girl, blooming cocktails are lethal, not like yer get at 'ome yer know, just a single measure of alcohol, 'ere it's just a measure of fruit juice and the rest is seventy percent alcohol, no wonder yer were legless".

"I'm not going to touch alcohol ever again, I'm lucky to be alive, I could have drowned on my own vomit, I have never, ever felt so ill, not going down that route again I can tell you".

Jay was feeling a little better now that she had some more non-alcoholic fluids inside her and the headache tablets had worked, for which she was grateful. She sat back and waited for the imminent arrival of the Rep, hoping that he wouldn't be too long as she was losing valuable sunbathing time.

Numerous guests were arriving and taking there seats in readiness for the talk and as they approached they nodded at Jay, some asking how she was feeling and others saying "See you having a good time last night, certainly now how to let your hair down, don't you?" She didn't know these people from Adam, yet they all seemed familiar with her, she dreaded to think what kind of fool she had made of herself and sunk down into her chair, trying to make herself inconspicuous and thereby avoiding any further comments about her antics last night, she'd rather remain oblivious to them!

The Rep, Umbawi, arrived five minutes late, a native of Kenya but with a good knowledge of the English language, he wasn't too bad with the humour either, managing to jolly up the audience, with several quips and various idiosyncrasies pertaining to the locals, tips on how to rid yourself of the unwanted attention of beggars and street traders, "Firstly you say no thank you, then you can say please go away I'm not interested and if that fails you just say "piss off", they usually get the message" and so he went on. He described various trips. A day trip to a well-known beachside restaurant on a stretch of beach known to be the most beautiful, unspoilt location in Kenya, you can have camel rides, sun bathe and swim in safety, then an evening meal in the best restaurant in the area etc. etc.

There was snorkelling, deep sea diving, riverboat trips and a variety of safaris. "Coo, don't 'alf fancy a safari, what abou' you Jay?" Gladys asked.

"Yes, it's something I've always fancied, mind you it's a lot of money, might think about a day safari".

"Nah" said Gladys, "No point in just a day, why

don't yer come with me and Fred, I fancy the three day with two nights in a luxury tent. Go on Jay, what yer going to do 'ere all by yerself, we can't trust yer on yer own yer know, come wiv us".

Jay deliberated for a moment, thinking that maybe Fred and Gladys were right. What would she do here all by herself? What the heck, that's what credit cards are for after all. "All right; in for a penny in for a pound; silly to come all this way and not go on one".

The three of them waited whilst Umbawi finished his talk, then they joined the queue to book their trip. When it came to their turn to pay they were told that if they were interested they could travel by light aircraft for an extra twenty pounds each. They would fly low over the savannah getting a different perspective on the animals, they would definitely see more. Umbawi highly recommended it, plus it would be more comfortable than the two-hour journey in a truck. Gladys was a game old bird and was definitely up for it, Fred wasn't so keen. "Just like paper maché those bloody planes, one puff of wind and they fall to pieces"

"Nothing like putting the fear of God in us, is there Fred" Jay replied.

Umbawi addressed their concerns and said it was one of the safest ways to travel; it was even safer than going by road as the drivers out here were all maniacs. "Agree wiv yer on that point. " Answered Fred. "Blooming taxi driver yesterday didn't know what side of the bleeding road to drive on. Go on then Gladys, book us up, can't be any 'arm in it", waving his stump at her.

"Fred yer bloody terrible you are." Gladys laughed at his jest.

"Ok, if you two are up for it, I won't be chicken either" Jay said as she handed her credit card over to Umbawi.

Credit cards zapped, there was no turning back, they would be leaving at five thirty the following the morning, a cab would take them to the airfield which was just a fifteen minute drive away and then it was up, up and away, it was all quite thrilling but at the same time a little scary.

"Exciting ain't it?" Said Gladys a grin on her face and her shoulders jigging up and down expressing just how excited she was.

"Yes, but in the meantime I have some serious sunbathing to do." Excusing herself saying "Catch up with you both later", Jay returned to her room to get her bikini, suntan oil, towel and a book, she was going to spend a leisurely day doing nothing.

Chapter 16

Jay's room still hadn't been cleaned, it was such a stinking mess that it was most probably being left to last; it may even need fumigating. Even though it was her mess, she couldn't stand the smell, it was making her come over all queasy again the sooner she got herself organised and out of there the better.

Quickly deciding on the pink floral bikini today, she stepped into the bottoms, thinking how lucky she had been in keeping her figure. Her tummy was fairly taut and her backside pert, not bad for almost fifty, she occasionally worked out but not to any rigid regime. When she put the top on however, she could have sworn it had shrunk, surely her boobs could not have got any bigger, if they increased any more, what with her being so tiny, she'd have trouble standing up straight, in fact they would most probably topple her over. She squeezed her breasts into the confining space, looked in the mirror and decided that although they were hanging over a bit, she was passable, nobody would take any notice of what she looked like anyway, perhaps she should consider a breast reduction as when they eventually headed south they may end up around her waist and she'd be able to tie them in a bow! She put on a long pink sarong and tied it up under her arms, thus covering her overflowing breasts, slipped on a pair of pale green leather mules, looked in the mirror. Satisfied that she looked half decent, picked up her beach bag leaving her room, shutting the door firmly on that God-awful smell.

At Reception, the girl behind the counter recognising from her frequent enquiries held out her hands in an apologetic gesture and shook her head, indicating that there were still no messages for her. She found it hard to believe that Steve had not telephoned he had seem so sincere in his feelings for her, but then she had been fooled by men before and decided she would try to put all thoughts of him out of her mind and attempt to enjoy her holiday, after all it had cost her an arm and a leg. She had always preferred male company, perhaps because she had been bought up with two brothers who were older than her and fashioned her behaviour on theirs, she grew up being a bit of a tomboy, her close friends were always boys, preferring to play Cowboys and Indians than with dolls. Her father however was the biggest influence in her life and she was proud to be called a Patterson rather than a Wilson (her mothers' maiden name), as the Wilson's were a bit stuck up, compared to her fathers' East London upbringing. He often said to her mum "Yer just like yer blooming muvver, a bloody Wilson, my humour is wasted on you", then after he had said something like this he would fling his arms about her and say "I luv yer, yer silly cow". Somehow they stayed together, it was a puzzle how they managed it though.

Reg, as her father was called, was an extremely

exuberant man, while only short at five feet six, he was big in reputation, always leaving an impression on the people he met, not always good, as dad enjoyed a drink and was often the worse for wear, again he always blamed her mother for driving him to it. There were not many people within a ten-mile radius of where we lived that did not know Reg Patterson and that included the men in blue! He had been born within the sound of Bow Bells and having settled and raised a family in the South of London had lost some of his cockney accent but he retained the saucy sense of humour that East Londoners possess, often going a little near the mark with his witticisms, managing with the assistance of his mischievous smile to get away with it. She was pleased to say that she had acquired some of his humour albeit a bit masculine. Jay always reminisced about her father when she was feeling down, wishing that he was still alive, so that he could brighten her day with some remark or other, she had loved her father so much and had never stopped missing him and his larger than life presence.

She had a wander around the hotel, checking out the quaint little shop, filled to capacity with native artefacts. There were all manner wild life such as elephants, lions, rhinos in various poses there was a particularly dramatic one of a lion and it's kill, the detail was phenomenal, the glory of the kill and the end of the Impala's life depicted in such detail that you could almost believe it was real. There were fine looking replicas of Masai warriors and naked ebony women, some with babies feeding at their breasts, every one intricately carved in ebony, mahogany or cedar, such craftsmanship and all the talented wood carvers got were a few pence for their labour, life was pretty unfair. Looking at the necklaces, bracelets and belts that had been painstakingly made up of thousands of minute colourful beads, which must have taken hours of patience, only to be bought by foreigners who would take them home for presents and they would be worn once or twice and when the novelty had worn off, thrown into obscurity somewhere, perhaps never to see the light of day again. The usual medicines, toiletries, refreshments and postcards were on display and Jay chose several postcards, knowing full well that they may not arrive at their destinations until after she had returned from holiday but was going to post them anyway. She purchased the cards, stamps and a large bottle of cold Perrier and placed them in her beach bag, she would write the cards this afternoon and the water would save her going to the bar for a drink as she didn't want to be tempted by any more of those lethal cocktails.

There was a little beauty parlour next door to the shop, the signs in the window advertising the various beauty treatments available. Henna tattoos, piercing, manicures, hair braiding to name but a few. Jay looked through the window, there was a blonde woman and she presumed her teenage daughter their nails done and their hair braided in the traditional way, their hair was being divided and plaited close to their scalps, so tight that it looked painful, apparently it can take several hours to complete a full head of hair but what a waste of a major part of a day and for what, to come out with hair looking like rats tails with beads on. She would see them both later in the evening at the disco, both thinking they looked the dogs' bollocks, but lacking the finesse of the local girls whose thick, black wiry hair was more suited to this hairstyle. She certainly wouldn't be going in for that, she had lovely thick hair and although a bit wild on occasion, once it was tied back in a ponytail it was no problem. She may consider a Henna tattoo though; deciding on an apt design would give her yet another objective to consider.

Walking until she reached the beachfront, she could hear the voices of traders plying their wares and offering their services as guides to those pale faced new arrivals that had ventured unwittingly onto the beach and whose Reps had not warned them that they would be easy prey to these wily and cunning schemers. She was grateful that they were prevented from entering any part of the hotel grounds, as she wasn't the type of woman who would be able to deter them and would probably end up with numerous knickknacks that she didn't really want. It was possible to get lucky and find a genuine guide that would be half the cost of those recommended but it was a risky business and as she was a woman on her own would not be prepared to take the risk for the sake of saving a few pennies.

Chapter 17

Jay found a quiet little spot with a man made stretch of beach within the hotel complex overlooking the sea, it appeared that everyone else had somewhere else to be, the traders and holiday makers on the main beach were not going to bother her and the presence of the hotel security guards were monitoring the entrances to ensure that they didn't. Jay stood for a while just looking out to sea, watching the activity on the beach, the lobster pink bodies, that had been subjected to too much sun, trying to no avail to discourage the unwanted attentions of the black faced traders who were literally pushing goods upon their latest victims, who eventually dug into their bum bags and paid over the odds for some useless bit of African tat just to break free, only to move on and be pursued by yet another opportunist. Her eyes wandered across the great expanse of pale turquoise sea, the sun reflecting on the crystal clear mirror, disturbed only by the by the breeze or occasional flying fish, far on the horizon were dozens of boats of all sizes, their white sails dotted about like cotton wool balls and seemed barely to be moving at all. Only a few birds braved the heat and were flying overhead, when spotting something in the sea below, they drew back their wings and dived gracefully into it's depths, retrieving something edible from within, these actions were continually repeated until at last, replete they flew off to the sanctuary of their nests, maybe to regurgitate the days catch into the gaping beaks of their chirruping eager chicks.

The heat from the sun was glorious; it beat down relentlessly upon her bare back and slender legs, she was pleased for the cool sea breeze that gently brushed against her skin and made the heat more bearable. Yes, this felt like a little bit of heaven and she would have loved to have stood for longer, looking at the wonders before her, but the affects of the nights bingeing had not quite worn off and her legs were beginning to feel a bit shaky, she wondered if this was what was called the DT's. The sun beds were a bit more up market than the plastic ones around the pool being of dark varnished mahogany, easily adjustable to various positions complete with a comfy mattress covered in an especially colourful linen type fabric. Browns, oranges, yellows, with African motifs dotted randomly and portrayed in black and interlaced with gold welcomed her eyes, it seemed a pity to have to cover it with her towel when it would have done justice to any living room wall. Feeling quite chuffed that she had found such an ideal location she claimed not one but two sun beds, seeing as there was nobody else about to occupy them, her beach bag on one and reluctantly laying her towel over the other. She opened the matching parasol and purposefully placed it alongside the sun bed, so it would shield her face from direct sunlight. Generously oiling her curvaceous body with Ambre Solair, Factor 4, no Factor 15 for her, Jay had an olive skin and therefore tanned easily, she slowly and sensuously smoothed it into her arms, then across her chest and stomach, managing quite successfully to apply it to her back, she put this down to the fact that Paul, her brother used to regularly put her in arm locks as a child, almost wrenching her arms out of their sockets, so that now she was quite able to contort her arms way up her back with ease. At the time she hated him for his actions never occurring to her that later in life this act of sadism would aid her in doing up hard to reach zips and applying oil etc. She lubricated her shapely legs, which were in dire need of a shave, the hairs now becoming quite apparent, the warm weather seemed to enhance the growth and strength to such an extent that they would definitely prove useful on a garden broom and do an able job to boot! Progressing upwards over the subtle rise of her knees and towards the widening of her thighs where there was a slight dimpling of cellulite, only be apparent upon closer inspection, would not be classed in males' eyes as an imperfection on such a delectable body. Her legs were not the only thing that was in need of attention, her bikini line also needed a trim as a few tell-tale, dark brown, curly hairs were escaping from the skimpy bottoms, she discretely tucked them back in her pants and providing she didn't spread her legs (chance would be a fine thing) they should stay in place until she got around to sprucing them up later that day. Once all her body was suitably covered, she wiped her hands on her towel, delved into her beach bag and retrieved the postcards and pen.

Sitting down, pulling her knees up and using a book to rest upon she started to write to her family.

Hi Rach,
Weather in the 100's, getting great tan, eat your heart out. Safari tomorrow, would you believe in a light aircraft? I disgraced myself on the first night – Got slaughtered, apparently I had a great time. See you soon, Love mum. XX

The remainder of the cards were written in a similar manner, just changing the words slightly, leaving out the bit about getting drunk when writing to her mother, otherwise she would have got a lecture on her return saying that she was just like her father couldn't hold a drink! Her duty done she adjusted the backrest so that she could lie flat, putting on her sunglasses she laid back, stretching her legs out, relaxing into the deep softness, feeling to all intent and purpose like the cat that had got the cream then carried on with the main task for the day, to complete the bronzing of her already darkening skin. This was superb, she looked up at the sky, not a cloud to be seen, the leaves on the palms frolicking in the breeze adding contrast to the clear and exceptionally blue sky, just like Steve's eyes, the now not so welcomed memory, still vivid, feeling once again disappointed that he hadn't the common decency to even send her message. Still, better off without him if that's how he treats women, just another male chauvinist, she had so looked forward to spending some of her holiday with him and now all she had was the unwanted attention of Dave, one of the worlds biggest rejects! Thankful that she had met Fred and Gladys, pleased they had persuaded her to go with them tomorrow, not that she needed much persuasion, she was really looking forward to it. She loved animals and to be able to see them in their natural habitat would be an experience she hoped she would carry with her for the rest of her life. Jay removed her sunglasses and closed her eyes, what sort of tattoo should she have, she didn't want anything big or flashy, something unassuming, she wasn't into flowers, so perhaps a small bird or a butterfly and she'd like it on her shoulder and who knows if she really liked it she may have a permanent one when she returned home.

She tried to imagine what the safari would be like and what she would need to pack for her little adventure, if the kids knew what she was up to, they would not believe it, she had practically become a recluse since her disastrous affair, now here she was in Kenya, all that was missing was the love of a good man and they seemed pretty thin on the ground. Listening to the twittering of the minute green and yellow birds flitting about in the trees, she lost herself in a dream world, enjoying the solitude that was hers, turning every so often and quenching her thirst with the occasional drop of water.

Chapter 18

Jay was aroused by a bong, bong, bong and a mellow voice near to her. "Excuse me madam, but the final sitting for lunch is now being served"

She looked up and saw a fine-looking brown faced waiter clad immaculately in a white cheesecloth shirt and white sarong, a badge on his left lapel spelling out his name "Joseph" with a rather large gong in one hand and a large mallet with what looked like a large golf ball attached to it, in the other, he looked poised to give it another bash.

"Thank you Joseph" she said reading his name "What time is it please?"

"It's almost 2.00 p.m. madam" His English was impeccable as it was with most of the staff at the hotel.

She'd been out for almost two hours and was astonished that the sun had not moved around and burnt her face, then she noticed that the parasol had been moved to protect her. Joseph noticing her surprise when she looked at the parasol explained that he had taken the liberty of moving the parasol, as she was sound asleep, he presumed that she would not want to get burnt, he hoped he done the right thing.

"Thank you so much Joseph, that was really considerate, your English is excellent by the way." She said by way of reassurance.

He went on to tell her how fortunate he was to have been educated in England, how hard his parents had found it to finance, but because he was an only child they wanted the best for him. She said how unusual to be an only child in this country and he told how he was of Christian faith and educated unlike the majority of Africans, thereby having the advantage of learning about birth control, health and how to succeed and avoid becoming poverty stricken. He hadn't stayed in England as he missed his family and the hot climate. He was studying to become a Doctor, hopefully qualifying the following year and felt he could be more use to his own countrymen. Jay wished him well with his studies, saying that with his attitude he would surely succeed then reaching into her bag she gave him a hefty tip, which unlike all the other members of staff he tried to refuse, but she insisted, in the end he succumbed, thanking her as he put it in the pocket of his shirt. "You enjoy your meal madam and if you need anything at any time, please ask for me"

"I will Joseph, I definitely will".

She filled her beach bag, put on her sarong and made off towards the restaurant, but first she would have a dip in the pool, she needed to cool off.

The pool area was now more occupied, some faces she recognised, she waved to them as she passed. Putting her bag and towel down, taking off her sarong she headed off towards the pool; she was really looking forward to this swim and to cooling off. Standing on the side of the pool and with all the elegance of a swallow, she took off from the side, the water barely rippling as her slender torso dived into the welcoming depths, she swam the length of the pool under water, rising exhilarated, gulping in the air, the water streaming from her hair and face. Jay wiped away the water that was blurring her vision only to open them to see Dave standing on the side of the pool watching her, his luminous pink swimming shorts fitting just below his bulging belly. "Hey Jay, that was quite impressive, watch this." He called to her, without further ado he flung himself off the side of the pool and with an enormous belly flop, worthy of any member of the whale family, caused a mini tidal wave and probably emptied the pool of a third of it's contents!

"Phew, that must have hurt" she winched, Why do men have to show off, I think that is my cue to go to lunch, she climbed out of the pool. She was drying herself and watching Dave, who was oblivious to the fact that she was no longer in the pool, continuing his one-man show, unsuccessfully attempting to do the butterfly, spending more time under the water than on the top. Then the backstroke, where the only thing that was really afloat was his belly, several times he had to put his feet down so he could rid himself of the water that he had swallowed. Deciding that he had best give the backstroke a miss he developed a style of his own, a combination of breaststroke and doggy paddle. Jay found it highly entertaining, watching this man show off his so-called masculinity, she felt a little sorry for him, but it didn't last long. She dried herself off, put on her sarong and went to the restaurant; she took a seat where she had a view of the pool. That poor, silly man, why didn't he realise that whatever he tried, he didn't have a hope in hell's chance of ever winning her affection. Dave finally gave up trying to impress and seeming a little disorientated spun around looking, then spun around again. It was obvious that he was looking for her as nobody else had attempted to enter the pool with him it; he looked a little defeated when he found that she had left the pool. Making a last ditched attempt at bravado, instead of using the steps to get out, he tried to haul his bulk over the side of the pool, managing to get himself stuck by his belly, one leg still in the pool and the other stuck on the side.

Jay, who had now been joined by Fred and Gladys, watched him and were absolutely wetting themselves with laughter, Gladys was doubled up and Fred was holding his ribs, well as best as he could with only 1.5 arms! The tears were rolling down Jay's face, yes it was wicked but it was just so very, very funny. Dave was still struggling, nobody went to his aid as everyone else was finding his failure to get out of the pool amusing too, they had no intention of stopping the fun. He managed to somehow slip back into the pool with yet another big splash, but instead of going to the steps he once again tried to haul himself out, this time with a bit more success, ending up on his knees and baring his backside to all and sundry in the restaurant as he had knelt on his shorts in the process pulling them down around his knees. Fortunately for Dave he did not hear the furore coming from the restaurant as everyone burst into fits of more laughter, if he did he certainly didn't show it. He simply stood up, pulled up his shorts, collected his towel then walked quickly off in the direction of the bar, to perhaps drown his disappointment, or to find some antiseptic to administer to his now very red and sore belly!

Jay wiped her eyes with a paper napkin. "I haven't laughed so much in ages, poor old Dave, if only he knew".

"Poor old Dave, my foot" said Gladys "That man would 'ave been in yer knickers as soon as yer could say 'ows ya farver. It serves 'im right randy ol' git!"

"Blooming good job we're off on Safari tomorra, ain't it Glad, that bugger won't leave the poor lil' cow alone", offered Fred.

"No, it's a pity 'e didn't bloody well castrate 'imself as 'e got out the pool".

They all fell about laughing once more, Jay was pleased she had found such great company, if she stuck with these two; she was going to have fun that was for sure. Once they had stopped laughing, which took a while, as it only took one of them to start to snigger and it would set the other two off again, they went and collected plates and helped themselves to the buffet, where there was a multitude of dishes to choose from. Jay still with a bit of a dickey tummy settled for a mushroom omelette and some toast. Gladys had a cheese omelette and chips but Fred had the works. He had what looked like chicken stew, beef ribs, yellow spicy rice, curried potatoes and numerous vegetables. His plate was piled high, Gladys had helped him by dishing it out but how he managed to traverse the tables without spilling any was an art. He tip-toed in and out and around the tables, like Fred Astaire at the London Palladium, Ginger (Gladys that is) had already tripped the light fantastic and was posed with knife and fork at the ready waiting for Jay and Fred to join her.

They chatted amicably over their meal, often referring to Dave remarking on what a twit he had looked, with Gladys describing his arse as "somewhere suitable to park yer bike", causing them to again erupt into fits of laughter.

"Wonder what the flight will be like", enquired Jay. "I've never been on a light aircraft before, bit nerve racking".

"We're going to make sure we've got our incontinence pads on, ain't we Fred?"

"Yeah, I'm wearing mine now, crapping meself at the thought already"

"Hundreds of people have done it before us, it must be safe enough" Jay said trying to instil confidence in them all, but knowing it didn't really instil any in her.

"We're more likely to kill our blooming selves laughing, if today is anything to go by. Don't yer worry lass, it will be quick, if the crash don't kill yer the bloody lions will".

Jay loved Gladys wit, it was similar to her own, the more she got to know this lovely old couple the more she grew attached to them, they were her guardian angels, perhaps God had finally decided to help her out! They finished their meal with a huge helping of banana ice cream.

"I'm stuffed," said Jay

"Well thank yer lucky stars it was food and not that Dave," joked Gladys giving Jay a saucy wink.

"Perish the thought, well I'm going to my private little beach that I have found, what are you two up to?"

"Now that would be telling, wouldn't it Fred? Yer won't be seeing us now until dinner"

"If you don't mind, can I meet you both in the bar at about seven. I'd prefer to join you both for dinner this evening".

"Be our pleasure dear, better make it six thirty though, as another load of guests are arriving this afternoon and we want to get there before the rush" Gladys informed Jay.

"OK, see you at six-thirty then"

"Alright luv." Said Gladys grabbing hold of Fred's only hand saying, "Come on then yer randy ol' bugger."

Fred turned and gave Jay the thumbs up as he was pulled along behind an eager Gladys. Jay smiled, shaking her head in wonder. Well, well, well and I thought they were going for a Siesta, lucky devils, just goes to prove you are never to old!

She spent a leisurely afternoon, sitting in her little piece of heaven, pleased that she was getting browner by the minute, staying there until five o'clock just as the sun was starting to go down, casting a orange hue over the calm sea, it would only be another hour until it got dark and she needed to go back to her room and get changed for dinner.

Chapter 19

As Jay opened the door to her room she was greeted by the smell of the rose petals scattered once more upon her bed, the dirty mosquito net and bed linen having been replaced with fresh, there was no sign of last nights stomach contents, the cleaner had done an excellent job, she must remember to leave a goody bag and tip at the end of her stay, for whoever they were certainly deserved it. Cecil was still in his web, for which she was relieved, he now had quite a sizeable larder, as insects of all shapes and sizes were bundled up into tight greyish shrouds. She wondered whether Cecil was on a diet, as he didn't seem to be eating, or could it be the smell of her vomit putting him off his appetite.

Jay stripped off, staring in the mirror admiring the nice bronzed figure reflected there. She was certainly getting very brown considering she had only been here a couple of days. White marks where her bikini had been, emphasised the size of her breasts even more, there were no strap marks as she had pulled them off her shoulders. Her bottom looked like porcelain as her back was a dark toffee colour, several more hours exposing the front to the sun and it wouldn't be long before that was the same colour. Her face, although protected from the sun, thanks to Joseph, was a lovely caramel, her cheeks were glowing, the colour of skin accentuating her tawny brown eyes. A few wisps of hair had succumbed to the sun's rays and had turned burnished red, yes; all in all, she was pleased with today's outcome.

She decided on the clothes for that evening laying them out on the bed, a strapless top of white lace, which would show of her newly, acquired tan. Tonight she would wear the pillar-box red pedal pushers, stretchy so they would cling to the contours of her body but still showing some bare bronzed leg. Pleased with her choice of clothes she ran the shower, making sure she remembered the razor for her well over due grooming. When the shower was at an acceptable level of warmth she put the plug in (taking no chances) and stepped in the water it hitting her head and cascading down her body. She looked even browner now, if that were at all possible. Lathering her body with the M & S shower gel, the sweet smell of almonds and orange blossom wafting up to greet her nostrils, she washed away the days Ambre Solaire. Adding more gel she lathered her armpits, shaving off the two days growth, then gave the same treatment to her legs. Her skin was now silky smooth and shone like satin, all she had to do now was to trim the pubes, which she did very carefully, satisfied that she had removed everything necessary she rinsed the soap suds off. Getting some baby oil she rubbed it into her skin whilst still letting the water run over her, this would stop her skin from drying and flaking preventing her losing the wonderful skin tone she was so proud of, the oil also made her pubic hair spring into a mass of tiny curls, they felt so soft as a result. She washed her hair, added conditioner and then rinsed it out. Feeling refreshed and now well groomed after having shaved off the bristles, she stepped out of the shower wrapping a clean towel about her body and another around her hair.

It was nearly six p.m. only another thirty minutes to go, she had better get a move on. She dried herself dabbing at her skin, applied deodorant and some talc to her nether regions. Rubbed her hair dry, tying it back into a roll at the back of her head, small tendrils of hair escaping and curling around her forehead and ears, giving a severe hairstyle a much softer look, pleased with the result, she put on her makeup. Tonight she would put on a bit of colour, a shiny bronze eye shadow, black eyeliner and lashings of mascara, accentuating her already long eyelashes. There was no need for foundation or rouge as the sun had taken care of that, her complexion was faultless and a pale pink lipstick with lashings of gloss complemented the colour of her skin. Dressing quickly as she was now pressed for time, but taking care not to smudge her make up, she put on her white top, she looked in the mirror and decided that she looked ok; opting for no knickers, she slipped into the red pedal pushers that fitted like a glove, the seat of them rising up into the crack of her pert little backside. For jewellery she put on large gold ringed Gypsy style earrings and a little black beaded choker. To finish her assemble she buckled a wide black leather belt around her tiny waist and put Roland Cartier black and white stilettos on her feet. She was very pleased with the result, a nineteen fifties style, looking not dissimilar to the girls that were in the movie Grease.

Clutching a small black evening bag she left her room, the heels of her Roland Cartiers tapping on the steps as she made her way down the stairs and along the stone path, the noise from the crickets seeming as though they were trying to keep in tune with her as she quickly made her way towards Fred and Gladys who were already at the bar, drinks in hand, who turned when they heard her approach.

"Wow look at you. Is this the same Jay that was wiv us earlier today?" remarked Gladys a look of surprise on her face. "Don't yer brush up well."

Fred stood up offering her his seat. "What would you like to drink then me dusky beauty?"

"Aw, come off it Fred, I've only put on a bit of war paint". Although knowing that make-up indeed improved her looks but didn't think enough that it warranted such surprised comments.

"Yeah, don't embarrass the girl Fred. 'E's trying to make me jealous Jay, keeping me on me toes and 'im wearing me out this afternoon an' all, that's gratitude fer yer!"

"On that note, I think I will have an orange juice please", said Jay, steering away from the way the conversation was headed.

"Yer seen that lot that arrived today, a couple of right tasty geezers amongst them, yer never know girl wish 'ard enough and yer may strike lucky".

"Yeah, right, I remember my dad saying, "Wish in one hand and shit in the other and see which one gets filled first".

“Jay, really, didn’t think yer were like that, goodo, nice to know yer’ve joined the club” and Gladys laughing took Jay’s hand shaking it vigorously in approval.

“Well, can I escort the two most butiful ladies in this joint to dinner”

Gladys took hold of Fred’s stump and Jay took his extended hand and the light-hearted trio, skipped merrily to dinner.

Chapter 20

Gladys was right about getting to the restaurant early as the influx of new guests was looking about wondering what the procedures were. The waiters as efficient as ever led them towards vacant tables and soon the newcomers were ordering their meals. They watched as the motley bunch filed in and sat down, it didn't take Gladys long before she had to pass judgement and as a result and between snatched mouthfuls of food, the evening was scattered with giggles and muffled laughter.

"'Ere look at that silly moo." What does she fink she looks like?" Mutton dressed as lamb, with a blooming toy boy in tow", indicating with a nod towards a woman who must have been in her sixties, the man trotting along behind her like a puppy dog looked half her age. This unlikely couple were shown to a table next to the critical trio, who were now smirking as their imaginations ran wild as to why these two were together.

Mrs Mutton, the deep lines on her face caked with powder giving her an ethereal mask, round circles of dark rose blusher on her cheeks, scarlet lipstick smudged over ungenerous lips, the apparent intention being to make them look more voluptuous and irresistible to the gigolo opposite her, whom she was now pouting at, the wrinkles above her lips becoming more evident. The gigolo played his part well and held her jewel encrusted hand in his and leaning forward whispered something in her ear, definitely suggestive by the coquettish look she gave him. Her heavy eyelids shadowed in violet plus false eyelashes that looked like caterpillars trying to mate as she fluttered them at her companion. A further attempt at defying the aging process was her hair which was dyed jet black and hung down in crimped waves over her shoulders, perhaps to camouflage her baggy neck, the skin of which hung in folds and would have been an asset to any British bulldog. She could have benefited from spending some of her evident wealth on plastic surgery. Leaning forward on his elbows, Fred whispered to the women, "Wonder what they're 'aving for desert?" jerking forward, forgetting that his stump was too short to support him adequately as he used his good arm to scratch his head in mock disbelief, Jay and Gladys could not suppress their gigglesand Fred took it well as usual.

"Can yer believe what's she's wearing, if her top was any lower yer'd be able to see her blooming navel!" Gladys' observation was second to none. "'Er skirt looks like a bleeding belt, 'ow she can walk in those 'eels, beggars belief".

"Wonder what he sees in her, he's not unattractive, in better shape than that Dave", piped up Jay.

"Don't yer go getting any ideas young lady, cos unless yer gotta loada wonga under yer mattress, that type of bloke wouldn't be interested" surmised Glad.

Jay's first impression was correct, he wasn't unattractive and immaculately turned out. Mutton at least had good taste in something. His hair wavy blue black hair had that just washed lustre about it and fell just below his ears, with his coffee coloured skin he looked of Mediterranean origin. He was quite slim, before he had taken his seat, Jay had noticed that he was not very tall either, however there a presence about him that oozed sex appeal and Jay kicked herself for not being loaded, as she could imagine that one night alone with this man would have been explosive and well worth the expense, after all it's a well known fact how hot blooded Mediterranean men are! Things were going from bad to worse now she was envying an old age pensioners' love life!

Overhearing some of their conversation Fred recognised the language as Italian and said, 'Ere, they're flipping I Ti's" Fred going on to explain about the time he had spent in Italy during the Second World War.

"You don't look old enough Fred," said Jay in all sincerity.

"Don't go pumping up his ego, 'e's got a big 'ead as it is".

"Now, now Glad don't go getting jealous just cos I look younger than you"

"Who, yer kidding yer ol' fool".

"Come on you two, behave," admonished Jay, wagging her finger at them.

"I was a boy soldier," reminisced Fred unperturbed by Gladys' ribbing, "I joined up when I was sixteen, lied about me age, the authorities never checked, they'd take any poor bugger that was willing. There were quite a few of us lads, some of 'em me mates. Eventually we were shipped off to Italy to back up our troops when the Nazis invaded. We stuck together through fick and thin, most of me mates got blown to pieces. I was lucky though, me best mate Jack, that's Jack Russell, we used to call him the terrier cos he was a real slip of a lad, used to be able to get into the smallest of places, 'e wasn't one of the lucky ones when the grenades went off. The silly bugger flung himself over me to protect me from the flying shrapnel, 'e was blown to smithereens, because of 'im I didn't lose me life I only lost this 'alf of me arm" he held his stump up to confirm his story. "'e was a bloody 'ero was Jack, I only 'ope 'es up there somewhere an' knows how grateful I am an' when I join 'im, I'll shake that silly bugger by the 'and" his voice cracked at the memory and a tear formed in the corner of his eye.

"OK, yer silly ol' devil that's enuf, don't go getting all maudlin on us now" with that Gladys got up and put her arms about his shoulders and gave him a reassuring squeeze. "I think it's about time we retired to the bar and got us a stiff drink, come on you two" and she pulled Fred up from his seat and they walked off arms about in other, in silence, closely followed by Jay.

Jay later learned from Gladys that Fred had spent a lot of time in an Italian hospital and that's where he had picked up the language. The rest of the war was spent convalescing. By the time they had reached the bar Gladys had raised Fred's spirits; it wasn't long before they were on the road to another evening of high spirits and laughter. Their conversation resumed, the solemnity of Fred's experience was not mentioned again. They ordered their drinks, Fred had a double whiskey, Gladys a port and lemon, Jay stuck with the orange juice and discussed their plans for the following and day, deciding it would be a good idea to ask Reception to give them all an early morning call at four-thirty, if they retired at around ten that night it should give them at least six hours sleep.

"I don't expect any more of yer shenanigans this evening you two, early to bed fer all of us, need ta be as fresh as daisies in the morning" Fred told them in a fatherly way.

"Yeah, an' no effing about for you either Fred, I need me beauty sleep".

"Yer can say that again".

"Yeah, an' no effing about for you either Fred", she reiterated.

"Ha, ha, very funny, I meant yer needed yer beauty sleep yer silly moo."

"Yer cheeky bugger" Gladys giving Fred a teasing clip about the ear.

"'Ere mind the barnet" he said as he ducked, obviously used to this type of retribution.

"Oooh, musn't muss the syrup. Yer big tart." Gladys carried on with the teasing. "Yer oughta see 'im, gets 'imself done up like a dogs dinner, 'ogs the bloody mirrer, I don't get a bleeding look in, if 'e weren't so 'ot in the bedroom department, I'd feel sure I'd married a blooming pansy".

Fred decided he wasn't going to win; Gladys' tongue was too quick, so he pretended he was in a sulk and huffing, downed his whiskey in one.

Chapter 21

As the previous evening, they took up position in the comfy chairs around the dance floor, a good observation point, drinks once more obtained they were ready for the floor show. Jay was relieved that there was no sign of Dave, Chris was there however; sitting at the bar, fag in one hand drink in the other in animated conversation with a plain faced teenager, who was a bit on the podgy side and by the look on her face totally besotted by him. Her giggling could be heard quite clearly, Chris had at last found someone who thought he was amusing. Poor little cow she thought.

The bar and dance area quickly filled up, several of the newcomers occupying the seats nearby. Most of them having that Mediterranean look about them. "Looks, like we're being taken over by 'em, still it might 'ave been worse, they could 'ave been bleeding German"!

"'Ere, now they look promising" Gladys nudged Jay drawing her attention to the two attractive men that had just come on the scene.

"You've got eyes like a hawk Gladys but I have to agree, they are quite tasty".

"Stop drooling you two, anyway Glad, yer spoken fer, so don't go getting yer knickers all wet with the excitement" Fred reminded Gladys of his presence.

"Gaw on wiv ya, there's no 'arm in looking, chance would be a fine thing any way".

They were temporarily drawn from their lecherous appraisal of two men upon the arrival of a young family, three children, all looked to be under the age of six, in tow. The middle one, a girl, was causing a right old rumpus, laying on the floor, thrashing about, screaming and hollering "I wanna ice-cweam, I wanna ice-cweam", mother had grabbed hold of the child's arm, pulling her across the dance floor, kicking and sobbing.

Gladys' immediately gave her opinion "What she needs is a bloody good 'iding, that's the trouble these days, no discipline".

The mother shook the child, who now had a stream of snot hanging from her nose and was gulping in air as though she was going to go into a convulsion. "If you don't stop it, you will go straight to bed and there will be no ice-cream for the rest of the holiday".

"Please, please, put the little brat to bed" Jay hoped, nothing spoilt a holiday like a load of snotty nosed, squawking kids. She didn't hate kids, providing they were not where she was; she'd had her quota of nappies, measles and chicken pox, there was no way she wanted to share in the trials and tribulations of other parents. Once again she was thankful that she was off tomorrow and wouldn't have to tolerate them for the next three days at least. The father stood by, he looked a bit of a wet blanket, watching whilst his wife admonished her daughter. The child screamed on.

"Right, that's it then, I've had enough, this is the

last time you come on holiday with us." The frustrated mother dragged her defeated looking child, back across the dance floor, floppy like a rag doll, who very so often would struggle and kick her heels in a last ditch attempt to get her own way. The father, head bowed, holding on to the other two, followed closely behind, looking rather sheepish. It was obvious who wore the trousers in that family.

"Thank goodness for that" Jay looked relieved. "I would have had to gone to bed myself if it had gone on any longer".

"You and me both" said Gladys then went back to the matter in hand.

Gladys had noticed that one of the two men at the bar had left, leaving the other on his own so she instructed Fred to go and strike up a conversation with him, eventually asking him to join them. Fred said that he was no blooming matchmaker and asked Gladys why she couldn't go, to which she replied that she didn't bloody well speak any I Ti. Fred once again defeated by Gladys agreed to go asking what he should say, to which Gladys told him to use a bit of common sense, ask him about Italy of something, then take it from there and not to be daft.

"Don't bother on my account." Piped up Jay feeling a little guilty as Fred reluctantly carried out his mission.

"You can shut up for a start, yer need some male company, listen to yer Aunt Glad. You", and turning to Fred "You can just go over and start a conversation wiv 'im, ask 'im where abouts in Italy 'e comes from, just make it up as yer go along, then when you've got a bit pally, ask 'im to join us. Simple ain't it yer great daft lump of lard?"

Jay wondered what Fred was saying, now that he had struck up conversation with the very attractive male specimen, hoping that he wasn't trying too hard on her behalf and making her seem like a desperate woman on the pull. The men were conversing quite freely, nodding at each other, Fred patting the chap heartily on the back at the same time turning and pointing towards Gladys and Jay. When Fred finally returned, much to Gladys' delight, he had the Italian in tow.

"There yer go, knew 'e wouldn't be able to resist once 'e saw yer. Yer never know yer may not be sleeping alone tonight".

"Gladys' you are incorrigible, what do you take me for?"

"Shut up and enjoy." Gladys commanded.

Fred was looking very pleased with himself "'Ere, guess what, 'e owns a blooming vineyard just outside of Rimini, that village where I was laid up, so we been catching up on what's been occurring there and 'ow it has changed". He then proceeded to introduce them "This is Hermes, Hermes this is me wife Gladys and the other charming lady is Jay"

"How do you do" said Jay shaking Hermes' hand.

"Very wella thank you" Hermes replied in a deep, sensuous clipped English accent, which resulted in Jay getting goose pimples.

Gladys followed suit, then the men sat down

and continued their conversation.

Jay found it quite refreshing that this man wasn't drooling all over her, so obviously a gentleman.

Whilst the men were talking Jay discretely appraised Hermes, he could have been aged somewhere between forty and forty-five, she could be wrong however as she was never any good at judging ages. Jay did not consider his angular features handsome but instead pleasantly interesting, he somehow intrigued her. Yes, she was attracted to him, possibly due to his accent as he spoke English in languorous way making the normally stiff words sound warm and seductive, like molten chocolate would be to a chocoholic. If he had said, "You smell like an elephants arse", it would still have sounded alluring in an odd sort of way.

Hermes had a dark complexion, a small scar evident on the upper part of his high cheekbone, just beneath his left eye. His eyes of brown, although quite small and close set were framed with thick dark lashes that alleviated the severity that's attributed to small eyes. His uncharacteristic fair hair was cropped short, just beginning to show signs of receding at either side of his temples. He was very debonair; with clothes that were expensively cut although casual. As he was talking to Fred he was, expressing himself freely with his hands, emphasising his words in a somewhat flamboyant theatrical way. The only jewellery he had on was a simple gold stud in his right ear and a gold band with a single diamond around the middle finger of his left hand. His long, slim, athletic limbs were not overlooked, although Jay was not too keen on the gold ear stud, she admitted to herself that he was strangely and undeniably attractive. Their conversation petering out, Fred turned to the ladies asking if they were ok for drinks and as they had almost emptied their glasses they both agreed that they would like top-ups. Fred got up from his seat to oblige, when Hermes got up to assist, Fred beckoned him to stay seated, "I'll be ok, I'll manage, will get a tray", and with that he went leaving the trio in uncomfortable silence staring into their drinks.

Gladys excused herself to go to the ladies, which left Jay and Hermes on their own at last. Jay having the sneaking suspicion that Gladys's visit to the loo was simply another one of her tactics as matchmaker, Jay would have to tick her off later. The silence lasted just a few moments, as she could not stand the uneasy atmosphere and tried to start up a conversation. "How long are you staying for Hermes?"

He looked up seemingly surprised that she had spoken and replied. "I am er 'ere, for de three weeksa."

"Three weeks, you lucky thing, I'm only here for seven days, off on Safari tomorrow for three days with Fred and Gladys".

"Thatsa good, I to ama going to Safari also witha my friend, whicha one are youa going?"

"I believe it is the Masai Mora Park or something like that, not very good with names."

"Whata, howa doa you say, coincidencez, we to are a going, itsa callda de Masai Mara Nationalez Reserve".

"Yes, that's it. Where is your friend this evening?"

"He hasa de sore 'ead, bad it make him sicka, 'e go to beda early".

"Migraine?"

"Yes, 'e getsa really bada 'ead, 'ope 'e ok for flighta tamorrow".

Fred with the tray full of drinks returned, followed shortly afterwards by Gladys, who just had to pass comment. "See you two are getting friendly." Grinning like a Cheshire cat.

Jay gave her a warning look as if to say don't you dare say anything more.

Chapter 22

The DJ who had only been playing low background music now upped the tempo and several people were on the dance floor. Music that sounded a faintly Hawaiian in an upbeat sort of way filled the air and Gladys grabbing hold of Fred, led him onto the dance floor and they began by spinning around each other in slow circles, Gladys imitating a hula-hula girl, waving her arms and hips to and fro as she circled Fred, they were both exceedingly spry for their age. Fred cheekily nipping Gladys' backside, whenever it was wiggled at him, Jay could see by the smile on her face that Gladys was enjoying it.

Nineteen fifties music was now blaring out of the loudspeakers. When Rock around the Clock came on Gladys and Fred came over to Jay and Hermes and not listening to their excuses dragged them both up onto the dance floor. Gladys danced with Hermes, who was insisting that "'e coulda notta danca" and Jay danced with Fred.

"Tell yer what," said Gladys "You two dance together, me and Fred enjoy a bit of rock and rolling, don't we love" and pushing Jay and Hermes together went over and started to jive enthusiastically with Fred.

Jay thought they were very impressive, to confirm her thoughts a circular audience formed about them and they clapped and cheered in appreciation at the expert display in front of them. Jay admired their stamina and zest for life, hoping that she would still be like it in twenty years time. They all stayed for the next dance, "Fifty ways to leave your lover". Hermes was right, he was a bloody useless dancer, he didn't hold Jay as she would have liked but instead they faced each other, Jay swaying gracefully in time to the music, he dancing rather floppily with hands by his side, his feet seemingly stuck to the floor as though they were super glued. So much for the hot blood that should be coursing through his veins he had a much life as a flaccid penis. Isn't it always the way, Jay was thinking, when ever you want the music to stop it just seems to go and on and on.

Gladys, thankfully, declared that she needed to sit down and have a drink; which gave Jay the excuse that she'd like to go and join her. All of them sat down except for Hermes, who said he had to get back to see if his friend was recovered, he would perhaps see them the next day at the Game Reserve.

. "He didn't seem to enjoy dancing very much did he Gladys?" said Jay feeling a smidgen of rejection.

"No 'e wasn't very good was 'e? Think 'e was worried about 'is mate, still never mind lass" patting Jay's knee "It's anuvver day tammorra".

It was almost time for them to retire for the night, when who should arrive in all his glory but Dave, dressed from head to toe in skin tight black trousers, black shirt and white shoes, his hair was slicked back with an attempt at a teddy boy quiff.

"Bloody 'ell, what the effing 'ell does 'e look like?" said Gladys with her usual expletives.

Dave headed towards them.

"Oh No" groaned Jay

As though prompted, You Are The One That I Want, song from Grease had started playing.

"Good evening ladies, Fred"

"'ello Dave" said Fred as the women didn't acknowledge him.

"Wow, look at you" addressing Jay and gaining her attention "Don't you look fantastic tonight, well looks like they are playing our song, I'll be your Danny and you can be my Sandy" and with that he whisked a protesting Jay onto the floor.

Unlike Hermes, Dave had no hesitation in placing his hands around her waist and holding her tight and then as though he had survitus dance, he let go of her, gyrated to the other side of the dance floor, spun on his heels and flung himself down on his knees and skidded across the floor ending up in front of her. "John Travolta hasn't got a patch on me, as he Jay?"

"No, Dave he hasn't" you great big twat she thought and made her way back to Gladys and Fred, who had obviously found it highly amusing as they were in hysterics.

"Thanks a bunch, I'm having serious doubts about you two, thought you were my guardian angels".

"Aw, come on, we're only 'aving a laugh, 'e looked so bloody stupid the big Jessy and 'e did it all for you", said Gladys.

"Maybe, but I think that little episode has

prompted me to go to my bed, it's passed our curfew anyway".

"Bloody 'ell, is that the time" said Fred "Come on Glad, we'll never get up in the morning"

"Yeah, ok, feeling a bit cream crackered"

They all made their way out and parted company at reception.

"See yer in the morning Jay, goodnight luv".

"Goodnight you two, sleep well and no hanky panky, you know I get jealous," Jay answered a little bit of truth creeping into her comment.

On her way back to her room Jay heard fluttering and squeaking above her head, she looked up and saw a spate of activity as dark bird like creatures, stiffed winged were swooping up and down in an erratic fashion, they were not much bigger than a sparrow. The light on the stairway was out and she had to fumble along the wall to find the switch, once illuminated there was an eruption of life. Geckos, small lizard type creatures, scurried willy nilly across the walls, trying desperately to find somewhere to hide, no sooner had she seen them than they had disappeared within the various nooks and crannies, harmless and incredibly shy, although they made her jump initially they didn't really bother her.

It dawned on her as she shut her door behind her that the flying creatures could possibly be bats, the noise they were making was ceaseless and continued to be so for the duration of the night, she hadn't heard them the previous night because she had been unconscious. Perhaps they were the reason there was no evidence of mosquitoes or any other creepy crawlies, Cecil, the monster spider, more than likely escaping their sharp little teeth because it was the same size as them, if not bigger.

She proceeded to ready herself bed, took off her clothes, brushed out her hair and tied it back into a ponytail then spread cream on her face to ease the removal of the evening's make-up, smoothing it away with cotton wool. She opted to have a complete wash down rather than a shower; now that she had some decent soap she could luxuriate in its frothy, rich consistency. Lifting each arm, she gently washed away that night's perspiration, which although not evident, would have become noticeable if left.

Her body had taken on a bronzed glow enhanced by the whiteness of the lather, massaging large breasts in circular movements, the nipples rising at the attention they were receiving. Rinsing off the soap from her upper body she continued down lingering a little longer than necessary around the yielding lips between her legs, the soapsuds making her fingers slide easily between them, stroking the now highly sensitive protuberance that had risen in anticipation of being convulsed into delight.

She continued manipulating and it wasn't long before she shuddered with pleasure, temporarily satisfying her need, only to leave her with a longing deep inside, for a man to hold in her arms and a throbbing cock deep inside that would bring her to the ultimate peak of complete and utter satisfaction. Tenderly she washed the soap away as though asking her body for forgiveness for not being able to appease entirely the want inside her.

Once dried, finding some tranquillity, her eyes, if not her body were ready for sleep, she brushed her teeth until they gleamed, rinsed, wiped the excess toothpaste from around her mouth, went to the bedroom, unfolded the mosquito net, slipped between the cool, crisp white sheets and fell into a dreamless sleep, not even the bats would disturb her.

Chapter 23

Knock, knock. Jay woke, wondering for a second where she was; the sun was not streaming through the shutters as normal. Knock, knock, knock. A little more demanding. Somebody was at the door to her room, still sleepy, she got out of bed fumbling for the towel she had flung over the back of the chair and quickly wrapped it around her body and opened the door.

"Your morning call madam, I took the liberty of bringing you coffee"

There stood Joseph, once again immaculately clad in white that dazzled her eyes against the darkness behind him.

"Oh, Hello Joseph, is it four-thirty already?"

"Afraid so madam."

She allowed him to enter her room to place coffee, a fresh roll and butter on her dressing table. She was aware that she only had a skimpy towel about her, causing her to be a little embarrassed, however Joseph was not perturbed and discretely kept his eyes cast downwards.

"Is there anything else I can get you?"

"No, that's fine, thank you Joseph"

"Have a good trip madam, you will enjoy it"

Turning on his heels he left her to drink the coffee. Switching the light on over the dressing table so she could see what she was doing then poured out the coffee.

"Oh Christ" Jay groaned when she saw a dark brown nipple protruding out of the towel. "Oh well, no point worrying about it now, hopefully it made Josephs' morning, no wonder he had his eyes averted".

Buttering the roll she took a big bite eating and drinking as she moved about the room, laying her clothes out in readiness for the trip. White t-Shirt, khaki shorts, white bra and pants. She hoped she had remembered to pack everything necessary, it was too late now to worry whether she had or not, she would have to make do; it was after all, only for two nights. Time was pressing on, she had a quick wash, brushed her teeth, tidied her hair then covered herself in sun cream. No need for make-up with her tanned faced she felt it wasn't necessary. She quickly got dressed, put on some comfy white moccasins, checked that everything she was leaving behind was locked away and left her room, shutting the door firmly behind her. As she walked out onto the balcony she was greeted by the dawn, it was breathtaking; the sun was now a ball of bloodshot orange, rising up from a bed of various hues of blue from cobalt to turquoise laced with the oranges and yellows emanating there from the ball of fire. The birds were well into their dawn chorus, the awakening of another day, what a view and what an excellent way to start out on what she considered her little adventure! Gladys and Fred were waiting patiently at Reception Gladys greeting her with "Whatcha, the cabs 'ere".

"Morning Fred, Gladys, did you get a good

nights sleep"

"It would 'ave been better if Glad didn't keep digging me in the ribs"

"Well, I wouldn't 'ave 'ad to if yer 'ad't kept bloody well snoring"

"What, I 'ardly snore at all, surprised yer could 'ear it anyway, yer deaf ol' bat"

Here we go again thought Jay, they're off again, their light hearted banter a joy to listen to, neither taking offence at the others comments, a gift that only those who are truly happy in each others company have. There was no doubt they were still in love, you only had to catch them unawares to see the way they looked at each other and how they were always making contact in some meaningful way or another. She wished she could find someone that she could be as happy with; she didn't relish the thought of being on her own for the rest of her life.

The driver, unable to speak English, only smiled at them as he put their luggage into the boot of the cab, Jay and Gladys sat in the back, Fred in the front. They left the hotel travelling along the craggy, dusty roads, their backsides leaving their seats when they went over the bumps. Fortunately there were only a few other vehicles on the road at this hour of the morning, so barely any danger of hitting anything as they were driven in a haphazard away, zigzagging across the road, if you could call it a road.

"This should help to get our backsides in trim Gladys, feel like I've had an hour in the gym already".

"Yeah, me arse will be black and blue by the time I get there"

"It'll match yer legs then" a muffled comment coming from Fred

"'Ere, whatya mean, yer cheeky bugger"

"Well, the varicose veins on 'em are like an ordnance map, if yer arse goes blue an all, then at least yer'll be colour-co-ordinated".

"You, bloody wait Fred Beasley, yer ain't too big to 'ave a clout".

They cab turned off the so-called main road and there before them was the poor excuse for a runway – Gatwick it was not!

"Oh, dear, what have we let ourselves in for Gladys?" asked a worried Jay.

They pulled up beside a small white plane an eagle in flight emblazoned on the side in blue, written in black and red were the words "Wings Over Africa"; it looked as though one puff of wind and this small aircraft would fall over – three white-faced passengers reluctantly left the cab putting their life's, or so they imagined, in the laps of the Gods.

"Hi there, take it you are on the Masai Mari trip," said a young man with an African accent, although very tanned he was undoubtedly Caucasian, with his white blonde hair and pale blue eyes. He jumped down from the aircraft, which wobbled back and forth, which only confirmed Jay's suspicion that it was a little too flimsy for her liking.

"That's right," said Fred replying to the blonde haired young man.

"Well you had better jump aboard then, is there only three of you?

"Yes, why you expecting more?" Fred asked him.

"Another two. We'll wait another ten minutes then we will have to go", he then unlatched the steps, pulled them down securing them in place saying "This way, if you please" and holding onto their arms (all except Fred of course), steadied them whilst they got into the plane.

There were six passenger seats inside, three rows of two, one behind the other, they had to keep their heads ducked until they were seated in the relatively small hard backed seats as the ceiling was low, a small window located beside each seat. The aircraft was remarkably clean inside; someone obviously took great care with it. Up front in the cockpit were the pilot and co-pilots seats.

Jay looked out the little porthole of a window, there was a cloud of dust in the distance and it was getting closer by the minute, another car.

"This must be the other two passengers" Jay offered the information to the young man as the cab pulled up and out got two men.

"Here Gladys you'd never guess, it's only Hermes and his friend".

"Well Jay, yer didn't 'ave much luck wiv that Hermes feller, now yer can try yer luck wiv the other!"

"Are yer being coarse again Gladys? Fred said obviously reading something more into her words.

"No, it's yer that filthy mind of yers again Fred".

"Well actually Gladys, I don't think I would

have much luck there either." Jay said interrupting them.

"Why not? A beautiful woman like you, a man would be a fool not to want yer."

"Just you have a look then." Jay urged and Gladys leant over Jay to look out the window.

Without thinking Gladys opened her mouth the words spilling out. "Effing 'ell, they're a couple of blooming poofs!"

There was Hermes, looking as dashing as ever in a khaki safari suit a pith helmet balanced on his head, leaning against him was his "friend". As they drew closer she took in the astonishing sight before her for Hermes' companion was wearing a large pink, floppy rimmed hat with a blue and green patterned chiffon scarf wrapped around the brim, the scarf hanging limply down until a breeze caught it and wafted it up into the air. Perched on his nose were horn-rimmed sunglasses, that when viewed close up would reveal sparkling coloured stones along the top of the frame, even Dame Edna would have been proud to wear them. He had a loose fitting; cream translucent shirt, pierced nipples. The tight pink three quarter length trousers clung to his crutch where there was not much evidence of any genitalia. Six-inch stilettos would not have looked out of place with his outfit but instead he had chosen flat turquoise canvas pumps. A gold stud earring in his right ear that was exactly the same as the one Hermes had in his. As he walked, tight cheeked towards them, he lifted his arm theatrically, the back of his hand held limply to his head as if feigning faintness. Hermes, looking concerned, had his arm about his "friend" protectively.

The young man once more alighted from the plane, ushering the odd couple on board towards the two vacant seats in front of Gladys and Jay.

"Hello, dida notta realise thata you a, were a, flying outa on de same a, flighta" Hermes speaking in Italian turned to his friend and introduced them.

"Franco, Signorina Jay"

"Hi" said Jay and in return Franco waved dismissively at her with his limp hand.

"You a willa excuse a Franco, he still 'asa de sore 'ead anda he speaka no English" Hermes said apologetically continuing the introductions in Italian.

Franco dismissed Gladys and Fred with a discourteous nod then placed his head on Hermes shoulder.

"Franco, isa mya, 'ow you say?

"Rear gunner" piped up Fred.

"Noa, he'sa. Whata de word"

"Gardener?" Fred offered at the same time whispering behind his hand to Jay "Up hill gardener that is". Jay covered her mouth to smother her laughter.

"Noa, Isa 'ave ita now. He'sa my lover." Now smiling because he remembered.

Gladys now unable to control herself said in a disparaging voice. "No, way, really we would never of guessed". Hermes did not appear to notice the disapproval and went back to patting Franco.

"OK, everyone time for take-off, fasten your seatbelts," said the young man.

"What about the pilot?" Asked Gladys.

"I am the pilot. Peter Fourie at your service. " The fair haired young man told the shocked passengers.

"Christ, he's hardly out of nappies," said Gladys, as usual, far too audibly.

"I can assure you madam that I am fully qualified pilot and have been so for several years. You will be pleased to know I very rarely make a crash landing"! He said with a wicked smile on his face.

"That'sa nota funny" said Hermes as Franco who must have understood some English after all, had gripped him tighter and was clearly shaking in his boots.

Peter went forward and took up his rightful place in the pilots seat.

Fred asked Peter "Shouldn't we 'ave a co-pilot?"

Peter explained that there was no need for a co-pilot for trips under four hours and Fred with a loud humph, grumbled that it wouldn't be allowed in England. Peter told him that protocol rarely exists in Africa, they make up their own rules, but for the sake of appearances why didn't the lady come up and join him. Jay said she didn't think she was brave enough, but Gladys had other thoughts and pushed Jay off her seat propelling her towards the front of the plane, telling her not to be a stupid beggar, she'd have a great view. Patting the seat next to her she told Fred to sit down. Jay sat down next to Peter, it was better than watching the two poofs canoodling, she would have more than likely ended up spewing and it would not have been due to the flight! She glanced around, she wasn't sure whether the aircraft could actually take off, let alone fly, loads of buttons, switches and dials, which she made a mental note not to touch under any circumstances.

Peter looked at her "Your names Jay isn't it?" "Make yourself comfortable."

"What type of plane is this Peter? She asked making an effort to converse under nerve-racking conditions.

"It's a single engine eight-seater, that is six passenger Piper Cherokee, I can assure you that you will have an enjoyable flight, you may never have the opportunity to sit in a cock pit again".

That sounded ominous she thought as she listened to him.

"The view of the Savannah will leave you breathless, make your pulse race with delight at the sheer excitement of this experience."

"Let's hope you're right," replied Jay thinking all that was missing from his description was the ultimate orgasm".

"OK, everyone fasten your seatbelts." Peter shouted back to the others. Jay sat rigid clinging onto the sides of the seat.

"Piper 1 to Tower, ready for take-off for Masai Mara, over" said Peter into the handset. "Tower to Piper 1, clear for take-off, over"

A resounding bang sounded as the Piper engine sprang into life, blue smoke wafted past the window, "Strap yourself in Jay", Peter instructed, as the radio crackled like popping corn. She quickly did up the belt and once again took up her poker like position, gripped the sides of her seat, clenched her teeth and closed her eyes.

The plane juddered into life slowly taxiing along the runway, which seemed interminable as the ancient Piper rattled and shook its way along the rutted surface. Jay peeked every so often to see what was happening only to quickly close them again. She could feel the plane start to leave the ground and bump back down again, making the cheeks of her arse tighten, making her wish that she had the foresight to have taken some Arret tablets beforehand, as she felt if the flight was anything like the take-off she would eventually shit herself! The plane once again attempted to leave the ground, this time successfully, the bumpy ride had stopped and the engine was now purring instead of choking.

"You can open your eyes now Jay, we are now flying at two thousand feet" said Peter encouragingly. Jay did as she was told, gingerly opening them, there in front of her was the wide-open space of the blue, blue sky reaching for miles in every direction, her fears at last gone as she gazed out at the truly amazing spectacle before her, she was lost for words.

She could hear Peter relaying to the tower that we were now on Charlie and he took his hand off the joystick and standing turned to speak to Hermes, the African Queen, Fred and Gladys. "Anyone like a cold drink?"

Well the African Queen nearly had a fit when he realised the pilot was not at the helm and muttered something Italian in his a high pitched effeminate voice, Hermes consoling him by patting his knee and whispering something into his ear, a little too close to be polite in company.

"Jay's not flying the plane is she?" said Fred

Gladys reacted with. "Bleeding 'ope not."

"It's ok chaps, we are on Charlie and to the uninitiated we are flying Beacon to Beacon, that's automatic pilot" Peter reassured them.

"Is it safe?" asked Gladys

"Don't be stupid Glad, would 'e use it if it weren't safe?"

Peter undid a heavy metal case filled with ice cubes and pulled out various bottles of soft drinks, removing the caps passed them around, the green-faced Queen looking down his nose as a bottle was handed to him, it didn't stop him sipping weakly from it though, after he had of course wiped the bottle neck. Peter nudged Jay's elbow with a bottle of 7Up, drawing her away from the panoramic view below, then sitting down beside her. "I told you it was breathtaking, didn't I Jay".

"You certainly did"

Switching off the automatic pilot he took hold of the controls again. "Ok, if you look out of the windows I will take you down for a closer look." Peter turned the plane and swooped down low. "Those are water buffalo, if you look closely you will see their young, they stay in herds, it's safer because there are plenty of predators out there".

"Look" shouted Fred "Elephants"

Below there was a small herd of about six elephants, one so huge it stood out from the rest. "Now that's a magnificent Tusker." Peter continued. "The head of the herd, beside him is his matriarch, I will see if I can get closer as she has a baby tagging along behind her." Peter swooped lower causing the elephants ears to flare back, their trunks rising in awareness of their presence. They started to run kicking up the dry earth until only their heads and backs were visible. "They are off to the water pan, we may be lucky and see some hippos to".

They were awestruck, glued to the wildlife below, the only interruption being Hermes translating Peter's dialogue to Franco. God, thought Jay, this is Africa, if only she had someone to share this experience with. The plane once more started to gain height, there not far from the plane were, as Peter explained, vultures and condors, they were soaring on the thermals, he noticed that the vultures were gathering towards the ground, so once more Peter took the plane down for a closer inspection telling them that they were gorging themselves on a carcass of a young Springbok that had probably been slain earlier that morning. Once more the radio crackled, the African language that came over the airwaves was gobbledegook to Jay but Peter seemed to understand what they were saying.

The plane dropped abruptly, according to the altimeter, by two hundred and fifty feet, it made Jay's stomach go up into her mouth. Thank goodness I only had a light breakfast, she thought.

"Hold tight," said Peter. "Hold tight," said everyone echoing Peter's words, all except Franco who was still clinging to Hermes like a bad rash. "We are coming in to land. You will see the Lodge shortly"

They flew down low over the campsite; there were about a dozen large tents dotted around a riverbed with two round thatched buildings set some way from them. Jay could just about make out some activity in the river, plenty of waterfowl and what Peter said were hippos. An abundance of greenery, huge trees that buzzed with life as they flew over disturbing the many white birds, looking like someone had thrown a barrow load of confetti into the air as they took flight. There was one long thatched building about half the length of the river, which Peter told her was The Lodge, with several white clad figures moving about, disappearing every so often under the building.

After circling a couple of times, the radio crackled again, this time the voice from the Tower was speaking English.

"Tower to Piper 1, Tower to Piper 1. Are you receiving me? Over"

"Piper 1 to Tower, reading, over"

"Tower to Piper 1, landing instructions, South, South East, full flaps, left rudder 180 degrees. Over"

"Piper 1 to Tower. Roger. Over"

Jay thought that the take-off was pretty scary but sitting in the co-pilots seat, whilst attempting to land on a ploughed field is nothing short of terror, the stuff nightmares are made of. She once more found herself gripping onto her seat, clenching her eyes tight and praying for a safe landing. The plane bumped up and down several times, then came to shuddering halt, clouds of dust covered the plane obliterating any view of the outside world. When the yellowy brown dust cloud had disappeared, Peter opened up the door and lowered the steps; they all alighted exhilarated but relieved that they were on terra firma. A dusty red, open topped Jeep was there at the end of the runway waiting to transport them to their accommodation; Peter accompanied them.

It was just a short drive, the scenery a drastic contrast to the beach resort that was stark in comparison. The dense foliage bristling and alive with noise, varying in tone and intensity, Jay was all eyes, peering out into the green depths hoping that she would see something. "Look, look Gladys." She said like an excited child "A monkey, it's got a baby hanging underneath".

"Coo, look Fred, ain't it great." Gladys said busily snapping photographs.

"Looks like it's coming down" Fred said just as excited.

The driver slowed the Jeep down, the rather large monkey made it's way down the tree and through the grass until it was walking with it's four long legs beside them, the baby clinging underneath for dear life. The driver stopped and Fred, digging deep in his pocket pulled out a boiled sweet, throwing it the monkey, who reached out and caught it with ease, placing it in it's mouth, sitting in front of them with the look of deep concentration sucking the sweet with evident enjoyment.

"That's a baboon, you can tell by its arse and long face"

"My yer very knowledgeable all of sudden Fred"

"Well, I should know, I've been blooming living with one fer long enough"

"That's it, no more hows ya farver fer you me lad"

"Right, and no more bananas for you"

"Don't yer go getting all smutty again", said Gladys once more ticking Fred off.

Their humour was lost on Hermes, Franco and the driver but Jay and Peter thought they were extremely comical. The driver continued to drive on slowly until they finally reached their destination, The Lodge, as it was called.

Chapter 24

They were greeted at The Lodge by a handful of willing, smartly clad porters who immediately took their luggage and smiling beckoned them to follow. They entered an extremely large thatched building, leading to the reception, the porters were handed their respective tent numbers taking the luggage they beckoned the little convoy to follow them through the open plan building. There was a wonderful aroma of freshly baked bread and other temptingly mouth watering smells emanating from what would be the kitchen. Several white clad waiters were standing by studying the newly arrived guests. A short tubby man approached them, he was dressed in white, though unlike the sarongs of the waiters, he was wearing trousers, he had a black bow tie and a gold oblong badge with black lettering upon his shirt pocket, identifying him as the Manager. His hair was almost black hair, although there wasn't much left of it as his dark brown scalp shone through the strands that were sleeked over it. However, the thick long handle bar moustache under his large bulbous nose, more than made up for the lack of hair on his head. His face was weathered looking like tanned hide, boasting two very rosy cheeks, as though he had been rushing around.

"Bonsoir Mesdames est Monsieur's, moi

nomme est Marcelle Dupres, I am pleased to be at your service and welcome you to The Lodge. You will be escorted to your accommodation and then return for petite déjeuner. I 'ope everything will be to your satisfaction. English or Continental breakfast will be served for you in fifteen minutes. Please be comfortable."

Marcelle's English was very clear but he still laced it with the odd smattering of French. Jay had always thought the French accent, elegant and romantic, she still did, even though it was coming from this funny, stout, little man. Again the small convoy set off, acknowledging Marcelle Dupres with a thank you, or a nod as they went by him. Peter had claimed a stool at the bar and was already downing a well-deserved lager. "See you later" he said, raising his glass to them.

They passed the garden where several large wooden tables and seats stood, the seats having crimson padded covers for comfort. The tables were set for breakfast with brilliant white tablecloths and crimson napkins fanned out at every place setting. Several arrays of flowers in small glass vases strategically placed and sparkling cutlery adorned the tables, belying the fact that the were, after all, only picnic tables. It all looked very luxurious, not at all what Jay had expected, she honestly thought that she would be roughing it in a camp site, maybe cooking baked potatoes over an open fire, like in her Girl Guide days but this exceeded her expectations. If she had any doubts at all about spending more than her allowance on this trip, they had soon disintegrated. The walk to their tents took them along a path beside the riverbank, where Herons were wading looking for a meal, Grebes diving below the water, monkeys chattering in the trees above and brightly coloured blue and yellow weaverbirds flitting back and forth in front of them, then diving into the abundance of exotic flowers, the bouquet of blossom wafting on the breeze, the scent was glorious. If this wasn't Eden then it must be pretty damn close to it, Jay decided. She couldn't wait to get to her tent, settle and then return quickly to the deliciously tempting smells that were awaiting them at breakfast. It was now gone nine o'clock and she was ravenous, having only eaten a roll that morning. They went over a tiny little bridge with larch tree branches interlocked forming sturdy handrails, to one side was a small waterfall, which cascaded down in a flurry of shimmering ribbons into the small babbling brook below them, tiny fish darting around in nonsensical display. As they crossed the bridge their shadows being cast upon the brook below, the little black and gold fish disappeared under the lily pads, which were the biggest and most beautiful that she had ever seen.

Jay didn't think things could get much better, she'd have been happy sleeping in a one-man tent in these surroundings and was again surprised when looming up in front of them were half a dozen enormous dark green tents that looked more like marquees and she was going to have whole one to herself. "Oh, Gladys, isn't it wonderful, I could spend my whole life here, pinch me I think I'm dreaming". "Ouch" screeched Jay as Gladys obliged.

"Yeah, it's outta this blooming world ain't it girl?"

Gladys and Fred were shown to their tent, Jay had the one next to theirs about twenty-five metres away, Hermes and Franco were in one on the opposite side.

There were two wooden seats outside with crimson cushions like the ones in the dining area, along with a small wooden table, a couple of what looked like oil lamps to either side. The coffee coloured, black haired porter, who escorted her didn't look much over twelve years of age, such a skinny slip of a lad. He unzipped the front of her tent and then undid the secondary zip, pulling back the flap back to allow her to enter. He indicated to her a flask on the long dressing table that would contain cool fresh water, plus The Lodge information guide.

Inside the tent were three single beds; one in the far corner and the other two alongside each other just as she entered, each bed had a bedside cabinet. A large rosewood chest of drawers and matching wardrobe stood against the sides of the tent, small gaily woven rugs were laid beside each bed, the floor being of the same resilient texture as the tent, was sealed at the bottom edges, so that once zipped the tent would cocoon the occupant in its security. Situated at the back was the bathroom, not a bucket or a hole in the ground as Jay had envisaged but a fully functional flushing toilet, sink and shower, all very tasteful in white, the shower curtain adding the only colour to the bathroom with its white herons on a blue background. Never in all her imaginings had she thought a tent could be so luxurious, she was highly delighted with her lot. She dismissed the porter with a tip, he said something to her in Swahili, which must have been thank you and he disappeared through the opening of tent.

Jay opened her bag, taking out her toiletries then placing them in the bathroom, splashing her face quickly with some cold water she dabbed it dry on one of the soft white towels, then went out into the sunshine, remembering to close the zippers on the tent to prevent the mosquitoes, spiders and snakes from gaining entry.

Chapter 25

.After making her way to Gladys and Fred's tent, as there was nowhere to knock, she called out enquiringly to them. "Hi, you in there?"

"Yeah, just on our way won't be a mo'"

She waited until they emerged. "Don't forget to zip up," she advised them, as they were just about to leave without doing so.

"That's something we'll 'ave to get used to, you can remember tha' can't yer Fred?"

"What do you think Gladys, isn't it wonderful, I didn't expect anything like this, it's superb." Jay could hardly wait to have a look around.

"It's certainly different, I'll warrant that, 'ow I'm going ta sleep with all this blooming twittering going on I don't know".

"You'll be alrigh', stop blooming moaning and let's get some breakfast down us" said Fred.

Off they went to satisfy their hunger. As they came towards the dining area, Marcelle greeted them. "Are you all 'appie with your accommodation ?"

"Yes, thankyou, it's marvellous, exceeding our expectations by far" Jay answered, her delight evident from the smile she presented him with.

"Très bien". "This way. Your table, Mesdames et Monsieur, sil vous plais" proceeding to pull out Gladys chair for her, when she had sat he shook open the fanned napkin, placing it over Gladys lap.

"Coo, luvva duck, see Fred, that's 'ow yer treat a lady".

"If yer were a blooming lady, I'd treat yer like one", Fred quipped.

Marcelle then duplicated his actions for Jay. "Merci beaucoup Marcelle" Jay smiled up at him.

"Ah, parlez-vous français, mademoiselle?"

"Oh, no, no, very little" she said holding her hand up in denial. "Only what I can remember from school and that was a long, long time ago", quickly reverting back to English "And I'm far from being a mademoiselle".

"You still look like a young girl to me mademoiselle".

"You French men, so charming" Jay replied a little flattered. "Now what's on the menu for breakfast?"

"Le fruit salard, cereals et le Continental breakfast. It is over there, a buffet service," he said pointing over her shoulder "This est le breakfast menu, if you would like something from this", handing her the crimson menu card. "Barbu will take your order, please to enjoy your meal". Marcelle then went to the table where Hermes and Queenie, who was still wearing his stupid pink hat, were already seated.

"Ere" said Gladys "Think that Marcelle bloke 'as a soft spot for you, nevver thought 'e'd go".

"Aw, shut up an' leave the girl alone," Fred groaned at Gladys.

"Right what we having then, I'm starving" intervened Jay.

"Well, I'm going to the buffet fer some fruit juice 'n' cereal, if that Barbie chap turns up, tell 'im I'll 'ave the scrambled eggs, bacon and toast".

"It's Barbu, Fred" Jay corrected him. "Yes, we'll tell him, would you mind bringing me an orange juice please?"

"Ok, luv. What abou' you then Glad, do you want a juice?"

"Yeah, I'll have grapefruit if they've got it, if not orange will do".

Off Fred trotted and the girls perused the menu once more deciding what took their fancy. "There's such a lot, can't make my mind up, that's the trouble when I'm hungry, I want to eat it all", said Jay.

Gladys decided on the Eggs Benedictine, the women had a little discussion about what they were and how they were cooked etc., Jay thought they sounded good so she decided to have the same.

Barbu arrived and took their order and duly departed. Fred returned, tray in hand, upon it were his cereal piled high in his rather large white bowl, several small pastries and their fruit juices. Fred passed them their drinks "Blimey Glad, yer oughta go and see the amount of food they've got up there, enuf to feed a blooming army".

"Looks like yer made a dent in it, sure yer got enuf?"

"Yes thanks". He proceeded to tuck in.

Perfectly timed, just as Fred wiped the surplus crumbs from his mouth, Barbu arrived with the Eggs Benedictine and Fred's breakfast. "This look scrumptious" said Jay.

They eagerly ate their meal; it was so good hardly a word was spoken until they had finished. "By the way", said Fred "I saw that Peter at the buffet, said we would see 'im alright later, 'e was pretty good after all said and done".

"That's fine with me, though I don't think we can speak for Hinge and Bracket over there".

"Stuff 'em, we'll steer well clear of 'em, blooming poofs, give me the willies, don't like to turn me back on 'em, nobody's going to oil my back gate, I can tell yer", Fred said shaking his head in disgust.

Gladys, quick as flash, "So they give yer the willies then do they? Told you I 'ad me doubts about 'im didn't I Jay?"

"Shut up yer silly moo, yer know what I meant".

They were just about to leave their table, to freshen up back at the tents, when Marcelle reappeared. "I 'ope you all enjoyed your meals."

"Yes thank you, very much, compliments to the chef," said Jay

Marcelle handed Jay a piece of paper with some writing on it, "From le management mademoiselle," and he briskly walked off.

"See, told ya, he bloomy fancies yer" said Gladys, dying to know what was written in the note.

Jay unfolded it, her eyes welling up with tears at the words she read:

Darling Jay,
I have searched for two whole days for you, only to find that you had gone on safari. I hope you don't mind but I followed you. I am waiting at the bar please join me. Steve. xx

"Come on, tell us, what 'e said? Has that Frenchie upset you, you wait til I see 'im".

"No, Gladys, it's not Marcelle. Don't you worry, these are tears of joy not unhappiness, you go back to your tent and get changed, I will catch up with you later and tell you all. Now don't worry about me".

Fred and Gladys, looking a little concerned did as she said, leaving her sitting alone.

When Jay knew they were out of sight she slowly turned, looking over her shoulder towards the bar, there staring straight back at her was Steve. In her excitement at seeing him she knocked over her seat as she got up to rush over to him; she crossed the expanse of ground between them with the speed of light. Steve standing up, caught her in his arms, holding her tight, then looking down he lifted her chin with his finger and kissed her tenderly on her trembling lips. "I never thought I would find you".

"I never thought you would either, I'd given up all hope of seeing you again". What happened?"

"The maid took my trousers to be cleaned and the slip of paper with your telephone number was still in them, when they came back, alas no number. I rang all the hotels I could, then I actually went to several of them until finally I found the right Sandy Beach Hotel, they told me you had left this morning at five-thirty and where you would be staying. I chartered an aircraft immediately, flying here straight away arriving only thirty minutes ago. I had a devil of a job stopping myself from running over to you and whisking you away from those two old age pensioners."

"Those two old age pensioners as you called them happen to be my guardian angels I have you know, they have been looking after me, they really are quite hilarious. Gladys is bursting to know what's going on".

Marcelle came over at that moment "Excusez moi Monsieur Steve, chef said whilst you are here can you have a word with him about the changed menus. Clarence had to call the vet out to Ollie, he'd cut his leg, so you may want to go and see him also".

"OK Marcelle, thanks, remember don't forget to do that little job I asked you to do, Miss Patterson will be wanting to freshen up soon".

"What's going on Steve? She said curiosity getting the better of her. Why does the chef want to see you? And who is Ollie?"

"It is such a big coincidence Jay, I could barely believe it myself when I was told where you were staying. This is one of the properties I set up five years ago; also I'm a major shareholder. As I think I told you I am currently in the process of organising a similar one to this in Zimbabwe. I usually visit here once or twice a year if my commitments allow. My impromptu visit has taken the staff by surprise, they will try and monopolise me whilst I am here but I am not going to allow that to happen as I have a lot of time to catch up with you. I will go and see chef whilst you are changing then I will introduce you to Ollie".

"I can't believe this, just wait till Gladys hears about it, she's been trying to pair me off with every

Tom, Dick and Harry, including those two over there" discreetly indicating with her eyes Hermes and Franco.

"You must be joking," said Steve.

"No, we didn't realise what they were until Hermes turned up with Franco for the flight, came as a bit of a shock I can tell you".

"I bet it did, that one with the pink hat would more than likely have had your eyes out if you had made a pass at his boyfriend. Well Jay, I believe we deserve a drink don't you? Benjamin, a bottle of Dom Perignon 57, please," he called to the bar tender, and looking at Jay he said, "Only the best will do for you my dear".

The champagne flutes filled, and Jay forgetting her resolution never to drink again, they toasted each other, Steve saying "To the most beautiful woman in The Masai Mara Lodge".

Jay reciprocated "To the most surprising man, here's to a great few days". The bubbles tickled Jays nose making her sneeze. This was now going to one bloody fantastic holiday.

"Now my dear sweet Jay, it's time for you to freshen up. I hope you don't mind but I have a little surprise for you".

"As long as it's a nice surprise," she said.

"Well I hope you think it is, I have upgraded your accommodation".

"But I thought what I had was excellent, surely there's nothing better".

"Believe me my dear, there is and you shall have it as you will be my guest for the remainder of your stay here".

"Marcelle," Steve called. "Get Samuel to show Miss Patterson to her new accommodation please. I take it that everything has been done that I have asked for".

"Absolument Monsieur Steve" said Marcelle.

Samuel arrived to take Jay; Steve bent down and kissed her on the forehead. "I will call for you in an hour, that should give you time to get ready for our little excursion, then on to our own private safari".

"I'll look forward to that," she said with feeling.

Chapter 26

Samuel led Jay up pass the tents where she saw Gladys and Fred, sitting outside and made a point of going over to them. Samuel waited patiently for her to finish her conversation.

"Hi, well I expect you are itching to know the gossip".

"We did wonder," said Fred.

"Well, I never mentioned it before, because I didn't think anything was going to come of it, but a met this chap called Steve on the flight over here, he said he would look me up and when he didn't I was really disappointed. Anyway, it turns out he has been looking for me and to cut a long story short, he's actually a shareholder in this place. He's upgraded me, haven't even been to see it yet and then he's taking me on a private safari, just the two of us. He's really luscious Gladys; you'd love him. He's picking me up in an hour so I have to dash and get ready, will catch up with you later. You both have a good time today". Waving goodbye she went to her tent to pick up her belongings.

"No, madam, everything has been taken care of" Samuel told her at the same time beckoning her to follow.

She followed him over yet another bridge to the other side of the river; looking in the direction they were going she could see two large round thatched buildings, they were even bigger than the tents and built on top of a small incline.

"Is this where I am staying"? She asked Samuel.

"Yes, madam, you are special guest of Mr Steve".

As they ascended she took in every detail. The black walls had burnished orange motifs, so typical of African art, painted around the circumference of the building, the thatched roof just overhanging the tops of the windows. The heavy dark oak door boasted a big round iron handle that Samuel turned, swinging the door open he allowed her to pass. Jay stood, her mouth agape in wonder at the sight that met her eyes for the room was filled with a plethora of long, green stemmed flowers with white tubular heads, the red stamen inside dusting the inside of the petals reddish pink, their sweet uplifting perfume filling the room. Steve had done this for her what a thoughtful, generous man he was.

Well, she thought the tent was magnificent but this was spectacular, like something out of Vogue. The luxury it afforded excelled even the best hotel that she had ever stayed in. It was so big that she could have swung an elephant around in it. The walls were painted white and hanging on them were large dark framed pictures of lions, elephants, impala and more that she couldn't put a name to. The ceiling was high, dark oak beams stretching upwards into the cavity of the pitched roof, various African artefacts hanging from them, she looked for the shrunken skulls and was thankful there was nothing like that around, what was there, was in exceedingly good taste.

An enormously large circular bed commandeered the centre of the room with a lavish gold and red bedspread adorning it; one corner of the bedspread was folded back revealing the creamy white silk sheets beneath as though tempting her within. A mosquito net was draped in scallops from the circular frame attached to the ceiling beams and tied back in red and gold ribbons that matched the bedspread. Either side of the bed were zebra skin rugs contrasting dramatically against the warm terracotta of the floor tiles. The matching ebony wardrobe, dressing table and chest of drawers were moulded so that they fitted snugly to the curved walls, all possessing ornate handles of ivory entwined with gold.

Her bag had been packed for her and it was lying near the chest of drawers. On top of the chest were several large boxes, on the dressing table where there should have been a flask of water, stood a bottle of Dom Perignon 57 and two crystal champagne glasses. Between the glasses stood a white card with distinctive black handwriting, which she immediately recognised as Steve's. Lifting the note Jay read the words.

Darling Jay,
I hope you like the Rondavo. I have supplied you with an outfit for this afternoon's excursion; I hope the size is ok. The smaller package is a special something I have envisaged you in, I hope you like them as much as I do.
I will call for you at 11.00 a.m., when we will break open the champagne.
Love, Steve xx

Wondering what he expected her to wear Jay rushed over to the boxes. There were four gold and white striped boxes in all, two large, one medium and one small. She opened one of the large ones first and there folded neatly inside was a light khaki safari type shirt, she took it out of the box and checked the size, it was a ten. The designer label inside was a name she didn't recognise but she just knew it was expensive. Under the shirt was what she thought were a pair of khaki trousers but when laid out on the bed she saw that they were a pair of culottes, very stylish. She then opened the next large box and inside was a pair of riding boots, dark brown leather kidskin, again the size, a four, was spot on. The medium box was next to be opened, inside was a beautifully crafted, ladies pith helmet, in a darker khaki, she slipped it onto her head, looked in the mirror saw her image and laughed. She didn't normally wear hats; the unaccustomed weight feeling strange, it fitted snugly though so if that's what Steve wanted she'd wear it to please him. Now for the last package, this is the "special something" that Steve said he had envisaged her in, she was intrigued, what else did this man up his sleeve. She opened it up and there were the most luxurious and tantalizing pair of black lace French knickers with matching brassiere. She smiled thinking "saucy beggar", but she could not wait to try everything on, never in her life had a man bought her underwear, she did not find it offensive, in fact, it endeared him to her all the more.

Jay went to the bathroom, her toiletries having

been laid out in the splendid bathroom, it couldn't have been anything but splendid now could it? There was a toilet, bidet, sink, massive glass panelled shower and an extremely large deep round bath, more like a small swimming pool, it had the many round vents attributable to a Jacuzzi, she'd love to find out if it was but there was no time to wallow in a bath, a shower would have to suffice. Turning the shower on she found it unexpectedly powerful and instantly warm, she took off her clammy clothes and stepped in, pulling the glass panels shut giving herself up to the enveloping warmth of the pummelling water, it was extremely invigorating. She quickly washed, and shampooed her hair, rinsed off, stopped the shower and stepped out, grabbing a buttercup yellow towel in the process, it was so big she could have wrapped it around her twice. Yes, she could easily get used to this lifestyle.

Her hair dried quickly so she pinned it up off her face, her body dry she put on deodorant and sprayed herself with smelly mosquito repellent, unfortunately it was necessary. She dabbed some perfume about her person to try and camouflage the smell, it was halfway successful. Now for the French knickers, she slid them on, pulling them up over her long slender legs and then over her tummy, wiggling her backside so that they fell right. They were so comfortable, especially in this weather she thought, they let the air circulate nicely. Now the big test, she put the bra on, not too bad, it did fit but it was slightly padded, she had no need for assistance in that department and thought that her boobs looked gigantic, the padding pushing her up and in, making an extremely deep and captivating cleavage. Still Steve had taken the trouble to buy her these exquisite garments the least she could do was to wear them. She put on the culottes, they fit perfectly and looked great, now the shirt, there was no problem doing the buttons up until it came to the top two, because of the added inches caused by the bra the shirt was a little constricting, she could maybe get one of the buttons done up, but the top one just would not be persuaded. She looked in the mirror, only a little bit of cleavage showing, she wondered whether she should change into a t-shirt when she heard footsteps approaching, then a knock on the door.

Chapter 27

"Is that you Steve"? She called through the door.
"Yes."

"Won't be a minute", she glanced in the mirror, well you will just have to do now, she thought, there's no time to change and she went and opened the door. There stood Steve, looking like Indiana Jones except better looking, she noticed that he had great legs; his calves were like granite and deeply tanned, an Adonis in khaki.

"Hi Honey, let me look at you" she stepped back and he grabbed her hands and lifted her arms out so to get a better look. "You look fantastic Jay, they fit perfectly?"

"Yes, who's a clever boy then?" She didn't have the heart to tell him that the bra was making her feel like Dolly Parton.

"Where's that champagne?" and he walked passed her into the Rondavo, picking up the bottle he popped the champagne, the cork ricocheting against one of the beams and hitting Jay in the thigh causing her to yelp. "Oh honey, I'm sorry, come here."

She sheepishly made her way over to Steve, rubbing her smarting leg. He lifted the edge of her culottes and inspected the damage "Looks like you are going to have a nasty bruise there," and with that he bent and placed a kiss upon it sending a shiver of delight throughout her whole being.

"I must get hit by corks more often, if that's the treatment I am going to get".

"Go on with you, let's sit outside in the sunshine and drink our 57, then you can get your boots on, because you may need them if we get out of the Jeep and you will definitely need the hat".

"Thanks Steve, for all the things you have done for me and all the wonderful presents you have bought, I feel like all my Christmases have come at once, I'm so pleased you managed to find me".

"I'm pleased I found you to and if I have my way Jay, everyday will be a Christmas Day for you".

They sat in the comfy little chairs and drank their champagne, Steve told her about The Lodge and how it had changed since he had got involved and he was going to show her around before they went off to the reserve. "I am definitely impressed and I know Fred and Gladys are, it's better than I could have ever imagined, this is going to be the best holiday ever".

"You'll be pleased to know that I have looked after them as well, I have sent them over a couple of bottles of champers and I have commissioned one of my best guides to take them on their own private safari, so they won't have to be bothered with the shirt lifters".

"Thanks again Steve, they will appreciate that and so do I, they have been such good fun to be with, if it wasn't for them I would have been right down in the dumps and maybe not even here".

"Why's that then?"

"Because I was pissed off with the fact that you hadn't contacted me, why else?"

Steve was pleased that the fact that he hadn't contacted her had such an affect of her, but he was also sorry that he had upset her; he would make things up to her. "Well, if you'd like to go and put your boots on, we'll be off now"

Jay went back inside the Rondavo, slipped on white socks and those so very, very soft leather boots, they fitted like a glove. She walked out and Steve tucked her arm through his as he proudly walked her to the rivers edge and described the lay-out of the land that he had nurtured.

"Darling over there is twenty-six hectares of some of the most arable land that money could buy, but we won't sell as we are going to introduce the black rhino, which as you may know is nearing extinction. On the other side of the river we have given over ten hectares to our staff and their families, to plant, tend and grow their crops. They live mainly on mealy meal."

"What is mealy meal?" she asked.

"Well, darling, you might know it as corn on the cob." "That's enough about the property, we have to get a move on time is fleeting and I want to introduce you to Ollie before we set out." He then led her by the hand to the back of The Lodge where there was a large open enclosure with several small thatched shelters to either side of it. "Ollie" he shouted, "Come on you old devil, look what I have for you and reaching into his pocket he pulled some pellets".

"Jay, you call him, he may respond to a

woman's' voice".

"Ollie" she called, not knowing what to expect, then a rustling and stirring came from within one of the shelters, then surprisingly a long, long neck with an inquisitive round, wide eyed, beaked head peered out at them.

"He'll be out in a minute, his curiosity will have got the better of him and if he thinks I have some of his favourite biscuits he will not be able to resist".

True to his word, one long leg with pronged toes came out, as though testing the water, then the other, bringing with it a body covered in glorious plumage and there stood Ollie, indeed he was a magnificent specimen of a male ostrich, stretching his wings, and stirring himself from his sleep.

"Isn't he fabulous" exclaimed Jay.

"Yes, he's one of the resident pets, he roams freely, a big softy, we rescued him as a chick and raised him after his mother was slaughtered by a pack of lions. He was obviously small fry and they had left him to his fate, poor little bugger, very dehydrated when we found him, lucky to be alive. We have a fantastic vet and he advised us what to do and now look at him, a wonderful creature and he loves people to bits, he would never be able to go back to the wild, he wouldn't survive, that goes for most of the animals you will see wondering about".

"What else have you got then?"

"We have a couple zebra, they are fairly shy, although they will come out early morning after that they keep a low profile. We have just acquired a baby pot bellied pig; we have named him Curly. Also waddling about the place you may see a Pelican, he's called Roddy because he's a great fisherman and last but not least two young giraffes, Tina and Gerry".

"Why Tina and Gerry?"

"Well we called Tina after Tina Turner as when she stood her legs used to be so far apart, just like Tina Turner's when she danced and of course she thinks she is "Simply the Best", bossing poor old Gerry around something chronic".

"And I suppose you named Gerry after Ginger Spice?"

"No, it just went well with Giraffe, Gerry Giraffe!"

Ollie, drawn by their laughter was edging nearer, powerful legs strutting out, stopping every so often to dip his neck, stretch it and turn his head almost 180 degrees, assessing all around him and when he was sure there was nothing coming at him from behind or from either side he would slowly and deliberately start his strutting again.

"Come on Ollie, we haven't got all day" and Steve shook the pellets in his hand holding them out and tempting Ollie.

Ollie obliged, crossing the last few feet swiftly in two gangly strides, coming to an abrupt halt, his head whip lashing back and forth on his infinite beanpole of a neck, and would have quite easily collided into Steve had he not been so agile in side-stepping out of the line of fire.

"That was close" Jay breathed a sigh of relief and took cover behind Steve, holding onto his hips, if she hadn't of been so concerned about Ollie's next move, she may have found pleasure from the fact the cheeks of his firm buttocks were pressed against her stomach. However that went unnoticed as Ollie's' head, having gobbled the pellets greedily from Steve's hand was now searching for more and he was now peering behind Steve and down into Jay's eyes. "Eeeek" she squealed, digging her nails into Steve's waist.

Steve tried to extricate himself from her clutches, pulling each hand off him, but no sooner had he removed one; then she would quickly attach it to him again. "Come on now Jay, nothing to be scared off, Ollie's a pussycat".

"Really? He's a blooming big pussycat!"

Steve laughed at her "Now let go, there's a good girl, I can feel you drawing blood now".

"Sorry, didn't mean to, just I'm a bit nervous"

"I would never of have guessed, now come here" he took her hand and pulled her to his side, opened her hand and put some pellets into her palm.

"Give them to Ollie and he will be your friend for life"

She held out her hand as far as it would reach and as Ollie approached she hid her head behind Steve, thinking that she would be lucky if she had a hand left once Ollie had finished. However, Ollie was surprisingly gentle and when Jay finally took the courage to come out from behind Steve, Ollie was standing looking pensive, tilting his from side to side giving her the once over.

"Go on you can pat him if you like" Steve urged her. She reached out and stroked the dense plumage on Ollie's muscular back, occasionally removing it when she thought Ollie was going to peck her as he looked down at her with those big black jet stones of eyes. "He's ok Jay, he won't hurt you, he's just curious, it's not often a beautiful woman strokes him" he reassured her. "Now aren't you the lucky one, for once I wish I were in your shoes", he contemplated as he too patted the now docile Ollie, deliberately brushing the softness of Jay's hands and noting the unpainted but well manicured nails, that had inflicted such bitter sweet pain upon him.

"Goodbye, Ollie, no doubt we will see you later around dinner time, but for the rest of the day my time is going to devoted to this delectable creature beside me" and Steve put his arms possessively about Jay and led her off back towards the Lodge and to the waiting Jeep.

Chapter 28

A smiling Marcelle was, as ever, conveniently present. "I have done as you requested Monsieur Steve, the hamper is in the back along with the camcorder and camera. If there is nothing else I can do then I must get on, the other guests will be returning in an hour for luncheon".

"No, that's fine Marcelle, you carry on, you have done an excellent job", Steve praised.

The Jeep was different to the one she had travelled in on her way to The Lodge; it was camouflaged in spiralling snakes of varying shades of green and brown, so as to blend in with the surroundings. Steve opened the passenger door for Jay and guided her into her seat of sumptuous dark brown leather, the yielding softness moulding itself to her contours. He skipped light footedly around the front of the Jeep and jumped into the drivers seat, planting a quick kiss on her lips before he settled back and fastened his seat belt at the same time indicating that she should do the same. "Now, hold onto your hat darling, we are in for one hell of a bumpy ride".

Steve started the engine and it roared into life, putting the Jeep into gear they moved off down the rock-strewn, potholed road. They drove in silence out onto, as Steve informed her, the main highway, she would never have guessed as this was just as untouched by tarmacadam as all the other roads she had experienced the discomfort of travelling upon. The only thing differentiating it from all the others was the amount of vehicles, varying in dilapidation. Lorries cram-packed with people, like sheep going to market, cars that could never have passed an M.O.T. in England as they had doors hanging off, rust corroding holes in the body work. Almost all were emitting dark grey diesel fumes appearing like ectoplasm out of every aperture and would catch the back of their throats when it gained access through the windows of the Jeep. Steve told her to wind her window up and although he had turned the air-conditioning on, the fumes still persisted in finding their way in. "Don't worry honey" Steve said patting her knee "Not long and we will be free of civilisation, it will get better, I promise".

Jay hoped so, she had packed up smoking several years ago, she'd hate for all her efforts at preserving her health to be unwarranted. There were various people walking alongside the road, women with supplies piled high on their heads, balancing them skilfully, not once did she see any of these women drop a single item. A man with a small herd of goats, their skins no longer white but a dirty, dusty grey, looking emaciated and lethargic, their bones of their rib cages clearly visible. He had a long stick in one hand, which he was using to continually prod them in the right direction, but they didn't look as though they had the energy to take flight or disobey. Jay would have liked to give him a prod; her heart went out to these poor creatures.

"Who are they?" said Jay looking through the window and pointing at two extremely tall men, their colourful garb draped about their persons. Their hair was plaited and hung down their backs, ornate jewellery about their necks and through pierced ears. Both carried long spears.

"Those are Masai warriors, they are a very proud race, noted as great warriors, although nowadays they are a great tourist attraction and make a good living out of that by selling the items that they make and putting on displays of tribal dancing. I find it all a bit tacky, if you go to their villages, they supposedly still live in mud huts, and you have to keep your hand on your wallet, as the youngsters are so slippery they could steal your radio and the leave the music behind. Tourists sometimes feel intimidated and are tricked into buying things. The Masai never seem to want for anything and I have the sneaking suspicion that most of it is for show and they more than likely go home to a lovely brick built house with all the modern conveniences at the end of the day. That's only my view though, I have acquired a suspicious nature since having worked in third world countries for many years, TRUST NO ONE, that's my motto". Lifting Jay's hand to his lips he kissed it saying, "I may of course make an exception of you," and taking his eyes of the road for a second, winked at her.

Jay, felt a warm sensation of tenderness flood through her entire body, she would have loved for him to have stopped the Jeep and take her there and then in wanton abandonment. Just that simple little action had awakened in her a yearning for this man; she didn't just want to hold hands and embrace, she wanted the whole shebang, she hoped in her heart that Steve felt the same way and that she wouldn't have long to wait.

"Hey, you look deep in thought, you ok?" Steve drew her out of her imaginings, little did he know that just the thought of being with him had caused a moistness between her legs, she hoped it wouldn't be evident on her clothes and fidgeted to pull the material away from her skin, she casually extended one long slim booted leg up onto the dashboard in the hope that the cool air-conditioning would circulate up the leg of her culottes and to the crutch of her knickers, hoping that it would assist in drying them out before she had occasion to get out of the Jeep, so there would be no tell-tale dampness visible.

"I'm fine, just got a bit of cramp in my leg, it will be ok in a mo" she lied rubbing her thigh, which was unwittingly provocative and Steve grabbed the opportunity to be slightly suggestive.

"I'd love to massage it for you honey, but I'm driving, perhaps you can arrange to have cramp later, when my hands are free".

"Steve", she said as though shocked by his words but quivering at the thought, and she bore in mind that if he didn't make a move later then perhaps she could be inflicted with cramp again.

Turning off the main highway and along yet another unmade driveway, Jay was grateful that the seats were amply padded, as her backside would have come in for some serious battering, as it was, it was feeling a little tender. They passed through a large wooden archway a big sign displaying the name UMGOWA RESERVE. "You may want to reach over and grab the camera or do you know how to work the recorder, you will definitely want to get something to remember."

Jay undid her seatbelt, leant over to the back of the Jeep, retrieving both the camera and the camcorder. Steve pointed at the buttons on the camcorder, taking his eyes of the road every few seconds to explain the operation of the camcorder. "It's very simple, that one turns it on, that one records and that lever there enables you to zoom in and out, just point and shoot".

She practiced with the camcorder, aiming it at Steve whilst he was driving, zooming in and out on the strong profile before her, she called his name and he turned, smiling at her in that endearing lopsided way, his blue dark lashed eyes twinkling with amusement. He was at ease in front of the camera and now she was ensnaring him forever, to eventually take pride of place in the library of her video collection.

"Yes, think I've got the hang of it, it's not rocket science."

"That's good because you are going to need it soon". He drew the Jeep to a halt and then opened up the top. "There, now you can stand up and shoot till you drop, lean forward and rest your arms on the top of the windscreen to steady yourself, that's right, ok brace yourself". Steve put his foot down and she almost toppled over on top of him, but she somehow managed to regain her stance, her elbows resting on the top of the windscreen and with camera steadied between her hands, she was now ready to do her David Attenborough bit and hoped that indeed her pants had dried out and there were no marks showing through the khaki culottes.

They drove on along the dusty, paprika coloured earth; it wasn't long before Steve had to stop as a group of Springbok moved in leaps and bounds in front of them, she captured their elegance on camera. As the group cleared they set off again, Impala grazing leisurely beside them. In the distance was a black mass, looking like millions of ants slowing moving about. Steve once again put his foot down. "Now this is a sight you don't want to miss, pointing at a mass of large animals."

"What are they?"

"Water buffalo, we may be able to drive through the herd, we must be careful we don't get a rogue male buffalo, they can be dangerous, you just carrying on filming, it's my job to keep a watchful eye out". They neared the now heaving group, there seemed to be hundreds of them, big black cow like creatures, enormous wet snouts and menacing looking curved horns, their tails swishing away the hoards of flies that were continually pestering them. They didn't mind having the tiny little birds sitting on their backs and pecking away at their hides, Steve explained that these were Oxpeckers and that they helped keep them free of tics and other pests, that's why they tolerated them. The buffalo were very wary of them being there and standing stock still stared at them showing the whites of their eyes, she felt she should be scared but Steve was so confident that she put her faith in him, she felt secure in the knowledge that he would do nothing to endanger their lives.

"Christ almighty, look at the bollocks on that one", she forgot herself for a moment, slapping her hand over her mouth because of the profanity that she had used. Steve wasn't shocked and understood her terminology as one enormous bull waddled off, his pendulous testicles the size of watermelons, knocking against his legs. No wonder he walked laboriously with those between his legs, she thought, however he didn't seem to be having any difficulty mounting the cow that was now under him, he was rumping away like a good-un, perhaps that was all he needed to rid himself of some excess protein and in turn reduce the cumbersome weight of those pendulous testicles.

"Some guys have all the luck," said Steve laughing.

"Well if you ask the poor cow, she may oblige if you're that desperate", she quickly retorted laughing.

"My, you are witty Miss Patterson." Laughing he shared in her amusement.

She was impressed with Steve's knowledge, he knew what all the animals were, giving a running commentary as they passed, from Wildebeest to dung beetle. There were so many varieties of deer, they saw Dik Dik's the smallest deer's in the world, they mated for life and if they lost their partners they would live out their lives alone, sometimes dying of a broken heart.

They were lucky enough to see a group of female lions with about eight cubs, the lionesses were laying under the shade of a tree and the cubs, were jumping on them and climbing up the trees above their heads and sometimes falling onto them and getting a smack down with a large paw in reprimand.

Steve told her that this was a Crèche where the younger females look after the cubs of varying ages from various lionesses, enabling the alpha females to hunt for food, of which the alpha male is always the first to eat after the prey has been killed. Steve then went on to explain there was a hierarchy amongst the female lions, the eldest being the alpha female then down the scale, aunts, nieces etc. Males usually had their own prides, which consisted of as many females as he could, not only cope with, but also defend.

Drawing up beside a large watering pan, so close she felt she could touch them were three elephants, one bull, one cow and a calf. Jay watched as the slowly entered the muddy water, rolling over covering their dusty brown bodies until the water washed over them leaving their hides dark and glistening. One by one they stood up and drawing the water up into their trunks they sprayed it over their heads as though they were showering. The bull elephant made his way out of the watering pan towards them, Steve started up the Jeep and gently pulled away. The bull turned his back on them and as though he was giving them two fingers, cocked his back leg up, looked over his shoulder to see them off and then went back to the cow and calf in the water.

Chapter 29

"Now, my dearest Jay", said Steve "Let's go and find our own private watering hole, I think it's time for some refreshments, don't you?"

"Yes, I'm parched." She moistened her dry lips with her tongue. "Hope it's somewhere safe and we aren't going to be on someone else's menu".

"No, we will be quite safe, the sun is getting stronger, animals are far more sensible than us, they will be having their siesta in some shady nook somewhere".

"Well, in that case what's keeping you?"

"OK, keep filming, we'll be there in five." As they drove on, the occasional red beaked, spindly legged, bird madly dashed across in front of them, how they never hit them, she would never know.

Through the view finder she saw coming into view an expanse of water, several trees sparsely lining the bank, a mini oasis, the only sign of life was a heron ducking its beak periodically under the murky pool, looking for his lunch. Steve parked near to a tree, the branches with a meagre covering of vegetation offering a little shelter from the sun. Jay stayed in the Jeep until he had prepared the ground for her to sit on. A green tarpaulin and a blue cotton sheet to cover it, he added a couple of cushions, she continued filming him at work until he patted a cushion, beckoning her to come and sit.

It was like discovering a whole new world and they were the only two people in it. "Now make yourself comfortable" Steve told her

"Can I help with anything?" she offered.

"No, I've told you, you are my guest and I will attend to your every whim"

A parasol was hammered into the hard ground beside her, he opened it and to add to her comfort made sure that it was in the optimum position. A hamper followed and when opened offered up all manner of delicacies. Canapés with various savoury toppings, sliced chicken breasts in aspic and a crisp green salad, there were several exotic fruits; mango, paw paw, prickly pears and a melon and yet another bottle of Dom Perignon, to wash it all down. Just as Marcelle had done that morning, Steve flicked open the serviette and laid it across her lap. He then reached down and picked up a canapé and placed it between her lips. "You can have that to be going on with"

"Mmmn, yummy, give me more"

"Patience my dear" with that he went and retrieved a small tripod from the Jeep to put the camcorder on, once he was satisfied that it was positioned correctly and the camera running, he went and sat down beside her. He popped the champagne, filled her glass and they toasted each other, after which he ordered her to eat, drink and be merry.

They ate, drank and were certainly merry. In fact Jay was feeling rather tipsy, wondering whether she could control the urges that were springing from within her as Steve was intermittently feeding Jay titbits and wiping the crumbs from her ripe lips with the serviette. He longed to kiss her but restrained himself from doing so, as she was visibly enjoying the spread before her and so was he, his eyes were looking at her culottes, the legs of which had ridden, exposing the tanned flesh of her thigh.

They ended the meal with the fruit; Jay laying back her head on the cushion, her eyes closed as Steve fed her the exotic fruits piece by piece. His mind wandering to more lustful feelings as he thought it would more appropriate to call them erotic fruit, rather than exotic as the long juicy slices of melon, conjured up images in his mind as each one slid between her eager lips, passed the tiny white teeth, to be lapped by a darting wet tongue, her saliva surrounding it, she swallowed, sliding it slowly down inside into the welcoming depths. To make his restraint even more difficult he noticed that now the top three buttons on her shirt had popped undone and he took advantage by taking a long look at the deep cleavage, so clearly defined by the black lace bra that pushed her breasts up until they overflowed. The temptation was great to push the shirt aside and uncover the nipple hidden beneath, he remembered vividly the moment when her nipples were almost revealed to him before, when the drink was spilt over her whilst they were on the plane. You delectable woman, I could eat you, he mulled over in his mind. A stirring in his loins made it plain to him that if she were to open her eyes, it would soon be evident what he was thinking and as much as he desired her, this was not the time or the place for passion and that is what he wanted, pure unadulterated passion. Jay's hat had fallen from her head and lay upturned behind her, dark curls breaking loose from the restraint of the pins that had tied it, he caught one between his fingers and wound it around his finger and lent forward and once more took in the fragrance of almonds and orange blossom, a perfume that he would always associate with Jay. She mewed like a pussycat, content after her meal and sleepy from the champagne. He kissed her tenderly on the lips, and then stood up and walked off in the direction of a tree some distance away, he had to relieve the tension that was building up in him and if he couldn't make love to Jay then there was only way left that he could think of.

He stood, leaning his back against the tree, taking a look over his shoulder to ensure that Jay was still asleep and when he was happy that she was, he undid the fly on his trousers and took his throbbing cock in hand, holding it for a long moment imagining that it was she that had it within her small palm. He gently massaged it back and forth moving the skin slowly over the throbbing helmet, squeezing it gently, adding some lubrication of spittle from his mouth, the movement flowed more easily, he closed his eyes and dreamt that she was wearing those French knickers, slipping them off one leg had then opened her wonderful legs and had taken him inside. His hand gathered speed at the thoughts tumbling from his mind until finally he reached his crescendo, moaning deeply, saying her name softly and spurting his juices onto the ground below.

“Steve, Steve, where are you” Jay was calling out to him.

“It’s ok, I’m over here” He quickly adjusted himself and did up his fly and with shaky legs, made his way towards Jay.

“I wondered where you were, thought something had happened to you”, she jumped up and flung her arms about him, holding him close.

“Don’t be silly, nature called, that’s all”, well he wasn’t exactly lying was he?

“Next time tell me, thought you’d be carted off by a hungry lion or something”.

“If this is the response I get when I disappear, I might do it more often”.

Jay let go of him “That’s not the least bit funny” she said.

“OK honey, sorry I worried you, but come back here I was enjoying that cuddle” and she went back into his arms and they stood holding each other, her dark brown head of curls close to his chest.

Come on let’s pack up and get back it’s getting late and the mosquitoes will be doing their rounds very shortly.

Chapter 30

They arrived back at The Lodge at six p.m., the sun now almost gone and the air not so stifling, both agreeing what a glorious day they had spent together. They had managed to fill in all the gaps about their lives, their likes and dislikes everything that they never had time to discuss whilst on the flight over, there was practically nothing left to tell, they now knew almost all there was to know about each other.

Jay decided that he was the perfect gentleman; he so obviously loved pampering her and she enjoyed being pampered, an attribute sorely missing in her previous partners. Her feelings towards him had deepened immensely today, not once had he attempted anything untoward and although she was a little disappointed, there was still the evening and the night ahead. Steve was having similar thoughts, Jay was delectable, funny, smart and stunning with the body of a woman half her age, she was truly fantastic company and had aroused feelings in him that had laid dormant for several years, yes he was an extremely lucky man and blessed the day that her tampon landed at his feet. "Can you find your way back to the Rondavo Jay, I just need to make a quick phone call to the vet to check on Ollie, although I didn't notice anything wrong with him when we saw him earlier did you?"

"No, he seemed full of beans to me. I'm sure I

will find it, I'll call in on Fred and Gladys to see if they enjoyed their day and then I will go and get freshened up".

"OK darling, do you want to come down here for dinner and join your friends or we can have something on the patio outside your Rondavo, what would you prefer?"

"I would enjoy just spending the time with you" she said still in a state of euphoria.

"OK then, I will call on you at seven-thirty, we will dine at eight". He kissed her for the umpteenth time that day and she hoped that the evenings kisses would be much more ardent, if Steve was still behaving like a gentleman she would do her utmost to convince him he needn't bother!

Gladys and Fred were sitting outside their tent, drinking long cool lagers.

"Well, 'ow d'ya do stranger?" said Gladys. "No don't bother telling me, I can see by that big Cheshire grin on yer gob that yer've 'ad a blooming good time. Fred go and get the spare chair, this young lady is going to tell us a story. Ain't yer lass?"

Jay excitedly told them about her day, reciting all she could remember about the animals, the picnic under the tree and more importantly about Steve. "Gladys, I cannot tell you how happy I am, it's been one of the best moments in my life, I never thought I would be so lucky as to meet anyone like him and I think he genuinely likes me to".

"A beautiful woman like you of course you deserve to have some 'appiness in yer life", Fred piped up.

"Yeah, you go for it love, 'e sounds a nice chap, 'e certainly did us proud today, we 'ad a fabulous time and we 'ad a bottle of champers each, not that we're keen on it, but it was a shame to let it go to waste, if yer get me drift, of course we 'aven't 'ad the privilege of being up on Snob Hill, like someone we know".

"There is another one next to mine, but there is only two. I may have a word with Steve later see if you can come up there and keep me company. You think these tents are great, wait until you see the Rondavos".

"Ooooh, Rondavos, is it? Now ain't that posh?"

"She's only joking Jay, take no notice of the silly ol' boot, we're 'appy enough where we are", said Fred a little embarrassed by Gladys jesting.

"No, Fred, I mean it, there's no harm in my asking Steve now is there? Anyway, I've got to dash, Steve is arranging dinner at my place, so I'm afraid you won't be having the pleasure of my company tonight. Now I must go and have a shower, I'm absolutely filthy".

"Don't think we didn't notice," said Gladys as Jay ran off laughing.

She was deliriously happy, the day had been absolutely fantastic and there was more to come, she could hardly contain her excitement. Steve made her feel so special, like she was a princess, bowing to her every whim and spoiling her rotten and she loved every God damn minute of it.

For once Jay didn't dally in the shower; she wanted to be ready for when Steve arrived. Hurriedly washing the dust from the day off her curly mop of hair and her ever-darkening skin Jay sang out joyfully, even though a bit of key.

"Cupid draw back your bow oh oh, and let your arrow go oh oh, straight to my lovers heart…",

Whenever she sang at home, her kids compared her singing to that of a cat being strangled, she didn't consider it was quite that bad, she enjoyed a sing song and although they would feign annoyance she would continue on regardless, choosing not to notice their groans, exaggerated pulled faces and fingers in their ears, anyway there was no need for her to worry up here, there was nobody around to hear her inharmonious screeching so she carried on.

"Cupid draw back your bow oh oh……."

She concluded her ablutions, giving her teeth a thorough brushing, looking in the small mirror, she rolled back her lips and bared her teeth for closer inspection, satisfied that there was no fragments of the afternoons food evident, she rinsed several times with mouthwash; wanting to be fresh for the kissing she intended to do that night. She sauntered into the bedroom, a big yellow bath towel wrapped about her. Blinded by the towel that she was drying hair with she flopped down on the bed, only to get a sharp dig in the backside, she stood up quickly rubbing her bum, looking around to see that she had sat upon yet another white and gold striped box. "Where did that come from?" A frown appearing on her forehead as she spoke aloud "It wasn't there when I came in!" Realisation dawned her; someone had entered her Rondavo whilst she was showering. "My God, whoever it was must have heard her making that racket," embarrassed at the thought. The embarrassment was lost quickly in her excitement to find out what was in the box and she hastily lifted the slightly battered lid, a little card again written in Steve's handwriting read:

My Darling Jay,
Thanks for a wonderful day as a token of my appreciation. I'd love it if you would please wear it this evening.
Fondest Love, Steve xx

She carefully undid the tissue and gently lifted the garment by the delicate diamante straps, her eyes wide with amazement, as the luxurious amber silk of an exquisite evening dress unfolded languidly before her. A lump formed in her throat and her eyes filled with emotion, the tears welling up and clogging her lashes, she had never possessed anything so gorgeous, Steve certainly knew how to pamper a woman, if there had been any doubt about her feelings towards him, they had now evaporated. It was evident that a lot of thought and attention had been given in selecting this exceptional dress for her and she felt a dire need to hold this very special man in her arms.

She laid the dress out lovingly on the bed and wiping her eyes with the back of her hand checked her watch. "Crumbs, it's seven o'clock." Grabbing a tissue, she blew her nose and then proceeded with her make-up; she would make more of an effort tonight and choose carefully so as to compliment her dress. A light brown shadow for her eyes and a slightly darker tone to define, as well as several layers of mascara making her lashes even longer and thicker than they already were. She brushed her still damp hair, detangling it and then crunching between her hands to tighten the curls, she would leave it down tonight, it was more seductive and she had plans to hopefully seduce Steve later. A touch of colour to her cheekbones and a pale lipstick with lots of gloss finished her look. Jay decided against the foul smelling mosquito repellent, wanting to smell divine tonight so she splashed on some of her favourite perfume, not too much, just enough to stimulate Steve's senses. She searched the chest for some underwear having only bought a couple of pairs of knickers with the full intention of washing them out at night so the only clean knickers available were the black French knickers that had almost smothered Steve on the flight. Not normally the colour she would have chosen to wear under such a beautiful amber dress, other than going without she had no option and hoped the material was dense enough for them not to show through. A bra was out of the question, not with those delicate straps, so she didn't have that worry and her breast were firm enough to do so.

She turned towards the knocking on her door at the same time glancing at her watch, it was seven-thirty; Steve was on time. "Hold on, I won't be moment", Jay shouted as she stepped into her knickers and, taking care not to get make up on it, slipped the cool amber silk dress over her now almost bare bronzed body. Taking one last look in the mirror, her eyes still sparkling from the tears of joy that she had shed earlier, approving very much of the dress clinging to her curves, yes she was extremely pleased with her reflection, the only downer was the white moccasins on her feet, even though the dress was long enough to cover them she was a little disappointed with them.

Chapter 31

Steve turned to look at her as she opened the door; she was a vision of loveliness, the amber dress he had chosen for her was perfect, the silk folds clinging to her fabulous body revealing every contour, leaving little to the imagination, an amber hue surrounded her giving her a radiance which took his breath away.

Jay stood transfixed at the sight that met her eyes, what seemed like hundreds of candles their dancing flames lighting up the darkness, never in her wildest dreams had she expected this. A large oblong table was now in place of the small square one and was immaculately set in colours of white and red, a silver candelabrum in the centre, the flickering flames from the candles reflecting on the rows of silver cutlery, sending tiny shafts of light into the night. Once more Jay welled up with emotion and looking at Steve, who looked magnificent in his cream tuxedo and black trousers, she stepped into his open arms, the heady, tangy aroma of his aftershave alerting her senses. "Oh Steve, how did you manage all this" she said huskily finding it difficult to speak.

"I had a little help from my friends".

"I never heard a thing".

"You were in the shower, I almost rushed in when I heard the wailing, then I realised you were attempting to sing and thought it best I leave".

"Are you inferring that I've got a terrible voice?"

"Let's just say I've heard better and leave it at that?"

"I think we better had".

"By the way I forgot to give you these" Steve produced a small box and handed it Jay.

"Steve, you shouldn't have, you've given me far too much already." Jay opened the box and inside was a pair of sparkling, gold coloured stiletto mules; she held them in her hands, and once more found she was fighting back the tears, she mustn't ruin her make-up.

"Well don't just stand there, try them on" ordered Steve.

She took off her white moccasins and flung them carelessly into the room and put on the gold shoes, lifting the dress and pointing her foot towards him for inspection. "They are so soft and so beautiful Steve, I feel like Cinderella".

"My dear Cinders, you will go to the ball," said Steve bowing low, one arm about his waist the other stretched out to the side, directing her towards the table and pulled out her chair and as Marcelle had done before he placed the napkin over her lap. Taking a bottle of the renowned Dom Perignon from the silver ice bucket, he expertly popped the cork and quickly filled the crystal champagne flutes, the effervescent liquid cascading over the sides and the bubbles damping the tablecloth. Steve then pulled out his chair at the opposite end of the table and sat down lifting his glass he toasted her. "To the start of our beautiful relationship, long may it continue"?

"To the wonderful man that every woman dreams of", Jay raised her glass to him. A candlelit dinner? Most men only thought about candlelit dinners when there was a power cut! He really was full of surprises.

"Now honey, look in front of you and you will see a menu, that Marcelle and I have contrived together, I hope you like it". Jay lifted the embossed white card and turned it over and read the handwritten words.

DINNER BY CANDLELIGHT
In honour of Jay
A very special lady
LANGOUSTINES
(in ginger butter)
~
NOISETTES OF PORK
(with prunes and calvados)
accompanied by
Gratin of Parsley Potatoes
A Julienne of baby vegetables
&
Asparagus Tips
~
CHILLED BANANA SOUFFLE
(with burnt orange sauce)

"It's perfect, absolutely perfect Steve" said Jay not being quite sure what Langoustines were, but he had painstakingly taken the time to make everything just so that she didn't have the heart to enquire.

“Well if madam is happy we’d better make a start” and he picked up the little silver bell and rang it as loud as he could, the door of the adjoining Rondavo opened and a white clad entourage, led by Marcelle, emerged, lidded silver salvers held aloft in their hands.

“Good evening, mademoiselle”

Marcelle clapped his hands and the waiters laid the silver salvers upon the table, he then lifted the lid on what looked like enormous prawns. “The finest Langoustines, cooked to perfection by Jacque our Parisian chef, please enjoy.”

Once he had placed six Langoustines, coated with ginger butter, upon each of their plates, offering them each a thin slice of brown bread, Marcelle then clapped his hands again and led the entourage back towards The Lodge. Steve and Jay watched as the white figures disappear into the blackness and once out of view, they started to relax and enjoy this marvellous meal that had been prepared and cooked in her honour. They were at last alone.

“I feel like royalty”, said Jay “The Langoustines melt in your mouth, I could get used to this.”

“I hope you can, because if you stick with me kid, this is just a sample of what will be showered upon you”. Steve said with sincerity. Jay’s head was spinning; she was intoxicated with the happenings of the whole day, it couldn’t just be put down to all the champagne she had drunk, could it?

They sat and drank, enjoying each other’s presence, one course followed the other, Steve acting as waiter, expertly spooning out helpings of the noisettes and vegetables, each time he served her he planted a kiss upon her lips and on one occasion licked a tiny piece of sauce from her chin saying, "We don't want it going on that beautiful dress now do we?"

The intimate action of his warm tongue lapping her chin made the yearning deep inside her stronger and although the food was superb she could not wait to finish the last course.

Steve watched as Jay spooned the banana soufflé slowly between her lips, closing them around the spoon and smoothing off the creamy substance as she removed it, her pink tongue slowly licking away the excess from the corners of her mouth. He found her simple actions highly erotic, through her long heavy lashes her eyes smiled at him from across the table unaware of the effect that she was having upon him. They chatted inconsequentially and laughed about how they met and the incidences that followed, which added to the jollity of the evening. Romance was certainly in the air. Steve served her coffee from the silver flask; they both had it black, as it helped to assuage the sweetness of the desert. Coffee finished, he led her across the patio and sat her down in one of the two large wicker chairs, something else that had materialised out of nowhere, a truly magical evening. Returning to the table Steve lifted the lid on the last silver salver revealing a red velvet bag with gold drawstrings and two brandy glasses. Steve opened the velvet bag and withdrew a quarter bottle of Napoleon Brandy. "To compliment the meal thirty year old brandy, the finest," and he poured them both a healthy amount, then took up occupation of the seat beside her, looking like the Lord of the Manor with his fine lady beside him, he crossed his legs and the flame from the flickering candles shone onto his well polished black brogues, the same ones he wore on that fateful morning at the airport. He reached for her hand and they sat in companionable silence, holding hands and sipping brandy, looking out into the universe of blue-black sky at the myriad of stars, twinkling brightly in a galaxy that was meant for love and romance. The scene was set, the mood was right and Jay wondered when he was going to make a move on her and Steve was wondering whether he should, he didn't want to spoil the evening by coming on too strong, now that he had found her, he didn't want to lose her, there was all the time in the world; he wanted everything to be perfect. Nothing was going to mess things up this time around.

The candles were burning low, Jay was unsure what time it was, the meal had been unhurried so it must be getting late. She decided that if Steve wasn't going to make a move then she would, trying to make things look as natural as possible and not rehearsed, she stood up and stretched, walking to the edge of the patio her back towards Steve, she breathed in the night air the scent from the various blossoms carried on the warm breeze, she wished the evening would never end.

Steve watched Jay as she stretched up her arms, listening to her breathe in the air, mistaking it for a sigh and presumed that she must be tired after all it has been a busy day. Her body looked so tempting, the silk rippling over her buttocks and clinging so that he could see the crevice of her bottom, he wanted to nip each pert little cheek between his teeth and bury himself in the sweetness of her skin. He did not approach her however, he wanted her to want him as much he wanted her, and he was obviously not reading the signals that she was sending out.

Jay stood for a few minutes in anticipation and when she did not feel his arms about her she turned and went towards him trying to be as slinky and seductive as possible, she leant over him one hand on each arm of his chair and using gentle pressure kissed him on the lips, his arms went around her and he drew her onto his lap and he returned her kiss tenderly, running his strong warm hands over her bare shoulders and down around her waist, she thought that she could feel a stirring beneath her thigh, his breath warm upon her cheek, the potent smell of brandy reaching her nostrils. Jay felt like putty in his hands and wondered what he was waiting for so decided that she would drop a big hint that it was time for bed. "It must be getting late" she said mewing like a cat and reluctantly getting up from his lap. "It must be time for bed," she continued urging him on.

Instead of taking her by the hand and leading her into the Rondavo, Steve stood up, kissed her tenderly once more on the lips saying, "My darling girl, I'm so sorry, how rude of me, you've had a busy day, of course you are tired and want your bed, I'll excuse myself and let you get your rest. I will be in the Rondavo next door and will give you an early morning call then we will go out on that dawn safari". With that he quickly turned on his heel and went off in the darkness towards his Rondavo, leaving Jay a little stunned. She watched until he turned and waved said, "The table will be cleared before you get up in the morning, sleep well".

Disheartened and thoroughly frustrated Jay entered the Rondavo and shut the door behind her, resting her back against it in dismay, how could he have misread the signs she was sending out, was she that rusty that she couldn't seduce a man anymore, she vowed to try harder tomorrow unless of course she had said or done something that had offended him.

Steve shut his door behind him and leant against it, disappointed and wishing that he hadn't packed so much into the day and tired her out. He longed to be with her and already missed being in her company. She had aroused him when she had sat on his lap, so much so that he was uncomfortable, his trousers restricting the growth within and although he hadn't wanted to let her go he was somewhat relieved when the pressure of her thigh was lifted and he could stand up. Tomorrow was another day however, he would ensure that it was not so crammed packed with activity, unless of course that activity was in the bedroom!

Chapter 32

Jay lay fully clothed on the large round bed, reliving the evening and the wonderful surprises that Steve had so unexpectedly arranged for her. She decided to put the fact that he hadn't accompanied her to bed down to respect for her and although extremely disappointed, admired him for his discretion. Jay was sure that Steve was attracted to her, why else would he have taken such care in making the day and evening such a memorable experience. Unable to forget the definite hardening against her leg, the memory of which was etched in her mind, made it difficult for her to settle making her yearn to see his body, to touch him, hold him close to her, bare flesh against bare flesh. Why hadn't she made it more obvious that she wanted him? If she had, perhaps he may have thought that she was an easy lay and been turned off by her advances, as he had said once before he was used to women coming on to him and he preferred to do the chasing, the last thing she wanted to do was scare him off, he was such a catch!

The memory of his kiss still upon her lips she moved her hands leisurely of over the very fine lustrous amber dress, caressing the skin beneath, the silky material moving easily with her touch. Closing her eyes, fantasising that it was Steve's hands exploring her sensitive body, cupping her breasts and manipulating the small conical projections until they were hard and erect pushing against the soft silky material, his fingers sliding beneath, searching out her burning nipples, squeezing and massaging until she moaned with delight. The moistness now evident within her ready to accept what was not there, craving to be satisfied; needing, wanting, aching. Jay could stand it no longer, she left the bed, stepping down onto the sensuous zebra skin on the floor and tiptoed across the cold terracotta tiles to her bag and withdrew the cause of the commotion at the airport security. The nine inch green jelly mock up of a penis, soft and wobbly and now in her hand! Returning to the bed and her make believe world where Steve was slowly stroking her legs the dress easily slipping up aver her smooth legs, uncovering her thighs until the material was around her waist, hands moving across her stomach, pushing down harder, stronger so as to feel more like Steve's eager hands, continuously moving until finding the top of her knickers, lifting the black lace temptingly until fingers found the downy mass of curls, procrastinating the inevitable, stroking the fleshy mounds either side of the little hard nodule that would eventually convulse in ecstasy. Groaning with pleasure, needing fulfilment, her body aching to be penetrated, she flicked the switch on the Green Giant, it sprang into life, shaking and wobbling in an erotic dance....

The noise it made was phenomenal, like a pneumatic drill starting up, it broke into the still silence which acted like an amplifier, echoing the disturbing buzz around the room, shaking her immediately out of the little fantasy world that she had created. The moment of ecstasy so near, now lost.

“Bloody contraption” she shouted, trying frantically to turn it off, hoping that the deafening sound would not be heard outside, but in the dim light she had difficulty locating the switch as the imitation green rubber dick tried to wriggle free from her grasp. She sat upright and grasped it with both hands and bashed it against the wall in an attempt to stop it, but to no avail.

“Aaarrgh” she shouted at it, throwing it to the floor where it bounced merrily up and down at her. If it had possessed a tongue she was sure it would have been poking fun at her. She went over to it and kicked it but still it droned on….

Chapter 33

Steve, still semi-hard from the warmth of Jay's thigh against him, was fighting the urge to take himself in hand, instead he hung his jacket up and started to unbutton his shirt, when it was undone to his waist, his mobile phone rang. "Hi, Steve Knight," he said answering the call. "Hello Rashid, how the devil are you?" "Oh I see, can't it wait for a few days?" "OK, no sweat I will sort it, leave it with me." "Yes, fine, ok." "Sorry Rashid, I've got to go there's a bit of a commotion next door." "Yes, ok. Bye" and he terminated the call.

The noise coming from Jay's Rondavo was disturbing, he could hear her banging about and there was another sound he couldn't quite make out. He hoped she was ok, opening his door, running out into the darkness he covered the few yards between them in seconds. As Steve reached the door to her Rondavo he was poised to knock only to be greeted with, "Aaarrgh", Jay was screaming. He anxiously knocked on the door. "Jay, Jay, what is it? Are you ok?" he shouted through the door.

"Christ, it's Steve" Jay now bewildered, grabbed the vibrator and danced about with it in her hand wondering where to put the persistent plastic penis. As a last resort, as Steve was bashing the door down, she lifted the pillow on the bed, placing it underneath the sound now muffled she called back to Steve. "I'm ok, everything is fine". Reluctantly hoping that he would go away, but he wasn't to be deterred.

"Come on, open the door, I want to see you. I want to make sure you are ok."

Jay went to door, sheepishly opening it, Steve stepped straight in looking around him to see what was the cause of the commotion, then taking her firmly in his arms, crushing her in his strength, so that she could hardly breathe. "What was that racket? I heard you screeching, I was so worried about you" he said concerned.

"Oh nothing, thought I saw a spider," she lied. "Sorry if I worried you."

"You are safe, that's all that matters," with that he swept her up in his arms and carried her to the bed, gently laying her down, her long dark brown curly hair splayed out across the creamy white of the pillow framing her tiny face, her lips beckoned and her arms welcomed him into them.

Steve laid down beside her and leaning on one elbow looked into her tawny brown eyes, the dim light adding to her mystery. "Jay" he said, his voice thick with emotion.

"Yes?"

"Jay, I want you so bad, would you think me awful if I asked if I could spend the night with you?"

"Oh, Steve, that's what I have wanted all night", her words trembling on her lips. "Didn't you realise?"

He flung his head back onto the pillow laughing with relief. "How stupid can I be? I thought you were tired and wanted to go to bed," "And what the bloody hell is that noise?"

Jay froze, stunned into silence.

Steve realising the noise was coming from under the pillow reached underneath removing the throbbing green member, the noise once again echoing about the large silent room. "OK Jay, explain this?" he said in mock annoyance.

"Well, I, I." She stammered, now extremely embarrassed that she had been caught out.

"I really am quite shocked Jay." He said now making her feel guilty as well as embarrassed. If the light had not been so dim she would have noticed his amusement. Steve managed to turn the vibrator off immediately and threw it across the room it rebounded against the wall. He sat astride her, pinning her arms up above her head telling her that she would not have a need for it anymore as now she could have the real thing!

Chapter 34

Steve kissed her with a passion that had been withheld for far too long, kissing her hair, her ears, eyes, nose and finally a deep penetrative kiss, their tongues finding each others, he drawing hers into his mouth, then sucking her lips that sent shivers of pleasure down her spine. Jay then found his tongue, drawing back and forth between her lips like a dress rehearsal of the intimacy that was to come. Steve let go of Jay's arms and sat up feasting on her beauty, she looked like a goddess, lying there, an Aphrodite. Her eyes appealing to him, her full pouting lips begging, nipples erect beneath the silk amber, he bent down taking one between his teeth and gently nibbled, his breath now hot through her dress. Jay moaned in delight, she found it so much more evocative and horny then being stripped completely bare. "Steve, oh, Steve, I want you in me so badly, please darling, please?"

That was enough for Steve; his resurrected organ now had the green light and was throbbing impatiently in his trousers. He slid her dress up even further exposing the tops of those tanned thighs he had glimpsed earlier, then pushing it further still until he reached those very, very sexy black French knickers, catching his breath at the sight, "Darling, you wore them all evening and I never knew, you just don't realise what a turn on they are" he said as he moved his hands over her hips and down to the edge of her knickers, sliding his hand easily up the wide leg, surprised by the softness of the hair there and the neat little mound of her lips. He slid a finger into her and knew that she was more than ready to accept him.

"Now, darling, now, fuck me", she moaned determinedly in his ear.

To hear her beg him, using that obscenity blew his mind and opened a whole new world to him, one that he had only read about in books and he took her lead, "Yes, my little bird, I will fuck you, by God am I going to fuck you".

Jay helped him undo his fly. Steve's pulsating cock was rock hard and big, as she knew it would be, it was seeking relief. He pulled her knickers to one side and she sucked him into her, hungry for him and he just like a homing pigeon flew home to roost. Jay let out a gasp as he entered her, he was so big, she felt so tight around him, the whole of her insides were alive, every thrust was an orgasmic experience and she wanted more.

"Fuck me darling, I want you all, give me more, give it all to me now," she screamed.

"So you want more do you, you greedy little devil, more you will get." He positioned her legs over his shoulders and she arched upwards, her moistness now allowing her to accept him fully, he was in up to the hilt!

"Oh Steve, this is fucking fantastic, your cock is so fucking huge and so hard," her lustful words egging him on he as thrust himself into her harder and harder and faster and faster pounding against the womanly roundness of her fleshy bottom.

"Steve I'm coming, I'm going to spurt all over your cock," her words were electrifying he could no longer control himself. They exploded together in cataclysmic triumph, Steve collapsing on top of her, breathing heavy, his heart pounding against her chest, oblivious to the fact that she was now doubled in half and as she had recovered from her spasms of delight, was now feeling uncomfortable. "Darling", she tried to stir him "Darling, I'm losing all feeling in my body."

"Oh, sorry babe, that was out of this world, you blew my mind". Gingerly withdrawing his still throbbing and almost flaccid cock he fell onto his back. "Are you ok honey?" "I so wanted the first time to be special and all I could do was act like an animal, I hope I didn't hurt you."

"Steve darling, please don't worry, I wanted it as bad as you. You were fantastic." Jay at last relieved from the constricting position, laid close to him throwing her arm about his waist and putting her head against his still madly beating heart, the wetness dripping from their loins cooling in the night air, but they didn't move to wipe it away, they were content to just lie there in each others arms, spent for the time being.

. Steve gently lifted her from him and turned on his side, looking deep into her gold-flecked eyes. "You are so beautiful, you are all I ever want in a woman; you are my dream."

"And you mine" she answered. She had given herself to him freely and with abandon and he had taken her roughly and readily. Jay had not only opened her body to accept him, but her heart and soul also.

They had been eager and hungry for each other, but now was the time for them to express their feelings in a more loving manner.

They kissed tenderly and although the words "I love you" had not been spoken, the time would come when their love for each other would become more evident.

Chapter 35

The silence between them had been one of contentment; he thought Jay felt slightly cold lying beside him so putting his lips on her brow he whispered "Darling, are you awake?"

"Mmmmn" Jay murmured and flung her leg across him to pull him closer, she was sleepy and relaxed apparently not feeling the night chill.

"Don't you think we should get undressed and slip under the sheet?"

"Mmmmn" she murmured again, not stirring.

Steve extricated himself from her leg-lock, she protesting in her semi-conscious state. "No, don't go."

"Sorry babe, but nature calls" and he headed for the bathroom, tripping on the vibrator that he thrown earlier. He picked it up; thinking that it would definitely not be needed again, took it to the bathroom and threw it in the bin. I wonder what the cleaners will make of that in the morning, he laughed.

Steve lifted the toilet seat; concentrating on the job in hand he relieved himself, thankful that in his wisdom he had insisted on the best quality toilet paper as he wiped away the drips. He filled the sink with hot water and using one of Jay's flannels wiped away the dried on secretions, sorry that he had to, as the scent of their lovemaking was still evident and he loved it, he could feel movement in his cock as if it were nodding in agreement. However it had become dry and uncomfortable and as he had every intention of making love to Jay again that night, especially after that damn phone call, he didn't want his tool to be rough. He rinsed the flannel and taking it into the bedroom, he slowly removed her knickers and lovingly wiped her clean. Jay woke to feel the warmth between her legs, finding the tenderness in Steve's actions very stimulating, it wasn't long before she was once more ready for him. No more the roughness and sexual expletives, only tender caresses and words of endearment as they once more went on their journey of discovery. Steve slipped his shirt from his shoulders, removed his shoes, socks and trousers, wondering whether he should leave on his Calvin Clines, thinking it was a bit late for modesty he removed them and laid his clothes neatly over the chair beside the cabinet. He knelt on the bed beside Jay, tenderly he lifted her until she was sitting in an upright position, pushing her dress up underneath her, then lifting her arms above her head slid the amber gown from her, placing it over his clothes on the chair.

Standing by the bed, Steve again drank in her beauty, she laid there arms outstretched above her head, the dim light making her skin look dark, the white outline where her bikini had been evidence that she did not sunbathe nude, her breasts although large were still rounded and stood out shimmering like opals, the red jewels of her nipples still erect. Jay's stomach was mounded ever so slightly possessing a tiny navel, which he would investigate later; her hips were wide for one so petite, making a perfect hourglass figure, her slender legs askew one bent outwards at the knee, making the entry into her heavenly body quite evident and his cock throb and harden. Looking at the dark opening between her legs made him want to take her again, but no, he wanted to make love to this woman, she deserved more than what he had given earlier, that was just pure unadulterated lust.

He lay down beside her again, pulling her to him holding her close, their naked bodies moulding into each other, she was so tiny in his arms; he wanted to protect and care for her without end. Once more she entwined her legs about his, pulling him closer still, it seemed as though she had waited forever for this moment, she wanted to get under his skin, to get as close to him as possible. Steve brushed her hair from her eyes and lifting her chin he kissed her tenderly and longingly on the lips, she returning his ardour. His lips went to her eyes where they lingered, she could feel his warm breath caressing them, all the time his hands were moving over her smooth soft skin, down her arms, over her back, not yet was he going to stroke her erogenous areas, he did not want to stimulate her overly, he wanted to tease and tempt her until she could bear it no longer and begged for him to take her.

Jay mirrored Steve; returning his kisses and caresses, feeling the hardness of the muscle on his chest against her breast, heart beating loudly beneath her hands stroking the rippling sinews of his back then downwards to his lean hips returning once more upwards.

"Oh, Jay, you are so beautiful" he groaned into her open lips her darting tongue finding his and once more their tongues were performing. She sucked his tongue it was such a sensual feeling, it was as though she was once again having a dummy run before she eventually took his ever hardening phallus within its warmth embrace.

Her lips now took on the shape of her most intimate regions the tip of her tongue the tiny hard nodule which he lapped at, poking it with his tongue under the softness inside, this was his rehearsal and he could tell by the way she rubbed her body against him that she knew the ecstasy that was awaiting her. Jay's hands tightened around the flexing muscles of his buttocks and she pulled him towards her, he cupped her tiny little bottom in his great hands and did likewise and then released her as they were reaching the point of no return. "No Jay, not yet sweetheart," he stopped her from reaching for him.

"Steve, please darling, please, I want you now." Jay arched her body towards him.

"No honey, I haven't even started yet," he said making her squirm and groan with delight.

He pulled away from her and placed his hands over her breasts, pinching the hard nipples between his fingers. "Oh, darling that is so nice," the words catching in her throat, as he took her higher, the stimulation to her nipples drifting downwards causing a pleasurable sensation to her sensitive femininity. Steve nipped and licked, stroking his tongue across the hardness making them protrude even further. Placing her hands on the top of his head Jay pushed him down, the yearning now deep within her. He licked his way down to her stomach, poking his tongue into her sweet little navel, still she pushed him down further, he held on tight to her hips, holding her down and kissed the downy mound. "My darling Jay, you smell so good, I know you want me, but I am going to make you wait".

His words aroused her even more; "Steve, don't be cruel," her body writhed under his weight. Jay's whole body was screaming for satisfaction Steve was a knowledgeable lover using skills, she'd never known before, summoning pleasure from her whole body, she wanted to pleasure him to and wriggling free went about the learning process, doing to him what he had done to her. Now it was Steve's turn to groan with delight. Jay learnt quickly, looking at and feeling the lean body now beneath her. Steve, like her, was in excellent shape for his age, just looking at the dark brown hair that curled down from his chest to his navel and beyond was a turn on. She could feel that she was now very wet in preparation for accepting the masculinity standing hard and proud between his legs, she would have loved to have sat upon it and slide it up inside her, but no, he wanted to wait then wait they should.

She nipped and sucked his nipples, a groan came from Steve's lips, she was delighted to think he enjoyed that to, she moved on down stroking the surprisingly silky-smooth hairs on his hard stomach and lower and lower until she kissed him teasingly around his hardness, his hips lifting from the bed in expectation. She licked the length of his rigid swollen organ, her warm wet tongue wetting it with her saliva. "Jay, oh Jay, that's good, that's damn good" and he propped his head up the pillow so he could watch her.

Holding his erection gently, moving her hand up and down over the skin, sliding easily having been lubricated by her spittle, she squeezed it tenderly, pouring love into it as it throbbed, this hard cock that had given her so much pleasure a brief while ago was now full of vigour again. She lowered her head to engulf him, but Steve stopped her. "No, darling, this is an experience we should share", bowing to his superiority she allowed herself to be manoeuvred by his strong arms just as though she was feather.

They now lay end to end looking at each other, touching and exploring, the longing to please each other knew no bounds. He looked at her neat full lips, spreading them apart and once he had found what he was looking for his tongue darted in and out like a humming bird looking for nectar, her malleable lips, the opening flower, welcoming him and gave in to him totally, the velvety smoothness his tongue had found and the sweet smell of overflowing juices were driving him wild. Jay accepted his rigidity into her mouth and sucked and licked, lapping around the sensitive top, sliding it in and out of her mouth grazing it slightly with her teeth, he moved back and forth enjoying the pleasure her mouth was giving him. Steve's tongue was skilful, licking and teasing until the powerful waves of sensation and love that she felt coalesced into ecstasy and Jay could contain herself no longer, her back arching his tongue entered her and he drank the juices that flowed from her body as it contorted and shuddered in orgasmic relief.

Steve moved around until he was in a position to take her in his arms, cosseting her until her trembling had subsided, kissing her with wet lips glistening with her juices, the potent sexual aroma being shared. "Steve I want you, I am so ready for you"

"I want you to darling, so very, very badly," straddling her he raised her buttocks once more, she opening her legs to accommodate him. Steve entered her slowly and easily, pushing down gently, her muscles tightening to accept him and hold him tight, they now possessed each other totally. He moved over her, she lifting herself onto him and in that way they set up a rhythm, carrying them further and further into the kingdom of desire until, as one, they reached the height of rapture, convulsing and erupting into each other, the power of her orgasm contorting the muscle within her clenching his spurting phallus and she in turn could feel his throbbing as he came inside her.

Their craving for each now satiated they lay completely spent in each others arms, locked together, his drained member still pulsating inside her. "I love you Jay, I love you so very, very much".

"I love you to Steve"

They fell into a deep, deep slumber locked in each other's embrace.

Chapter 36

Jay awoke needing a pee, blinked for several moments to bring the room into focus and lithely skipped out of bed, only to find her body ached, she felt as though she had done ten rounds with Mike Tyson, a smile played upon her lips as remembered the lovemaking last night.

She was desperate for the toilet and ran as fast as she was able and sat down on the pan relieving herself at the same time listening to the sound of life outside the window. She could hear splashing which must be from the river below, bellowing that could be the resident hippos, more than likely taking their early morning dip and of course the usual chirruping of the numerous birds that nested in the many beautiful trees growing in the land about The Lodge. She wiped herself, washed her hands and quickly washed between her legs, looking in the little mirror she stared at herself with disgust, she hadn't removed her make-up last night and now she looked like a member of the cast from the Rocky Horror Show. She quickly soaped her face taking off the majority until she looked reasonably respectable, she didn't want to spend too long in the bathroom she had every intention of snuggling up to Steve and repeating the nights performances, if he was willing, she sure with a little bit of persuasion he would be. Giving her teeth a mandatory brush and a quick rinse, she walked comically her legs bowed, as though she had been riding a horse all night instead of Steve mind you he was hung like a stallion, make no mistake, she sniggered happily. She had almost reached the bed where she stopped dead in her tracks; the bed was empty! Looking about the room there was no sign of him having been there, other than the indentation in the pillow where his head had been. She ran to the door, opening it and looking out, there was no sign of Steve. Going to Rondavo next door the door was locked and there was no answer when she knocked. Jay went back inside the bedroom; her head bowed in despondency, sitting heavily down on the edge of the bed, her head now in her hands, wondering where he had gone to, why hadn't he woken her? Why did he leave? Her imagination ran wild. Perhaps he had to get up early and sort something out at The Lodge, no he said he was taking her on a dawn safari, but the sun was streaming through the window dawn was well and truly gone. Had she done something that he disapproved of? Should she not have sworn at him during the initial period of lust? No, he had followed her lead and was just as expressive and he said he had enjoyed their lovemaking. Where was he? Had she imagined his words declaring his love for her?

Her heart heavy with despair at Steve's sudden departure she flung herself down on the bed, tears welling up in her eyes, this time not with joy but with sadness. She crawled over to the pillow where his head had lain, placing hers in the indention where traces of Steve still remained, the tangy smell of his aftershave still apparent as she absorbed the aroma up into her nostrils, hugging the pillow about her head. Something was sticking into her cheek; she raised her hand and removed a sheet of paper, now crumpled where she had lain upon it. She unfolded it, wondering where it had come from and when she saw the writing, knew that Steve had left her a message, flattening it out, her heart once more plummeted as she read his words.

My Darling Jay,
Please forgive me, I should have told you last night but I was being selfish, I didn't want anything to mar our night together and I didn't have the heart to wake you this morning, you looked so beautiful lying there, it was a terrific wrench to leave you like that. I'm sorry but I cannot be with you for the next few days I've been called away on business. I hope you understand, enjoy your stay at The Lodge. Marcelle has been instructed to give you and your friends everything you require, the expense has been taken care of. I have left a mobile phone for your use on the chest, keep it with you, I will ring you when I land at Chinoi. Try to enjoy the rest of your stay; you will never know how sorry I am that I cannot be with you. Last night you were terrific and I do truly love you Jay and I know I will for the rest of my life.
Yours and only yours,
Steve xxxx
PS: By the time you read this I will be flying somewhere high above you, looking down and showering you with love.

Jay was deeply saddened that she was not going to see him until it was almost time for her to leave for the UK, but she was mollified by his words spelling out declaration of love for her. He said he was going to ring her and looked to the chest of drawers where on top she saw the mobile with a single long white-stemmed flower alongside. Yes, she too loved this man with all her heart.

Chapter 37

Jay checked her watch, it was seven-twenty, she would get showered and dressed then join Fred and Gladys for breakfast and find out what they could arrange for the day, she would speak to Marcelle. The sound of a light aircraft was passing overhead, she immediately thought of Steve and rushed out of the door, forgetting her nakedness, standing outside in her full glory she waved frantically at the plane, hoping that it was him. It was. Remarkably Steve had seen her and in acknowledgement the plane circled above and flew back swooping low over the Rondavo's leaving a fluffy white smoke trail in its wake. Overcome with emotion she stood there watching the plane until it was a tiny dot and the white trail of smoke had dissipated into the air, only then did she become aware that she was buck naked so, slapping an arm over her boobs and cupping a hand between her legs, she ran back inside, having a quick look about to see if she had shamed herself, but it was ok the coast was clear and she thanked Steve inwardly for moving her to the Rondavo's and the privacy afforded them by being up on a hill and away from prying eyes.

Quickly showering, reluctantly washing away the signs of the evening's lovemaking from between her legs, feeling a bit sore due to the long overdue sexual activity and remembering the enthusiastic way that Steve had gorged himself upon her, his strong jaw line pushed against her. Still, being a little sore was a small price to pay for the immense pleasure that he had given her. She brushed her teeth thoroughly, noticing that her lips were fuller than usual, they too were sore and bruised making them appear a little blue in places, but the kissing had been well worth it. After drying herself she put on a pair of shorts and a t-shirt, tied her hair back, searched for her white moccasins that she had thrown in last night and put them on and not forgetting the mobile she left the Rondavo, shutting the door behind her, noticing, as she hadn't when she had been outside earlier, that there were no longer any signs of the candlelit dinner, it was back to how it was when she arrived, with the exception of the two large wicker chairs that had been left.

Jay made her way down to the tents to call for Fred and Gladys but they must have already left for breakfast. Walking over the little bridge by the waterfall, she stopped for a few seconds and watched the little fish and wondered how the servants had managed to clear everything a way with very little noise. Then, of course, her and Steve were in their own little world, lost to everything but themselves; her cheeks pinked at what the servants may have heard.

On reaching The Lodge she found Gladys and Fred sitting down eating breakfast. Gladys greeted her, "'Ello stranger, didn't think we'd see yer up this morning"

"Yeah, thought yer'd be 'aving a lie in," grinned

Fred.

Jay explained that she awoke alone, disappointment evident on her face, telling them that unfortunately Steve had to go away on business and he would ring her later. Showing them the mobile phone that Steve had left her, Fred mumbled something about them being blooming contraptions. Jay went on to describe the candlelit dinner for two, with exquisite French cuisine, how she was treated like a princess and the beautiful amber silk dress and shoes, how her and Steve had talked into the night, relaxing with a very fine brandy.

"Then what?" Gladys inquisitively cupped her ear as though expecting Jay to whisper some secret message.

"Then? Well that's for me to know and for you to find out."

"Oooh. 'E 'ad is wicked way wiv yer then"?

"I'm going to get some cereal," and off she went, escaping Gladys's prying questions.

She saw Marcelle, at reception, his back to her in conversation with Hermes and she approached them waiting for Hermes to leave, overhearing him ask for breakfast to be taken to Franco, who was laid up again with one of his "sore heads"! Hermes nodded good morning to her as he went off to tend to the invalid.

"Ah mademoiselle Jay," Marcelle said as he turned and saw her standing there. "I hope you enjoyed le déjeuner last night, Monsieur Steve was so disappointed that he had to leave and has left instructions that I am to take care of you. Is there anything you require?"

Jay thanked him for all the hard work that he had put in to make the evening so splendid and could he pass on her gratitude to the waiters and the servants that had cleared up after them, then looking over her shoulder to check that Gladys and Fred were out of earshot, she then asked him if they could be moved to the Rondavo that Steve had vacated.

"Qui, certainement, I will get les garçons to attend tout de suite".

Marcelle asked her to give him at least forty-five minutes to arrange and carry out the move. She was pleased he wasn't going to dally, as she didn't want Fred and Gladys to get wind of her surprise. Jay also wanted some ideas on what to do for the day seeing as she had missed out on the dawn safari with Steve. Marcelle went on to explain that there was entertainment that day, national dancers in traditional dress would be at The Lodge from eleven and that it was a spectacle she should see, then went on to say that Steve had left the camcorder and camera for her use and would give it to her later. The entertainment would be followed by lunch; afterwards she could go and explore the grounds, assuring her that it was quite safe, the only dangerous animal being the hippopotami but they stayed on the other side of the river, rarely coming out during the day. The other animals were all tame and used to people, he said she could get some carrot and pellets from the kitchen so that she could feed them if she so wished.

Jay requested that tea and cakes be delivered to the Rondavo's at around four o'clock. Marcelle that would not be a problem, she and her friends would have time to relax before dinner at seven, following that was the night safari and if they wanted to go, he would arrange it for them. She thought his ideas were perfect, thanked him and then went to the buffet to get some cornflakes and mango juice.

"You took yer blooming time, we've nearly finished" admonished Gladys.

"Hold your horses, Gladys, I was making plans for the day, they include you and Fred if you've got nothing better to do".

"What yer gone an' done now then?" Enquired Fred.

"You'll just have to wait until I've finished my breakfast, have some more coffee", she said trying keeping them in suspense, in order to delay them.

Coming over Barbu asked her for her order. "I think I will have scrambled eggs on toast and a couple of slices of bacon and maybe some mushrooms too and can you get some more coffee please?" She asked.

Barbu nodded and went off to get her order arriving not long after with a steaming plate of scrambled eggs along with bacon, mushrooms, a rack of lightly toasted brown bread and bowl with butter in it. He also placed a silver pot on the table divided into 4 sections, each section had a lid and on inspection the contents revealed a selection of conserves.

"Blimey, who'd they fink yer are the bloody queen?" said Gladys jokingly.

"Steve has said I can have whatever I want and

he has obviously passed this on to the staff. Great ain't it?" she smiled with delight.

"Come on then, dish the dirt" Gladys probed her.

"Well", said Jay procrastinating, "Franco has another one of his migraines".

"Franco, bloody Franco" Fred exploded "No wonder 'e's got a blooming 'eadache, they were up bonking all night!"

"Yeah, the blooming racket, moaning and groaning all effing night" Gladys explained, offering more information than was necessary.

"Yeah, dirty bastards" swore Fred "Anyway we don't want to 'ear about those two, tell us about your evening again".

So between mouthfuls of scrambled egg, she told them of her evening and how brilliant it was and how special Steve had made her feel and what an absolute gentleman he, leaving out what took place after dinner, that was between her and Steve alone.

"So you 'ad a good time then?" asked Fred.

"Yes, you could say that." It was obvious Jay was not going to enlighten them any further but they could tell by the glow in her cheeks and the twinkle in her eye that a lot more happened than she was letting on, but they chose to abide by her wish to keep that private and didn't query her any further.

Jay finished her breakfast, wiping her lips daintily with the serviette and pouring herself a cup of coffee, checking her watch to see how much more time she had to waste. Just another ten minutes, she could eek things out until then by telling them about the plans for the day, then asking if that sounded ok to them.

"Blimey, yer got it all planned, ain't yer girl?" Gladys said surprised that Jay had included them in her day. "Sounds good to me, 'ow's about you Fred, you up to it?" she asked.

"What do yer mean am I up for it?" Replied Fred feigning offence.

"Well yer knocking on a bit ain't yer?"

"Cheeky cow" and turning to Jay "It's sound great love, we'll look forward to it".

They arranged to meet at ten-thirty getting drinks for the bar before the entertainment commenced to which Gladys replied as she stood up "Now if yer finished, I want ta go back an' wash me smalls while I've got the time."

Jay looked at her watch, she had succeeded it was well over the forty-five minutes she had promised Marcelle, it was now nine-thirty.

Chapter 38

Fred unzipped the tent and Gladys looking a little puzzled scratched her head saying, "I felt sure I left me slippers out 'ere, did you take 'em in Fred?"

"No, what do I wanna touch yer blooming smelly slippers fer?"

"Well that's funny, could have sworn they were out 'ere".

"Nothing so blooming funny as this" he said as he went into the tent. "'Ave we got the right tent?"

"Yeah" said Gladys checking the number outside. "Why, what's up?"

"All our blooming stuff 'as gone, we've been wiped out, well I ain't standing fer this, can't trust these foreigners, thieving little buggers" and he stormed out of the tent catching Jay out of the corner of his eye, her back to him and her shoulders heaving in laughter.

"Ok, what's so blooming funny, sorry Jay but it ain't no joking matter", he said reproaching her.

"What's tickled 'er?" asked Gladys coming out of the tent with a worried look on her face.

"Don't ask me" said Fred shrugging his shoulders and making off towards The Lodge shaking his head disbelievingly.

"Hold on Fred" shouted Jay still giggling unable to contain herself. "You're going in the wrong direction".

"No I ain't, I'm going to get to the bottom of this, once and fer all" and once again he set off, but stopping in his tracks when he heard Jay say:

"You are Fred, I can assure you that you are, you are to be my new neighbours". Jay went on to explain what she had done whilst they were having their breakfast. Fred was happy that they hadn't been robbed but Gladys was concerned.

"What?" "Do ya mean I've 'ad 'em rummaging around wiv me stuff, what about me dirty drawers, 'eavens above Jay, it doesn't bear finking about. We'll forgive you though." Going over to Jay and putting her arms about her, giving her a huge hug, "Ta" was all she managed to say as she was now a little choked; she didn't want anyone to know how soft she really was.

"Come on then you two" and Jay led them up the hill to their new lodgings. When Gladys saw inside she showed her appreciation by saying." Bloody 'ell, it's like a blooming palace."

The pictures were different to those in Jays and the furniture was in a slightly different position, but other than that they were the same.

The mobile in Jay's hand had started to ring; leaving Gladys to wash her smalls she walked off, pressing the button on the phone to accept the call.

"Steve, is that you?"

"Who else would be ringing you then my darling sweet woman?

"Oh, Steve, I was so upset to have missed you".

"No, I suppose I should have woken you, I'm sorry."

"I'll forgive you."

"By the way Jay, do you often run about with no clothes on in view of low flying aircraft, you're not a closet naturist by any chance are you?"

"I know, terrible aren't I? I so wanted to wave goodbye, completely forgot I had no clothes on".

"Well, don't do it again, your body is for my eyes only. I get very jealous you know".

Jay wanted to know where he was and Steve told her that he had just arrived at Chinoi airport in Zimbabwe where he had another project going on. His partner had flown over early the day before and wanted Steve to meet up him to survey the land which would take up much of the day and the following one, then Saturday he was off to an Auction where he was going to purchase some live-stock as they wanted to create a game reserve for the resort they were planning.

"Oh Steve, I'm flying back home early Sunday morning" the disappointment evident in her voice.

"I know honey, believe me you don't know how sorry I am, if I could get out of it I would, can't you stay on at The Lodge for a few more days? You don't have to worry about the expense, in fact you will find that the money you've paid for your stay there has been credited to your card and the same goes for Fred and Gladys to".

"Steve, you are too generous, but thank you so much, I do love you so very much".

"I love you to honey, it seems like only yesterday that you flung that tampon at me" she could hear the amusement in his voice.

"Don't remind me".

"Well, why don't you stay on as my guest"?

"I'd love to Steve, but I have to get back, my daughter is graduating from University on Tuesday, she's got an English Degree and I must be there".

"I understand babe, I tell you what though, providing it's ok with you. How's about my catching a flight Monday evening, then I can accompany you to the University, I'd love to meet your kids, it would be an ideal opportunity".

"Darling, I'd love for you to meet my kids too, now I love you more if it is at all possible".

"Well, darling I'd love to talk to you all day but duty calls. I will try and ring you but it may be difficult, I'll be really busy, but text me, I can always discretely text you back, you've got my number now, got to go, love you darling".

"Love you to Steve".

And the call was terminated.

Jay was so disappointed that she wouldn't share any more of holiday with Steve, but he was actually flying back to London to be with her and her family on Tuesday, she never thought she would say it, but she couldn't wait for the next few days to go as each day would bring her nearer to being in his arms once more.

Chapter 39

Jay rallied herself; she didn't want to get despondent, she needed to keep busy and so she took a leaf out of Gladys's book and washed her underwear, a pair of shorts and a t-shirt, hanging them over the shower rail, the heat of the day would dry it out by the evening. The Rondavo had been cleaned whilst she was at breakfast, so there wasn't very much left for her to do, other than to pack the clothes that she wouldn't be wearing for the rest of her stay at the Lodge. She poured herself a long cool glass of fresh water from the flask and finding some literature on The Lodge and Kenya, she went out and sat in one of the wicker chairs so that she could enjoy the sunshine. It didn't seem long until Gladys and Fred emerged asking if she was ready for that drink, could it be ten-thirty already, she checked her watch, yes it was. Good, the time was going fast, she then rebuked herself for wishing her life away.

Gladys and Fred were highly delighted with their new surroundings and when Jay told them Steve had refunded the cost of this trip, they were overcome by his generosity and asked her to thank him next time she spoke to him. She explained that he was going to be fully occupied for the remainder of her holiday but that he was going to join her in London and they were so pleased for her, asking that they be invited to the wedding to which Jay replied, it was early days yet, but she would be forever optimistic. They had all gone to the bar and having got their drinks went and sat in the grassed area where the entertainment was going to be. Franco had recovered and he and Hermes were canoodling down by the river. As The Lodge was fairly exclusive it only catered for the maximum of up to twenty guests at a time, therefore there were only a few other guests evident and they kept themselves to themselves. The dancers were arriving and placing their instruments in a semi-circle in front of them, leaving space for the dancers who appeared in all their painted and feathered glory, whooping and wailing in time to the bongos and what looked like a violin. The display was sometimes frightening with the male dancers jumping at them, flaying their arms and hollering. Then the half naked ebony bodies of the women came out chanting, their pendulous breasts swinging to and fro as they beckoned members of the audience to dance with them. Gladys and Fred were up like a shot, being game for anything but Jay refrained, preferring to observe, remembering the camcorder she rushed to reception where Marcelle had premeditated her intention as he was holding out in readiness for her to collect. Jay returned to the jigging throng and standing up to steady the camcorder, captured Gladys and Fred making fools of themselves, being totally out of sync with the native dancers as it was a little bit different to what they were used to however they were thoroughly enjoying themselves.

The entertainment finished Gladys and Fred returned slightly breathless to their seats. Jay beckoned a waiter over so that they could order more drinks to help them re-hydrate themselves as both were perspiring profusely. The entertainment had lasted a remarkable two hours, Jay wondered how the entertainers had managed to sing and dance for so long in this heat, some of them even wearing heavy headdresses and thick costumes.

Although the tables were laid for lunch, Gladys and Fred needed to sit for another ten minutes to recover from their exertions, after all they were getting on a bit, as Gladys informed her, so they carried on sitting watching the entertainers pack up their bits and pieces. They finished their drinks before they made their way to their usual table, this time they had two waiters fussing over them as well as Marcelle who said that Monsieur Steve has given instructions that everything must be 'just so' for his guests, and it was. They had a leisurely lunch, choosing not to have a starter, just the main course of chicken, rice and salad along with ice cream with tropical fruits for desert. Marcelle had insisted that they had a good French wine to accompanying the meal, continually filling their glasses when they became empty. They chatted about various things, their observations of the other guests and the dancing, pointing out the little weaverbirds that were busy flitting in and the magnificent site of the white egrets perched on the branches of a blue gum tree. There were so many of them that they looked to all intent and purpose like the blossom of a well-endowed magnolia.

All three of them were getting rather silly due to the amount of wine they had drunk, laughing out loud especially at the expense of Franco, who had started hip hopping over the grass, a small handbag in his hand because a small lizard had jumped out of the bushes near him.

"Big Pansy" was Fred's comment they were doubled up giggling, making their sides hurt with the strain. The wine had taken it's toll and when Jay said she was going for a walk, Fred and Gladys declined saying they were going for a siesta, so they went their separate ways, agreeing they would have coffee together later on Jay's patio.

Although Jay was a little tipsy she thought the ensuing walk may clear her head and so she picked up the camcorder, hung it around her neck and went over to one of the waiters to get her some carrots etc., for the animals she was going to visit. He arrived back with canvas bag full of pellets and carrots then Jay retraced the steps she had taken with Steve the previous day.

Ollie was already out and strutting his stuff, along with the two zebras. She called Ollie, who as though recognising her voice came bounding over and remembering what happened to Steve she sidestepped quickly, teetering a little in her inebriated state. She needn't of worried as Ollie came to an abrupt halt in front of her, bending his head to inspect the bag held in her hand, knowing full well there was something in it for him. Initially she was nervous not having Steve with her to protect her, but Ollie was so gentle, fluttering his long lashes over those big black pools of eyes that she immediately forgot her wariness and petted him, talking to him whilst at the same time feeding him the tasty pellets. She wanted to see the zebras and as she couldn't remember their names she walked off in their direction, Ollie following close on her heels, it appeared that she had made a friend. The zebras although they didn't run off, stood still, wary of her approach and were looking at her from the corners of their eyes, ears twitching constantly. She reached into her bag and pulled out some carrots, waving them temptingly but unlike Ollie, who had bounded over, they took their time approaching her, their heads going up and down in deep nodding movements until they finally reached her, gently taking the carrots from her outstretched hand, chomping away merrily and when finished immediately nudged her for another.

She spent a great afternoon with these three animals taking several photographs and filming them as they frolicked about; she believed they were putting on a performance just for the camera. The giraffes were a bit more nonchalant, staying at a distance, deciding not to grace her with their presence, preferring to pull the leaves from the trees than to have carrots. She finally said goodbye to her new found friends, they followed her a fair way but when they realised she had no more goodies for them they skittered back away from her. That's what's called cupboard love, she thought to herself, they loved her all the time she had something for them, but now all the food had gone they chose to ignore her and if she had time she may visit them again tomorrow.

Jay arrived back at the Rondavo the coffee and cake having already arrived, Fred and Gladys having taken the opportunity to sit in the comfy wicker chairs.

"Now who's the Lord and Lady of the manor, are you quite comfortable?" she said sarcastically.

"Yes, thanks very much, now go an' freshened up an' then we can 'ave some coffee, we've waited fer yer long enuff". Gladys waved her in through the door.

Ten minutes later she emerged refreshed, the coffee was poured the cakes quickly devoured, Fred produced a pack of cards and they spent the rest of the afternoon playing rummy and drinking coffee. The sun started to go down at five-thirty, they sat chatting until the sun had almost disappeared on the horizon and the moon appearing, then they went into their respective Rondavo's to shower and change for the evening. Before she left for dinner she sent a quick text to Steve.

LUV U, DARLING, MISSING U, YRS & ONLY YRS, JAY, XXX

Dinner was a lot more elaborate than lunch, the Chef, Jacques, had excelled yet again, nothing however, would ever compare to the meal and the evening that she had spent with Steve.

Jay's new mobile bleeped insistently. She had a text.

Fred and Gladys were intrigued as Jay pushed the buttons on her small phone at the same time telling them that she had a message from Steve.

DARLING, MISING U 2, STIL AT MTNG, LUV U. XX

"Well?" asked Gladys.

"It was Steve, he's still at this meeting and he's missing me, not that it's any of your business, you nosey old devil", she said pointing her to nose and laughing in a good-humoured way.

"'Ere not so much of the old," taking Jay's comment in the way it was meant.

They tucked into pâté and French toast, then lobster thermidor, followed by an Ameretti and Ice cream loaf, absolutely delicious, what with the food and all the wine that Marcelle was plying them with, if she stayed for longer than three days, she would certainly end up a porker! Whilst they were finishing the meal off with a brandy liqueur coffee, Marcelle advised them that their jeep would be arriving in ten minutes.

"I'm really looking forward to this aren't you Gladys? I hope the camcorder can operate in the dark".

"Yeah, we've smuvvered ourselves in repellent, 'ope you ain't forgotten".

"No, I remembered," she said.

Chapter 40

Their guide was a large beefy African and very chatty his name was Chantigwa, Fred and Gladys had already met him as he had taken them on their safari the day before. He was accompanied by Bolus an older version of himself, Chantigwa explained that he was his papa and knew the route blindfolded, which was just as well as it was pitch black Bolus would be keeping a watchful eye and was in charge of the very necessary spotlight. It was extremely dark in the jeep the blackness of the night closing around them, as they drove off, the headlights jeep cast a mystical light, leading the way as they left The Lodge, which was now disappearing from view behind them. Chantigwa was an excellent guide and extremely adept at manoeuvring the vehicle, how Bolus guided him along the unlit tracks was really remarkable. They had been on travelling for fifteen minutes or so when, a frightful screeching broke the deathly silence that engulfed them, causing Gladys to cling tightly onto Fred, her head buried into his chest.

"Christ what was that?" The normally brave Gladys expressing her fear of the unknown, in a voice flat filled with trepidation.

Chantigwa, in his heavily accented, but easily comprehensible English, explained that it would more than likely be a Jackal and Gladys was not to worry, as it would have a different type of prey in mind. Gladys relaxed her hold on poor Fred's stump and sat rigidly back in her chair. Jay thought it amusing that this usually rumbustious woman had been quaking in her boots and, was for once, sitting quietly afraid to speak. They carried along the bumpy road, Jay wishing she had bought a pillow with her to sit on as her nether region were still a bit bruised from the pummelling she had received the previous night when she and Steve could not control their desire for sexual gratification, the memory still vivid she found it hard to comprehend that she had abandoned herself so freely all inhibitions gone.

Her thoughts disturbed as the jeep drew abruptly to a halt and Chantigwa, finger to his lips requested them to hush. Leaving the engine turning over, they couldn't at first hear anything, then beside the Jeep, as though it were only inches away they heard a heavy thud, there was obviously something large in the undergrowth, disturbed by their approach. It was all they could do to stop from shouting out, but once again Chantigwa put his finger to his lips. Bolus, spotlight in hand, placed it into position through the opening on top of the Jeep; he directed the lamp towards the noise that was now increasing in volume. Turning the spotlight on it illuminated an incredible sight before them, for there in front of them, was a cow elephant and her baby, so close it made them breath in deeply with the wonder of this close encounter. Jay managed to catch them on film just as the mother reared her trunk and bellowed at them, warning them off expanding and flapping her large ears and walking towards them menacingly.

"Time to go" said Chantigwa and he masterfully dropped back into position, putting the Jeep into gear they left as quickly as they possibly could over the undulating track, which was even more dangerous at night. Jay could just about make out the dark shape of the protective mother, standing in the spot that they had just vacated.

"That was close" Jay said, wiping a little bead of perspiration from her lip.

"Any closer and it's 'ead would 'ave been up me arse" added Gladys who had now been shaken from her silence.

Chantigwa told them that the Cow elephant would not have chased them any further; she would not have wanted to leave her calf. They eventually slowed down when they were a safe distance away and proceeded along the rough unmade tracks, Chantigwa intermittently stopping and Bolus shining the spotlight, occasionally catching sight of something scurrying away, fireflies dancing towards the light and antelopes meandering off in far the distance.

The Jeep slowed, Bolus once more shone the light in a sweeping movement towards the trees that illuminated far into the distance bringing to life the dark silhouettes of trees, dozens upon dozens of round yellow lights flickered on and off and flittered about the eerie branches that reached out into the ominous blackness, it was a spectacular sight. Chantigwa told them that these yellow lights were the eyes of Bush Babies, cute, shy creatures and the spotlight was reflecting on their eyes as though they were made of glass. Bolus moved the flashlight scouring the ground before them, indicating that he had found something in the long grasses. Looking over the side of the Jeep, there, frozen, blinded by the light was an actual Bush Baby, tiny, wide-eyed and bushy tailed. Chantigwa explained that the Bush Baby would remain frozen until they moved the light from it's eyes, as it was now temporarily blinded, this was meant by Gladys and Jay saying "Aw, don't be cruel, let it go."

Bolus quickly moved the light away from the Bush Baby's eyes, quickly turning back to the spot where it had been sitting just catching it as it leapt directly up in the air and then propelled itself forward, its tail following on behind, he bounded off and disappeared into the safety of a nearby tree. Jay was overjoyed, she now had some great footage, something that she would be able to share with Steve and of course the children, who would not have believed what their mother had seen, if she had not had the evidence via the camcorder. They had been out almost two hours now and Chantigwa with the aid of Bolus drove back towards The Lodge, with three extremely awestruck passengers.

They arrived back at The Lodge absolutely worn out "knackered" as Gladys so rightly put it. They couldn't thank Chantigwa and Bolus enough for the exciting time they had given them. Once again the obligatory tip was given but this time Jay told the two men that she would make sure that Mr Steve knew how excellently they had looked after them all, who would, no doubt, be extremely pleased with them.

Before they went to their respective Rondavos, they requested a nightcap be sent up to them, Fred and Gladys would almost certainly be going straight to bed afterwards. The nightcap of hot chocolate that they ordered arrived almost immediately after they did and they all sat and drank together outside on Jay's patio. The hurricane lamps glowing, casting a dim light over the patio, Jay went and stood as she did the night before on the edge of the patio looking out at the night sky, once more the moon and the stars were a joy to behold, but somehow they were not the same, the love and the romance were sadly missing.

When Gladys's eyes could stay open no longer, her and Fred retired for the night, saying "Good night, don't let the bed bugs bite", torch in hand they walked the short distance to what had been Steve's Rondavo.

Jay entered her room, turning her torch on so that she could see better in the dim light, noticing the amber silk dress that Steve had bought her and stripped her of the previous evening, it was still draped over the chair where he had put it, the shoes neatly beside each other underneath. She folded it tenderly, holding it lovingly and brushing it against her cheek, the scent of sex still evident, small stains evident around the bodice where he had suckled her nipples. She would not be able to wear it again until it had been cleaned, she hoped the marks from their secretions could be easily removed; she'd hate never to be able to wear it again. She packed it neatly into her bag along with the shoes and most of her other items of clothes, ready for her departure tomorrow. She laid out what she was going to wear for the morning, then she quickly undressed, brushed her teeth and ran the bath, she was tired, but she wanted to take advantage of the Jacuzzi before it was too late, she wouldn't get a chance tomorrow, it would be a great way to end her day and may help towards easing the bruising to her body.

Bath now ready, she tested the water, it was just right, placing the mobile on the edge of the bath, she slid into its warmth, releasing a long sigh of pleasure as her shoulders were engulfed. She flicked the switch to start the Jacuzzi and the aerated bubbling commenced, gently caressing the aches and pains away, it was so relaxing she was worried she may fall asleep, so grabbing hold of the mobile she proceeded to text Steve.

> HI DARLING, HAD WONDERFUL DAY, SAW ELEPHANTS, BUSH BABIES & LOTS MOR. WISH U HAD BIN WITH ME. MISS U, LUV U. XX

The response was almost immediate.

> MISSED U 2. THINKING OF U EVRY MINIT. CANT WAIT UNTIL TUES. WISH I WAS WITH U NOW & MAKING LUV. XX PS: DO U NO WHAT TIME IT IS?

She sent another straight back.

> YES. HOPED U WAS AWAKE. I AM IN THE JACUZZI.

Beep beep, beep beep went her mobile again.

> HOPE U R BHAVING YRSELF, JST HVING NITECAP WITH RASHID.

She replied.

> I WISH U WAS LUVING ME 2, THERE IS ALWAYS THE VIBE. X

Her phone beeped again.

> SORRY HUN, IN BIN, GONE 4EVER. U MUST WAIT 4 ME. LUV U. NITE. XX

Her reply.

> YOU CHEEKY BUGGER. NITE HONEY. XX

She laughed at his cheek, turning off the Jacuzzi and pulling the plug, stepped out of the bath, wrapping the big sumptuous bath towel up under her arms, she went and checked the waste bin. It was empty; she went to the bedroom to check the bin there that too was empty. Of course the cleaners had been. What on earth must they think, hopefully they don't have things like that in Africa and they won't have realised what it was. There was no point worrying, it was gone, what she needed now was to get some sleep, fortunately she was dropping on her feet the bath having relaxed her as with Steve on her mind she may have found it difficult to nod off, she needed to sleep immediately as she had to get up at five o'clock for the dawn safari.

She set her small travel alarm, placed it beside the bed and pulling back the red and gold cover, slid between the cool welcoming silk sheets, and after several minutes fell into a restless sleep.

Chapter 41

The buzzing of the alarm clock woke Jay; she sat up abruptly; her eyes being unable to focus in the darkness, feeling as though she had hardly slept at all. The only light available was coming from the hurricane lamps outside, filtering through the surrounds of the heavy oak door. She reached for the large torch beside the bed, turning it on illuminating the room, sufficiently enough for her to wash and quickly ready herself for the dawn safari. She checked her watch, it was five-twenty, just enough time to brush her hair and put her clothes on. She grabbed a thin cardigan to put about her shoulders, as it might be a bit chilly, picking up the camcorder, mobile and torch she made her way out, shutting the door firmly behind her. Jay knocked on Fred and Gladys's door. "Morning you two, I'll meet you down at Reception, I have some things to sort out".

"OK luv, will be down in ten minutes, running a bit late, Fred couldn't find 'is pants", shouted Gladys through the door.

"Don't forget your torch, it's dark out here", Jay warned them and walked off towards The Lodge, thinking that maybe she should have waited for them as it was pretty dark, and a little scary the torch casting eerie shadows, making her unsettled and nervous. Various little creatures were darting across the ground in front of her as she shone her light out in front. She was relieved when she reached The Lodge, her heart could now stop pounding. She was welcomed Chantigwa; Bolus was apparently waiting in the Jeep. Marcelle was nowhere to be seen, he must be having some well-deserved time-off; he always appeared to be on duty whenever she was around. As she hoped there was some activity in the kitchen, another chef, not Jacques was busily preparing to cook breakfast for the guests, beating eggs and dicing up fruit, he looked up as she entered and although he spoke little English with sign language he managed to understand her request for coffee and croissants for the trip. By the time Gladys and Fred had arrived, a flask of coffee and a container with croissants had been handed to her. She could not fault the service at all.

The sun was just starting to rise and once more they set off, this time into the semi-darkness, Jay pleased that she had the foresight to put on a cardigan as the early morning chill was still in the air. They appeared to be taking a different route from that taken the evening before, although she could not be sure in the darkness. Chantigwa was again giving them commentary as they drove alone, the roads, just starting to show signs life. Those people that were gainfully employed were up and about travelling to either an office, if they were lucky, or labouring, either in the fields or on building sites. He told them they were on their way to the Rift Valley where they would see Flamingos, cranes and maybe even crocodiles. The Rift Valley was a wonder to see, lush grass, bush and desert all in one. They saw dawn break in all its glory, shedding shards of sunshine down on the valley and warming them up within the Jeep, it wouldn't be long before the temperature was back in the nineties. Chantigwa told them that the Rift Valley ran all the way from Mombassa up to and including the Nyiri desert, past Nairobi and continued up to Lake Turk, touching the edges of Lake Victoria.

True to his word, the Valley was teaming with wildlife. There were hundreds of Flamingos, Cranes and Herons making their way towards Lake Turk, the sky a heaving mass of wings. Then there was the extraordinary sight of Wildebeest crossing the river, migrating to their winter-feeding grounds. The noise of their bellowing echoed through the valley, the crocodiles lay in wait, aware that a feast was near to hand their expectation of easy prey in the form of old, young or infirm Wildebeest soon to realised, as the unsuspecting animals wandered toward the now well worn crossing to reach the opposite side of the river some to end their lives within the lethal jaws and the death roll of the crocodiles. It was just like the Survival documentaries that she had seen on the TV but better although more gruesome, this is what safaris were all about she thought!

They drove on leaving the cries of distress coming from the unsuspecting Wildebeest as the crocs' succeeded in their quest, Jay found the experience moving; unfortunately that was what life in the wild was all about!

The lushness of the valley now receding into the

background they were once more travelling towards the barren landscape, the deep paprika red of the earth heating up with the morning sunlight and offering little in the way of shelter for the animals, other than the odd sparse tree and some dried out bushes. The picture book safari now far behind them, Chantigwa drove them back to The Lodge where breakfast was being served and going to be gratefully received, they all had hearty appetites since arriving at the Lodge. They ate a large cooked breakfast of eggs, bacon and mushrooms; followed by thick toast and chef's speciality marmalade, it was delicious. They washed it all down with two cups of coffee each. They then half-heartedly made their way back to their respective Rondavos to prepare themselves for the flight back to The Sandy Beach Hotel. It was a prospect they were not looking forward to.

Chapter 42

Jay closed the door to the Rondavo for the last time, hoping that one day she would return with Steve, but now she had to go. Leaving her bags on the patio for one of the boys to pick up later, it was all part of the service she had now come to expect, thanks to Steve and his generosity, she was treated extremely well. Fred and Gladys had done the same, leaving their bags outside, then the sad trio walked over the little bridge, taking in once more the absolute beauty of the place, none of them wanted to leave.

Marcelle was once more about his duties and greeted them. "Bonsoir mes amies. I hope you enjoyed your stay and will come back and visit us again".

"I hope so Marcelle, I sincerely hope so", Jay said.

"Yes, we second that", said Fred in a neutral tone, the spark having left him.

"Arh, but you sound so sad Monsieur"

"Only sad to be leaving" Fred answered.

"Mai qui, I almost forget, please take these with the Managements compliments" and gave them each a bottle of Dom Perignon 57.

"Thank you Marcelle, that is most kind, Steve will be so pleased with the way you have looked after us."

"My pleasure Mademoiselle Jay, it has been an honour and I hope that you and Monsieur Steve are very happy together."

They, including Hermes and Franco, got in the Jeep and were driven to the runway where Peter was waiting to fly them back.

The flight back did not hold the same excitement for Jay and she insisted that Fred sat at the front Peter, whilst she sat with Gladys, she alone with her thoughts and Gladys staring out at the scenery below. Hermes and Franco were quiet too, sitting silently at the back of the aircraft. Peter was his same cheery self, once again given them a running commentary, but he too could sense their lack of enthusiasm and eventually lapsed into silence, the rest of the journey which seemed endless, went without comment, eventually they were approaching the runway and were coming in to land, the only conversation being Peter transmitting to the tower for landing instructions. They had a reasonable smooth landing and Peter saw them alight safely, wishing them well and hoping that the remainder of their holiday was just as enjoyable as their stay at The Lodge, which they all very much doubted, nothing could compare to the luxury and exceptional treatment they had received. They all thanked him and gave him a healthy sized tip, saying what a terrific pilot he was and who knows their paths may cross again if ever they returned to Kenya.

Two cabs were at the end of the runway already, the drivers waiting patiently and on their approach got out of the cab and opened the passenger door for them to get in, Gladys, Fred and Jay in one and Hermes and Franco in the other. Fifteen minutes on and they were back at the Sandy Beach Hotel; it paled into insignificance compared to what they had left. They collected their keys, agreeing to meet for lunch at twelve-thirty. Jay opted to make her own way back to her room, but before she could leave reception a smiling Receptionist stopped her saying, "These arrived this morning for you madam." And handed a medium sized package wrapped in brown paper to her. She stuck it under her arm, knowing that it could only be for Steve, for the first time since breakfast she was eager to get to her old room.

Jay opened the door to her room, everything was as she had left it, Cecil was still there in his web and it looked as though he had eaten as his web was now practically empty. She plonked her bag on the floor and sat on the bed and started to undo the brown paper package, ripping off the paper and throwing on the bed, she opened the plain cardboard and she undid this to three black velvet boxes. Steve had attached a little card to each, she opened the one up that read, This is for luck, inside was a strange looking black bangle, there was a description telling her that it was of woven elephants hair. The next note read, This is for good health and fortune, opening the velvet box there was a beautiful ivory and gold bangle, which she immediately put on and admired it's delicacy upon her wrist, tears of joy at such wonderful gifts were now oozing from her eyes. The note on the last and smallest box read, This is From my heart, inside was a gold ring with the biggest diamond she had ever seen, attached to it by a thread of gold was the message Will you marry me? She gasped with delight, putting the ring on her finger it fitted perfectly, the tears now falling in torrents upon her cheeks, all her dreams had been realised, she had at last met a wonderful that loved her as much as she loved him and he wanted to spend the rest of his life with her and all in a matter of days. Were they mad? No, they were desperately in love.

Jay immediately sent a text message to Steve with just the one word.

YES.

Her mobile rang and it was Steve, declaring his love again, the plans he had for them even down to where they would get married. He promised to ring her that evening. They were so happy.

Chapter 43

She rushed to get showered and changed; she couldn't wait to tell Fred and Gladys her news, they would definitely be getting an invitation to the wedding. She haphazardly put on a pair of shorts and a t-shirt, not even thinking to brush her hair in the rush to get out. Putting on her now slightly grey moccasins she grabbed the bottle of Dom Perignon that Marcelle had given her and sped off towards the bar to find Gladys and Fred. She felt a little deflated that they hadn't arrived at the bar yet, as she was bursting to tell them and to see the look on their faces. She wandered out into the sunshine and stood basking in its warmth, looking out over the beach and the turquoise sea mulling over everything that Steve had said to her. His plans to take her to Hawaii and marry her on a sun-drenched beach, as soon as next month if all went to plan, he had even offered to pay for her son and daughter to join them and any other close relatives and friends that she would want with them on the day. There was not a great deal of people for her to ask so it would be a fairly small gathering, which suited her as she'd had the big white wedding in the local church. This time she wanted it to be something entirely different so Steve's plan was a dream come true. Then they would spend a week with their family and friends so everyone could get to know each other, Steve was then going to whisk Jay off to a secret location for a proper honeymoon, to spend another two weeks without any interruption, she knew it was going to be out of this world. Jay kept looking at the ring sparkling on her finger, just to confirm that it was actually happening to her, the whole thing seemed too good to be true. Gladys's voice could now be heard in the background, she was telling everyone about The Lodge and what they had done there, so Jay made her way towards the bar and her friends. When Gladys saw Jay approaching them with a huge beaming smile on her face she called out to her, "What you got to smile about then, and yer blooming 'air is in a mess, it's all over the show?"

Jay simply put the bottle of champagne down on the bar with her left hand knowing full well that the diamond ring would not be missed and it wasn't as Gladys exclaimed, "Coo, luvver duck, what 'ave you been an' gone an' done?"

Asking the bartender if he would kindly uncork the champagne for them and supply three glasses Jay explained that they were celebrating, he readily obliged, popped the cork which made an enormous bang and soared up into the air, he quickly poured the overflowing liquid into one of the glasses, then passed the bottle to Fred and put the glasses on the bar. Jay put Fred and Gladys in the picture about everything that happened and once again Jay's emotions overcome her, even Gladys shed a few tears as she put her arms around Jay, saying what silly buggers they were, even Fred looked a little choked. They were so pleased for her and even more delighted when she informed them that they were invited to the wedding in Hawaii, all expenses paid, courtesy of her wonderful Steve.

"My, you've landed on yer feet there girl", Gladys said, "We'll certainly be looking forward to this wedding, won't we Fred?"

It went without saying that Fred agreed as he finished pouring the champagne and did the honours of making a small speech, toasting her happiness, saying that they may as well open the other two bottles of champagne that evening as they would make her last evening her engagement party, it was just a shame that Steve could not be there, however Jay was swamped in happiness knowing that in just over four days she would once again be with him and looked forward to her "so called" engagement party with her friends.

The three of them, arm in arm, went off happily to lunch and once they had eaten, Gladys and Fred went off for their usual siesta leaving Jay to go back to her room to change for a dip in the pool and a bit of sunbathing, before that she had a little wander around the complex, which was once again comparatively quiet and unpopulated. It was becoming apparent that the hotel was just being used as a base by the majority of the guests, somewhere to come back to after an expedition to somewhere of other. When she approached the pool she was thankful that Dave and Chris were nowhere to be seen, had a leisurely swim in the pool and afterwards made her way to her haven by the sea, where she spent the remainder of the afternoon sunbathing and catching up on the sleep she felt she hadn't had the night before.

An alarm clock must of gone off in Jay's head as she woke at five o'clock, she always seemed to unconsciously wake up at this time, which was just as well as she would have hated waking up in the dark. Another dip in the pool was called for as she extremely hot and as she reached the edge she was put out to see Dave who was just getting out of the pool, this time in fluorescent yellow shorts. The water had made these eye-catching shorts translucent and when he approached Jay to say hello she couldn't help but notice and compare, Steve's when limp was twice the size of Dave's little dick and it made her reflect on what a lucky girl she was. She was feeling exceedingly happy so, trying to keep her eyes averted from the view in his shorts, she told him about the party that evening and invited him to join them. When he asked what the party was in aid of, she took great pleasure in telling him it was her engagement party, then dived in the pool, thinking - put that in your pipe and smoke it! Leaving Dave standing with a surprised look on his face.

After her swim Jay had a little bit of time on her hands so she decided she would go and have the henna tattoo after all and made her way to the beauty salon. She was handed a book of pictures of all the tattoos on offer, she eventually chose a small butterfly and the young girl painted it onto her left shoulder, it only took about fifteen minutes and Jay was very pleased with the result, wondering whether Steve would like it, if he did then she would go and have it done permanently when she got home. Now it was time for her to get ready for dinner and the evening ahead.

Chapter 44

Dinner was a little disappointing; there was no French cuisine. They had all thought the food at The Sandy Beach hotel was good until they had experienced Jacques culinary skills now Jay thought the hotel resembled a Butlins holiday resort! Was she becoming a bit of a snob? She asked herself. In those three short days she had become accustomed to the good life and a taste of all the things that Steve offered her. Jay made a mental note not to forget her roots and get ideas above her station, she despised people like that and she didn't want to become one of them.

Gladys tapped Jay gently on the arm drawing her attention, indicating the elderly woman "mutton", who was once again with her gigolo boyfriend, surmising that the old girl must be spending most of her days in bed as she still looked as white as a ghost. Hermes and Franco were also in the dining room having dinner, Franco was picking over his food like a fussy child and he was wearing another of his outrageous outfits, this time a skintight turquoise jump suit with sequins, the sort that perhaps a male ice skater would wear and get away with. Tonight though he had made a change from the large floppy pink hat and was wearing a gold turban. Jay wondered whether Franco had something wrong with his hair or indeed whether he had any at all as she had never seen him without some kind of extreme headgear on.

Thankfully far on the other side of the restaurant, were the parents of the child that was causing the rumpus the day before; she was now sitting quietly just like a little angel alongside her two siblings who were busily tucking into their food. Perhaps she had learnt her lesson.

After Fred, Gladys and Jay had finished their dessert they skipped coffee and went straight to the bar to retrieve the two bottles of champagne that Fred had, as promised, bought down and left behind the bar in readiness for the celebration. Once the champagne had been popped, glasses collected, unfortunately not champagne flutes, they went and sat in their usual seats next to the dance floor.

They spent an enjoyable few hours discussing Jay's future plans the arrangements for the wedding and of course Steve and her family. The dancing had commenced earlier but they were too busy drinking the champagne and getting merry but with the alcohol now taking affect and the sound of DANCING QUEEN blaring out, they decided it was time to strut their stuff, of course on the way to the dance floor Gladys had to comment that they were playing Franco and Hermes' song. However, the gay duo were nowhere to be seen.

"How have you two stayed so happy together, let me know your secret", she said to Gladys and Fred as they danced alongside her.

"Secrets?" "Well that's it girl, there shouldn't be

any secrets between yer, should there Fred?"

"If that's the case then Glad, perhaps I should 'ave told yer, yer dress is stuck up yer arse."

Gladys quickly pulled her dress down, annoyed with Fred because he had found it amusing and hadn't told her before, Jay said she would have told her but she hadn't noticed.

"The other thing yer need is trust. Speaking of trust Fred Beasley, I don't bloody trust you anymore. I want a bloody divorce?"

"Shut up yer silly moo," he replied and grabbed hold of her and waltzed her around the dance floor until she was almost dropping with exhaustion, then they all went and sat down and polished off the rest of the champagne, chatting amicably when all of a sudden the music stopped and the DJ called for attention, asking everyone to raise their glasses to the lady on the left, Jay, who's been knocking the champagne back all night. Jay was then urged to stand up and when she did everyone raised their glasses and shouted congratulations. The next song the DJ put on was, believe it or not, CONGRATULATIONS, by good old Cliff and practically everyone got up to dance, sharing in her enjoyment. Gladys said that Dave was conspicuous by his absence but Jay hadn't noticed any way, she wasn't bothered, in fact nothing bothered her anymore.

As Gladys, Fred and Jay left the dance floor to retire for the night, Jay was met with cheers of "good luck" and "congratulations", making a lovely end to what had been a momentous day for Jay. She was now engaged to the most terrific, caring man in the world. He still hadn't sent her a text though, so she bid goodnight to her friends and went to her room, the first thing she did was text Steve.

"HOW R U HUNY? MISS U. LOVE U SO MUCH."

There was no immediate answer so she got herself washed and ready for bed, just as she was pulling down the sheets the mobile rang.

"Hello Darling", she said into the phone.

"Hi babe, sorry didn't ring you straight away I needed to speak to you and had to get away from Rashid, I'm now in my room. What you been up to?" he asked.

She told him about the evening's events, that she had invited Fred and Gladys to their wedding and they were highly delighted and they wished them both luck, also she passed on their thanks to him for everything he had done. Steve told her it was his pleasure, anything that made her happy made him happy too. He was pleased that she had a good evening and then he asked where she was.

"I'm in bed darling, yearning for you," she told him.

"What are you wearing? Those horny black French knickers I love so much"

"No, I'm naked. Does the thought turn you on?"

"Yeah too right, wish I was there, just thinking of you and I'm getting a hard on. Can you help me Miss Patterson." He said suggestively.

"I'm so sorry Mr Knight, I'd love to assist, if only I could, but I'm afraid it is out of my hands." She quipped. "Perhaps you should try the five fingered widow."

"No, think I will give her a miss, if I can't have your personal assistance then I will settle for a game of cards, I'm very good at the five knuckle shuffle".

They carried on in this vein, making suggestive and comical remarks to one another, both getting horny, until finally they decided they must end the conversation as Steve had a busy day ahead of him at the Auction.

"Goodnight, then darling, I love you so much, will text you tomorrow and expect your call sometime in the evening, I know how busy you are sweetheart. Goodnight babe."

Steve answered. "I love you so much baby it hurts, sleep well my princess per chance to dream, love is so sweet it takes my breath away, you are a hive producing permanent honey, I want you so badly I can't wait for Tuesday. Goodnight darling." The phone went dead as he terminated the call.

Jay's head was swimming; he said the most wonderful things, he was also a bit poetic, now all she could do was dream the night away. Tomorrow was another day closer to them being reunited?

Chapter 45

Saturday was a non-consequential type of day for Jay; it was just a case of making it go as quickly as possible. A coach trip was planned to go to a market in somewhere out of town in the hope of getting some keepsakes and presents for the children, other than that she would spend the day sunning herself, she was beginning to look like a native now, another couple of hours and she would able to draw benefit when she got home.

Jay met Gladys and Fred at reception where they boarded the coach along with about twenty other people. Their mode of transport was just as dilapidated as the one she had travelled in on her first day, this one however had the added benefit of air conditioning, which was a bonus seeing as the day was going to be another scorcher.

The driver and his colleague, who introduced himself as Seipho their guide for the day, were both dressed in green uniforms, slightly shabby but they were clean and reasonably smart in comparison to all the other drivers she had encountered. The dark green of the uniform did not hide the fact that they were both sweating copiously from their bodies, especially under their armpits which also had the white salt marks left by the dried sweat. Deodorant seemed to be sorely lacking in Africa, very unfortunate for anyone within close proximity of a native African, which proved the case on this occasion as their odour wafted through the coach aided by the air conditioning. The choice therefore was either to suffocate in the heat or put up with the stench and of course being British everyone put on a brave face and suffered. Fortunately Jay had some perfumed wipes, which her and Gladys held under their noses, Fred refused or course, he was a man! They drove for about thirty minutes along the dusty roads, pass small villages that should have been condemned, once more children lined the streets waving in the hope of having sweets thrown out the window, unfortunately this time Jay didn't have any so they drove on leaving disappointed faces behind them. Eventually they reached the river and the ferry that they were about to board. There were literally hundreds of brown faces hanging over the rails of the two-tiered ferry, most looked sad, dirty and bedraggled. Faces peered in at the windows of the coach offering to sell them bags of nuts, drinks or newspapers. The guide's advice was not to open the windows as it was best to ignore these people, which seemed a bit harsh, as they were only trying to make a living the only way they knew how.

Jay did have her doubts that the ferry would float at all, seeing as it was overcrowded, with every car or person that boarded it seemed to sink lower and lower into the water and just like every other form of transport in Africa it was very rundown. It did float ok, a remarkably smooth crossing all considered and before they knew it they had alighted the ferry and were driving along the main road making their way to what was to prove an Aladdin's cave with more than just the forty thieves!

The coach pulled up alongside the covered market, their guide, Seipho, told the passengers they had one hour to look around and barter for whatever they wanted to buy and to stick together, any problem and he would be on hand to help. Fred and Gladys waited for Jay as she alighted from the coach then they made their way across the road towards the market and were being constantly tugged and pulled by black urchins, begging or asking them to buy something. Jay was, on this occasion, pleased that she had the hated bum bag around her waist, so that she could keep her money safe, as once they were inside the market, they were jostled and separated. As Jay now found that she was on her own she felt very uneasy because if she happened to look at anything she was immediately pushed into the confines of the market traders enclosure, where they would try to pressurise her into buying something. With great difficulty she would make her escape only to be dragged protesting into another enclosure, the final straw was when an argument broke out and a knife was drawn. Where was the guide when she needed him? As soon as she was able she high-tailed it out of there and just like a rugby player that's about to be tackled she headed for the touch-line, reaching the coach to find that most of the passengers had the same idea and were sitting (along with the guide), waiting to go back to the hotel, most of them without any purchases, including Fred and Gladys.

They were so relieved to see Jay, they had searched for her in vain until finally they had found it too much to handle. Everyone insisted that they would be happier if they were taken straight back to the safety of the hotel, deciding it would be safer, albeit a little more expensive, to buy what they needed in the hotel shop. As soon as they arrived back that is exactly what Jay did, she bought a beautiful ebony panther climbing a tree for her son, an elephant for her daughter and a magnificent lioness and cubs for Steve, she guessed he more than likely had loads of these ornaments at his home in London, but she wanted to buy something for him and as she was a Leo lady she thought the gift would be appropriate. She also bought a hand woven basket to put them in, to make it easier for her to take home.

Taking her purchases back to her room she wrapped them securely in t-shirts that she had worn, so they wouldn't get broken in transit, then tightly packed them in the basket ready for her departure in the morning. As usual she went to lunch with Fred and Gladys, then sat by the pool for the rest of the afternoon, reading her book, taking a dip every so often to cool herself down. It looked as though most of the guests had either gone home or were out for a trip somewhere or perhaps gone on one of the many safaris on offer as the pool area was deserted. Jay was grateful that there weren't many people about, as she wanted a restful afternoon without having to make conversation with people she didn't know. It was five o'clock when she next looked at her watch, the sun would be going down in about thirty minutes, which meant there was still about half an hour left for sunbathing before the sun finally disappeared behind the restaurant building. Jay took this peaceful thirty minutes to send Steve a text and then sat back in the hope that he would answer.

> "HI, DARLING, JUST HAD 2 SAY HELLO, BIN SUNNIN ALL PM NOW LOOK LIKE A NATIVE. I MISS U SO MUCH, MY FLIGHT LEAVES 8.00 AM, LEAVING HOTEL 5.30, HAVIN EARLY NITE, WILL TEXT U LATER. LUV U. XXX"

The reply was almost immediate.

> "AM SO BUSY, AUCTION IS CRAMED WITH PEPLE & LIVESTOCK, JUST BOUGHT M & F LION CUBS U'D LUV THEM. GOT 2 DASH. LUV U HUNY. XX

It made Jay happy that he had found the time to text her and as the sun had almost gone down she decided to go and complete her packing in readiness for an early morning start.

When Jay had finished the majority of her packing she showered, dressed and then went to meet Fred and Gladys for their last meal together. It was sad that she was leaving them behind, she would miss them, they were not going home until the following Saturday, she'd be pleased to see them both again when her and Steve married in June.

Eating their meal they went over the week they

had spent together, saying how fortunate they were to have met and how much they would miss her during their final weeks holiday as she was like the daughter they had never had. Gladys was not able to have children due to her having a hysterectomy early on in her life, she didn't go into the reason why she had to have this major operation and Jay didn't ask, some things needed to be kept private. Fred had wanted to adopt but Gladys was against the idea, instead they had devoted their lives to one another and it was very clear they were still very much in love. They called Jay their adopted daughter and in return Jay asked Fred if he would like to give her away if Richard her son didn't want to as he was a shy lad and if he had to stand up and make a speech he would die, so he may decide against it but Jay felt she had to give him the option. Fred was absolutely delighted that she had asked him and Gladys was already deciding what she should wear for the wedding in Hawaii.

The meal finished, it had taken longer than normal with all the talk of the wedding and so they decided upon having a few drinks at the bar and then they would walk Jay back to her room to say goodbye. It was a sad moment when they arrived at Jay's room, Gladys and Fred went in with her and she made them a cup of coffee and then they went outside and sat on the balcony where addresses were exchanged. Jay promised to send a proper wedding invitation to them, saying it would definitely be on their doormat when they arrived home. Gladys said they would ring her as soon as they arrived back in London and then they left her to finish her packing.

Steve had said he would ring that evening but so far she hadn't heard from him, she decided to wait until after she had showered and then she would text him.

After her shower, Jay had nothing else to pack in her suitcase, no need to worry about the vibrator as Steve had put paid to that, the cheek of him she thought, I could have made use of that tonight, then again maybe she wouldn't have. Jay wanted to be rampant by the time he reached her Tuesday morning, she would make sure the coast was clear and as soon as he walked through the door she would frog march him to the bedroom and make mad passionate love to him, whether he wanted to or not, her guess was that he would. If she was as randy as she thought she was going to be perhaps they might not even make it the bedroom!

It was now five minutes past eleven; she set her alarm clock for five in the morning, got into bed, the cool sheets welcoming then picked up the mobile and tapped in a text message to Steve.

DARLING AM IN BED, UP AT 5. WILL KEEP PHONE BSIDE ME IF U WANT 2 TEX ME. LUV U, EACH DAY BRINGS US CLOSER 2GETHER. IF DON'T HEAR FROM U WILL TEX U BE4 GET PLANE, WON'T B ABLE 2 TEX UNTIL REACH LONDON WHICH WILL B 8 KENYA TIME. LUV U CAN'T WAIT 2 C U. YOURS & ONLY YOURS JAY. XX

Jay lay awake for what seemed hours just waiting for a reply but Steve was obviously busy, possibly with Rashid, however sleep finally overcame her and she drifted off, waking almost every hour on the hour as she felt that she had a text message from Steve but on checking her phone only to find that she hadn't. Ultimately her alarm went off but she didn't want to get up, still feeling tired from a restless night, sleepily checking her mobile, but again there were still no messages. Steve had obviously thought it too late to text her or his meeting may have gone on for longer than expected, either way she was still disappointed.

Chapter 46

Jay carried her hand luggage down to reception, lo' and behold who should be standing there waiting for her but Gladys and Fred, the little darlings had got up extra early just to see her off, she was so pleased to see them. The limousine that Steve had arranged was waiting to take her to the airport and the porter who had collected her suitcase from her now vacated room placed it in the boot of the limo, for which she tipped him with her remaining Kenyan Pounds. She had left a goody bag in the room for the cleaner that contained all her excess toiletries, plus a pair of old sandals and a couple of t-shirts, apparently this was the custom for ex-guests and was an expected and most welcome bonus for the staff who could not afford such luxuries.

Once again, Jay said goodbye to a tearful Gladys and Fred, they kissed her on each cheek squeezing her tight. The chauffeur opened the passenger door and she stepped into a world of luxury that she could quite easily become accustomed to. Once married to Steve it may become the norm, looking forward to that time, perhaps never having to go out to work to earn a living again. Jay had gathered by now that Steve was a very wealthy man, even though he hadn't actually told her point blank, it was fairly obvious by the way he had treated her.

Waving out the rear window to her now adoptive parents, the limo drove off; she waved until she turned the corner and they were no longer in sight, sitting back in the comfortable tanned leather interior of the silver Daimler, she sent a text message to her daughter telling her she didn't need to meet her at the airport as transport had been arranged, the she sent Steve a text.

> MORNING MY DARLING, NOW IN LIMO. THANX. B AT AIRPORT 6. FLIGHT 8. TEX U LON, LUV U. XX

Chapter 47

Jay arrived in London on time; she had picked up her luggage and was making her way through to the arrival area to where yet another chauffeur would be waiting. She didn't have to look very hard for he was standing right at the front, very smart in his pale grey uniform, holding a notice board with Ms JAY PATTERSON written upon it. Jay approached him and introduced herself to whom he gave a little bow of his head in acknowledgement, he smiled at her and said his name was John and relieved her of her luggage, putting it on a trolley. John then led her to the parked car, this time it was a beige stretch rolls. Jay felt so special, people were milling around going about their business, some occasionally stopping to see who this woman was who could afford a chauffeur limousine, wondering if she was famous making Jay wish she had put on something a little more suited to her, soon to be, new position in life - the wife of Mr Stephen Knight. Jay hadn't considered meeting anyone quite like Steve and had only packed an old and very comfortable black puffer jacket, she was wearing the pale blue jeans that she had worn on her outward journey, when what she should have been wearing was a sable or a mink that would have complimented the magnificent diamond ring that was now adorning her finger.

Lounging back in the red leather interior of the car, enjoying the comfort she decided she must text Steve and let him know she had arrived safely.

HI DARLING, BACK SAFE, FLIGHT HOME JUST A BLUR, MY HEAD WAS TRULY UP IN CLOUDS IN MORE WAYS THAN 1. HOMEWARD NOT AS EVENTFUL AS OUTWARD JOURNEY, I MISSED U SO MUCH, TOMORROW WE WILL BE TOGETHER. LOVE YOU XXX

John spoke to her through a microphone that was connected so that she could hear him plainly in the back, he told her to pull down the cabinet in front of her, where she found a small bar with the inevitable bottle of champagne, which she miraculously managed to open without it going everywhere and then poured herself a glass, taking several sips of the now customary Dom Perignon. There was also caviar with small round savoury biscuits and beside them a long, thin, navy blue leather box with her name on it. She opened the box, her eyes dazzled by the contents; it was exquisite diamond choker necklace. Steve had once again written a message in that now well-known wonderful scripted handwriting of his –

My Darling Jay, This is to wear on our wedding day, however it will dull in comparison to your beauty. All my love Steve, see you soon.

Also inside was a white envelope and inside was a

white and gold embossed wedding invitation.

An invitation to celebrate
The marriage of
Steve & Jay
Saturday 30th June 2002
@ 2 o'clock
Kiaora Beach, Hawaii
R.S.V.P
The Penthouse, Cannismore Court
Park Lane, London, ...

Her future started here.

John had obviously been given instructions as to where she lived as he pulled up thirty minutes later outside her flat in Surrey, not being able to find her keys she rang on the bell. Rachel, who had come over from Brixton especially to see her came out to greet her whilst John took her luggage inside and placed it in the hallway. Richard came out shortly afterwards and gave Jay a quick hug "Nice to have you home mum".

"Mum, you look so well," said Rachel "Come on tell us all the gossip."

"Wait until I get through the door" and turning to John, she thanked him, offered him a coffee, but he had another pick-up in town so refused. He also refused to accept a tip from her saying that Mr Knight had taken care of everything; he then drove off, leaving Jay with her children, who were itching to find out all the details and about the wonderful man that she had told them she was about to marry. Rachel offered the opinion that he must be something really special if within a week they had got engaged and were getting married within a matter of months. Jay explained that when people got to that certain age time was of the essence and there was no point in wasting it.

Jay unzipped her bag saying she would show them the video first, then they could see for themselves what a gorgeous man she was going to marry, at the same time showing them the ring and the jewellery that Steve had given her. Rachel was more interested than Richard; as per normal Rachel's eyes twinkled at the thought of what she could borrow and once Jay had given Richard his ebony panther (which he was delighted with), he went and sat down in front of the television. He wasn't interested in "girly" talk he informed them. Rachel loved the elephant but Jay could see by the envious look in her eye she would rather have the diamond choker, and who could blame her!

On finding the video they went and joined Richard in the living room, Jay turned the television on and played it back to them. There was Steve when they first started out on the Safari as she was practicing using the camcorder, the picture was a bit shaky but Rachel was still impressed with his good looks, telling Jay how lucky she was to have found him and couldn't wait to meet him. Richard just said he looked ok. Jay's heart was doing somersaults just looking at him; she loved this man so much. Then came the picnic, where they were both on the video, it was a particularly poignant moment watching Steve feeding her the fruit, it had even caught Steve in the act of looking at her cleavage and bare thighs, which made her laugh. Jay quickly stopped the video saying the rest was just the different safaris that she had been on and a lovely old couple called Fred and Gladys who had adopted her; they would meet them at the wedding. The rest of the video could be played later; she wanted to check the rest of the video first just in case there was anything they ought not see.

The plans of the wedding were revealed and Jay took pleasure in showing them the invitation card, they were particularly pleased when they knew that it was going to be an all expenses paid holiday for them. Richard, as Jay thought, declined giving her away due to his shyness, but she knew she had a reserve in dear old Fred. The children now updated were now sitting down watching television so Jay returned to her bedroom to unpack. She sent Steve a text to say she had arrived home safely, that she had told the children, watched the video of him and now more than ever she couldn't wait for Tuesday to arrive.

Staring at her ring, the bracelet and her diamond necklace, which were now laid out in front of her, she was reliving some of those special moments she had spent with Steve and wondering why he hadn't answered her text, but she'd forgive him because she knew that he would more than make up for it when she saw him.

"Mum, mum", Rachel calling to her excitedly bought her back to reality.

"What do you want darling?" she asked as she walked back into the living room.

"Isn't that a picture of your Steve"? she said

pointing at the TV screen.

"Yes, what's he doing on TV," she was surprised, turning the volume up and standing back to watch and then she heard the dreadful words pouring from the newsreaders mouth.

AT 8.00 P.M. KENYA TIME, STEVE KNIGHT, MILLIONNAIRE PLAYBOY AND ENTREPPRENEUR WAS TRAGICALLY KILLED.....

Jay's legs went from under her she sat in disbelief as the story was unfolded by the Newsreader.

THE ACCIDENT HAPPENED AT CHINOI WILD LIFE AUCTION; A RHINO ESCAPED THE CONFINES OF ITS ENCLOSURE. MR KNIGHT HEROICALLY PUT HIS OWN LIFE IN DANGER AS A YOUNG CHILD RAN INTO THE PATH OF THE RAMPAGING RHINO. MR KNIGHT TOOK THE FULL IMPACT AS HE THREW HIMSELF OVER THE CHILD WHO, THANKS TO MR KNIGHT, ONLY HAS MINOR INJURIES. UNFORTUNATELY MR KNIGHT WAS BADLY CRUSHED, SUSTAINING MULTIPLE INJURIES TO HIS HEAD AND BODY. HE LATER DIED IN HOSPITAL, NEVER REGAINING CONCIOUSNESS...

THE END

By popular request Jasmin Pink has written a sequel "Reality Is A Killer", which is available to purchase now